D1527680

DEC 0 0 2014

PRAISE FOR

UNSEAMING

Throughout *Unseaming*, reality is usually in bad shape right from the start—and from there things proceed to go downhill. Such is the general background and trajectory of life in Mike Allen's fictional world. More could be said, of course, but there's one thing that I feel especially urged to say: these stories are *fun*. Not "good" fun, and certainly not "good clean" fun. They are too unnerving for those modifiers, too serious, like laughter in the dark—unnerving, serious laughter that leads you through Mr. Allen's funhouse. The reality in there is also in bad shape, deliberately so, just for the seriously unnerving fun of it. The prose is poetic, except it's nonsense poetry, the poetry of deteriorating realities, intermingling realities, realities without Reality. And all the while that unnerving, serious laughter keeps getting louder and louder. Are we having fun yet?
—Thomas Ligotti, author of *Teatro Grottesco* and *The Spectral Link*

WITHDRAWN

Allen's 14-story debut collection saturates alternate dimensions with literal horrific fleshiness. His unsettling Nebula-nominated "The Button Bin" is as disorienting as it is disturbing; it neatly sets the stage for the blood-soaked dreamscape vision of an overstuffed sin-eater in "The Blessed Days," as well as the more direct but no less chilling creature that crawls onto the Appalachian Trail in "The Hiker's Tale." In prose both lyrical and unvarnished, Allen depicts haunting regret in "Stone Flowers" and disembodied shrieking rage and grief in "Let There Be Darkness." When he combines both emotions in "The Quiltmaker," a continuation of "The Button Bin," he transforms that original tale in ways that resonate throughout the collection. Never obvious, sometimes impenetrable, Allen's stories deliver solid shivering terror tinged with melancholy sorrow over the fragility of humankind.
—*Publishers Weekly*, starred review

Mike Allen's ability as a poet is evident throughout this fever dream of a book. Brutal, elegant, and shocking, the stories in *Unseaming* are snapshots of a beautiful Hell.
—Nathan Ballingrud, author of *North American Lake Monsters: Stories*

Mike Allen's *Unseaming* is wonderfully, wickedly labyrinthine in nature—which is to say, where you start with each story is nowhere close to the destination he has in mind for you. Just when you think you have a handle on the journey he's sending you on, Allen masterfully leads you down an entirely new path, just as wondrous and terrifying as the previous twist in the road. These are beautiful, complex, unsettling tales of love, loss, and pain that will stay in your head long after you put down the pages, stitching their way through all the dark corners of your soul.
—Livia Llewellyn, author of *Engines of Desire: Tales of Love & Other Horrors*

Mike Allen blends a poet's attention to language with a crime reporter's instinct for the darker precincts of human behavior. Lush, phantasmagorical, his stories match the monsters outside with the monsters inside, B-movie tropes opening into psychological and spiritual desolation. These stories glow with demonic energy, and what they illuminate are the faces of our secret selves, screaming back at us from the mirror's depths.
—John Langan, author of *The Wide, Carnivorous Sky and Other Monstrous Geographies*

Mike Allen's *Unseaming* confirms his status as a poet who writes in dread and awe rather than ink. His most recurrent themes are those of wrenching loss and transformative retribution, with a liberal helping of the literal fear of God(s); sowing out a hundred different apocalypses, personal and otherwise, these stories reap an unforgettable crop of nightmares, sketching a chimeric universe in which shape-changing is less a rumour or an option than a sad, simple inevitability. Not to be missed.
—Gemma Files, author of *We Will All Go Down Together*

After you travel these often blistering and always fantastic poetic nightmares with Mike Allen, the darkness owns your soul . . . *and you rejoice in it!*
—Joseph S. Pulver, Sr., author of *Portraits of Ruin* and editor of *A Season in Carcosa* and *The Grimscribe's Puppets*

Mike Allen has put together a first-class collection of horror and dark fantasy. *Unseaming* burns bright as hell among its peers.
—Laird Barron, author of *The Beautiful Thing That Awaits Us All*

UNSEAMING

Also by Mike Allen

Novels

The Black Fire Concerto
The Ghoulmaker's Aria (forthcoming)

Poetry Collections

Hungry Constellations
The Journey to Kailash
Strange Wisdoms of the Dead
Disturbing Muses
Petting the Time Shark
Defacing the Moon

As Editor

Mythic Delirium (with Anita Allen)

Clockwork Phoenix 4

Clockwork Phoenix 3:
New Tales of Beauty and Strangeness

Clockwork Phoenix 2:
More Tales of Beauty and Strangeness

Clockwork Phoenix:
Tales of Beauty and Strangeness

Mythic 2

Mythic

The Alchemy of Stars:
Rhysling Award Winners Showcase (with Roger Dutcher)

New Dominions:
Fantasy Stories by Virginia Writers

UNSEAMING

MIKE ALLEN

INTRODUCTION BY
LAIRD BARRON

ANTIMATTER PRESS
COLUMBUS, OHIO

ANTIMATTERPRESS.COM

Unseaming

Copyright © 2014 by Mike Allen

All rights reserved. No part of this book may be reproduced or utilized in any form or by any means, electronic or mechanical, including photocopying, recording, or by any information storage and retrieval system, without permission in writing from the publisher.

Cover photograph © 2014 by Danielle Tunstall, danielletunstall.com.

Interior art © 2014 by Paula Arwen Friedlander, arwendesigns.net.

This book is a work of fiction. All characters, names, locations, and events portrayed in this book are fictional or used in an imaginary manner to entertain, and any resemblance to any real people, situations, or incidents is purely coincidental.

ISBN-10: 0988912414
ISBN-13: 978-0-9889124-1-0

FIRST EDITION
Oct. 7, 2014

Published by Antimatter Press, LLC
Columbus, Ohio
http://antimatterpress.com

"Introduction: A Stitch in Darkness" copyright © 2014 by Laird Barron
"The Button Bin" first appeared in *Helix: Speculative Fiction Quarterly*, October 2007.
"The Blessed Days" first appeared in *Tales of the Talisman* 4, No. 4, Spring 2009.
"Humpty" first appeared in *Flesh & Blood* 9, 2002.
"Her Acres of Pastoral Playground" first appeared in *Cthulhu's Reign*, ed. Darrell Schweitzer, DAW, 2010.
"An Invitation via E-mail" first appeared in *Weird Tales* 350, July–August 2008.
"The Hiker's Tale" first appeared in *Cabinet des Fées* 1, No. 2–3, 2007.
"The Music of Bremen Farm" first appeared in *Cabinet des Fées* 1, No. 1, 2006.
"The Lead Between the Panes" first appeared in *Lakeside Circus* 1, No. 1, 2014.
"Stone Flowers" first appeared in *Scheherezade's Bequest* 8, October 2009.
"Gutter" is original to this collection.
"Condolences" is original to this collection.
"Let There Be Darkness" first appeared in *Penny Dreadful* No. 6, 1998.
"The Quiltmaker" is original to this collection.
"Monster" first appeared in *Nameless* 2, No. 1, 2014.

ACKNOWLEDGEMENTS

The stories collected in this book span a period of sixteen years, so it's inevitable that I will leave out someone important in my list of those who contributed to the creation and publication of these stories, and who encouraged me to write more of them. With apologies to any so omitted, my gratitude goes to Laird Barron, Jason Brock, Erzebet YellowBoy Carr, Claire Cooney, Jennifer Crow, Ellen Datlow, Shawn Garrett, John Glover, Shalon Hurlbert, Izzy Jamaluddin, Rose Lemberg, Tom Ligotti, Virginia Mohlere, Jaime Lee Moyer, Tim Mullins, Dominik Parisien, Michael Pendragon, Ben Phillips, Cathy Reniere, Julia Rios, Anne Sampson, Charlie Saplak, Ekaterina Sedia, Ken Schneyer, Darrell Schweitzer, Stephen Segal, Jon Smallwood, Tony Smith, Christina Sng, Ferrett Steinmetz, Sonya Taaffe, Shveta Thakrar, Catherynne M. Valente, Ann VanderMeer, Ian Watson, Lawrence Watt-Evans, Bud Webster, and Jacqueline West; and the music of Black Sabbath, Sepultura, Motörhead, and Slayer, to name just a few.

I regret that Larry Santoro, who did much to help me promote this book, never got to see the finished product. I am glad that *Tales to Terrify* continues, but Larry will be missed.

Special thanks must absolutely go to Elizabeth Campbell, whose invaluable contributions to this book's existence can hardly be enumerated; providing this long-wandering project with a good home is just one of them. Also to Francesca Forrest, who braved her first experience with cosmic horror to copyedit this book into something presentable, and to Nicole Kornher-Stace, for dragging her typonet through these words.

And it goes without saying—though it must be said—without Anita, my partner in crime, not one bit of this would have happened.

For Shalon Hurlbert

CONTENTS

INTRODUCTION
A STITCH IN DARKNESS
LAIRD BARRON

For years we've known Mike Allen as a celebrated poet and editor. He's been involved in the Rhysling Award for some time, and his work with the Clockwork Phoenix series has met with acclaim. We always knew he could write poetry. He's had books published, he's been profiled by the *Philadelphia Inquirer*, he's won awards. Same deal with his editorial record. Meanwhile, quietly, a story here, a story there, Allen has steadily made inroads into the speculative fiction field.

Matters began to shift in earnest several years ago when he published "The Button Bin" in a small ezine called *Helix*. It's a subversive piece of body horror and noir-infused dark fantasy that dealt with themes of abuse and betrayal. Written in second person present tense, it instantly attracted controversy. By the end of the year it wound up on the Nebula ballot; no mean feat for a horror story. One got the sense that after years of flying under the radar, he'd arrived. I suspect this book is going to take many folks who haven't been paying attention by the scruff of the neck and shake them.

The timing seems appropriate. It has been said by anthologist and editor Ellen Datlow that the horror genre is undergoing a golden age. I can't help but agree. The confluence of talented authors and editors juxtaposed with the rise of the small press and independent publishers has sparked something of a renaissance. Particularly gratifying is the general youth movement that has accompanied this creative surge. Many horror and dark fantasy writers working today are in their thirties and forties; callow youth by industry standards. This new wave is typified by powerhouses: Sarah Langan, Kaaron Warren, Joe Pulver, Livia Llewellyn, Ennis Drake, Richard Gavin, Gemma Files, Steve Duffy, Stephen

Graham Jones, Matt Cardin, Michael Cisco, and Gary McMahon, to name a handful. Pick up a book by any of these authors and you'll immediately understand Datlow's enthusiasm regarding the future of the genre. In my estimation it's not a golden age solely in terms of literary quality or abundance, either: it's also golden for innovation—an age of genre-bending, splicing, folding, and spindling. Creatively and artistically speaking, I don't know that horror fiction has ever seen an era more supercharged with exciting and important work.

Mike Allen has, with this debut collection, immediately made a case for his inclusion at the forefront of the New New Wave. *Unseaming* is representative of the finest work being done today. It combines elements of science fiction, fantasy, crime, and horror with an icy exuberance that is reflective of Michael Shea, Don Webb, and, in certain instances, of Cronenberg. Allen's a child of the 1980s, and the influence of horror cinema as purveyed by the aforementioned Cronenberg, with perhaps a dash of John Carpenter, seems evident as streaks of dark coloration in the bubbling froth of Allen's concoctions. There are images within these pages that once glimpsed will imprint themselves upon your consciousness, etch themselves into your soft brain matter. For such a nice man (and make no mistake, I've met Mike Allen, and he's one of the good guys), he doesn't pull any punches when it comes to his art. His darkest fascinations rival anything committed to paper by the likes of contemporary masters such as Clive Barker, Ramsey Campbell, or Caitlín Kiernan. This is raw, visceral, and sometimes bloody stuff. Primal stuff.

Allen's prose is among the more elegant and fluid among contemporary authors, yet at times clipped and lean. His skills as a poet, author, and journalist have synthesized into a voice quite distinct from his peers. Another strength that marks him out is his versatility. He skillfully adopts the mode best suited to the individual piece, be it anecdotal or lyrical. Whether he's conveying the mind-bending terrors of "The Button Bin," the bloody phantasmagoria of "The Blessed Days," or downshifting into the more naturalistic dread of "The Hiker's Tale," Allen is in command of tone and development. He reaches into your mind and plucks the strings, smiling his jovial, avuncular smile as he manipulates the prosaic until it begins to change. Until it turns to jelly.

English professor and acclaimed author John Langan recently commented to me that one of the great strengths of horror is that it simply is, a thing unto itself that cannot be duplicated by any other literary mode. There's something profound in that simple declaration. The essential uniqueness of horror is a quality embraced by *Unseaming*. Allen's narrative concerns strike at what horror does best—illumination of the hidden, exploration of the taboo and the transgressive. Time and again he returns to themes of physical transformation, the disintegration of identity, and the mutability of mundane reality. How flimsy it all is, this universe we float through like seeds upon a tide! When immersed in Allen's cosmos, you'll gradually discover that nothing is safe; everything is permitted. Your family, your friends, your childhood toys all conspire against you; the universe itself roils and seethes beneath a smooth, cool varnish, ever changeable, ever malignant in its appetite. There is a real sense of isolation, estrangement, and jeopardy in these stories.

So, with these few words, the moment draws nigh for me to step aside and cede the stage to the man of the hour. If you are a casual fan of the dark fantastic, prepare for a few jolts of shock and amazement and, I daresay, a new appreciation of a genre that is all too often defined by its lowest common denominator. On the other claw, if you happen to be counted among the rare breed of horror aficionados ever on the hunt for something fresh, something worthy of the tradition set down by the Straubs and the Blochs and the Wagners, then get ready to have your fuses blown. With that, I bid you all a fond adieu as you venture into the gathering darkness…

THREADS FRAYED AND BROKEN

THE BUTTON BIN

You know he's the one who made your beloved niece disappear.

He's come out of his shop now, fussing with gloves that look expensive, a match to his long glossy overcoat. Glare from the streetlight glints on his bare scalp. Above that light, impotent clouds wall away the moon, render the sky a blank carbon sheet.

His odd little assistant left moments ago, her hose-sheathed ankles still overflowing her shoes as she waddled across the lot to her van. His car squats directly under the light, smart—except for these few minutes there's no one to see him but you. Yet why would he worry? In a throwback town like this, with every house from a 1950s-era postcard, crime remains distant, alien, a single murder strange as an apocalypse.

You stand from behind the trash cans with your arm held out as if you're warding off a demon, pointing the black pistol you took from your father's gun safe.

You're lucky. Mr. Lenahan sees you but doesn't understand. In his moment of incomprehension you close the distance, press the nose of the Glock against the soft underside of his chin. He's a big man, Lenahan, you're looking up into his surprised round face.

Back in the store, you say.

He starts to speak, he wants to tell you he'll give you the money, there's no need to get rough, but something stops him.

It's not the first time he's looked you in the eye. Once last week, he helped you choose a bolt of fabric for a baby blanket, covered with baseballs and bats and mitts, you told him you wanted your fiancée to make it, he responded to your tale with rote coos and congratulations. And today, an hour before closing, you asked him to help you find a replacement button for one you ripped off your shirt just for the ruse.

Don't see too many men come in here more than once, he said, with a smile full of hints and questions.

And he's recognized you again. His eyes move as if scanning an inner catalog. He whispers, Your eyes are the same. Denise.

If you could silence your own heart to listen more closely, you would. Sweat drools down his wide forehead.

I can tell you where she is, he says.

You say, I know you can.

THIS IS WHAT she means to you:

Wide green eyes that mirror your own, peering shyly at you from the doorway of the den in your parents' basement: you stretched out full length on the sofa, paging through T.S. Eliot's silly book on cats. You catch her watching, a scrawny girl in overalls and a pink T-shirt, dark hair clipped back with a pink plastic bow, all this pink inflicted on her by your basket-case half-sister. She tells you that—My mom makes me—when you hold up your right hand, smallest finger extended, and say with infinite amusement, Hi, Pinky!

You see she's about to retreat, so you wave the book. Ever read this before?

Dumbstruck, she shakes her head. She is ten, you are fourteen.

Wanna hear from it?

She nods.

So it starts. You become her warrior-poet, showing her nuggets to be found in your parents' dusty academic volumes of Eliot and Poe, Yeats and Auden, Plath and Byron. Warrior, because you're a killer of deer, ducks, squirrel, which repulses and fascinates her all at once. She comes along with you and your dad on one such trip that fall, you figure it's going to be a boring stakeout in the woods, and you brought Wallace Stevens in your back pocket, because you want to creep her out with "The Emperor of Ice Cream" (you love the way she watches when you read, the way she shudders when you sneak something scary in on her) but it's a bad day for boredom, a three-point buck wanders into view and she gets to see your father kill it, watches silent and thoughtful as you help clean the carcass. You wonder what she thinks of the blood on your hands.

She has her own life apart from yours, school, a few school friends, softball. You see her in her softball uniform a lot, and go with your parents to several games, though they don't hold your attention you cheer loud for her whenever the chance arises, make sure she hears you. What you look forward to, face it, is her time with you, admiring your clever words—it's not hard to seem constantly clever to someone four years younger—with those eyes so much like your own but prettier. It's intoxicating. Exhilarating. Your drug of choice.

But her mother's blood pumps through her heart. Your father's wild first child, eighteen years older than you by a woman long vanished, whose very existence your own mom tolerates with pained, saintly silence. Your crazy half-sister, who accepted her fiancé's marriage proposal as he sat behind the protective glass at the jail intake, the day after the cops brought him in for beating her. They never did marry—she found her senses for a brief time three years later, when he forced his fist into her mouth and made her lips split. And when she found those senses, went into the shelter, your father and mother agreed with stoic grace to help watch Denise. And because it didn't take long for your sister to find trouble again, Denise spends a lot of time in your house, sleeping in the extra bedroom upstairs, polite little ghost with a burning curiosity stowed quietly inside, eating supper in the cluttered dining room while her mother shacks up with this bad man or that.

You shouldered your burden of guilt: she's thirteen, you're seventeen, charged with watching her while mom and dad spend Sunday out with those church friends, the ones your mom likes and your dad always bitches about. But you have a couple of your own friends over, sneaky middle-class hellions like yourself, sitting at the back patio table beneath the tacky umbrella, the three of you already high when Denise walks up. She asks what you're doing, but she has an idea already.

Being the good son is all about what your parents don't know.

She knows what you'll do, because you're the coolest uncle ever. She stares with thoughtful silence at the mystic smoke swirling inside the blue glass bong. You show her how to breathe it in. You and your chums giggle at her coughing fit.

You keep thinking about that moment, those giggles, her hurt frown, mortified she failed to impress you. You think about it two years later, when she runs away and your mom finds the needle hidden in the tape deck of your niece's CD player. The way she's scratching herself all over when the cops bring her back. The two of you together in the back seat during the ride to rehab, you as angry as mom and dad. You snap at her: I can't believe you.

That same hurt look in her eyes, so like yours. Then her gaze flicks your way again. Read me something, she says.

I don't have a book.

Can't you remember something?

Bring me back, her eyes say. And you try. You recite what you remember: Fearful symmetry. The center cannot hold. Rage against the dying of the light.

She does come back, but never for long. And the last boy she takes up with, Billy Willett, that sorry sack of shit, he takes her somewhere that neither can come back from.

What they found of him wasn't much. But he could still talk.

The county deputies think he was in a crash, his damned motorcycle struck in a hit-and-run during a late night kiss-your-own-ass curve on a mountain road. They found the wrecked hog, they found him down the slope, still alive despite all odds, most of him that was below the waist missing. Dragged off by animals, they think. His eyes gone too, pecked out by crows perhaps, while he lay unconscious on the old hillside. How he lived they don't understand, he must heal up like Jesus.

Denise was with him, now missing. Can't charge the boy with manslaughter with no body, and knowing her, so like her mom, she could be anywhere.

She was nineteen. You were twenty-three.

Willett gives you Lenahan's name. He never gave it to the police. Just to you.

WE CAN TALK down here, Lenahan says. Just let me get the lights.

I see you fine in the dark. Keep the lights off.

How about this one? Just a desk lamp. No one outside will see it.

Go ahead, then.

The lamp's slender fluorescent tubes do little to penetrate the gloom in the basement warehouse, a space much bigger than you expected from outside.

Lenahan's shop used to be a schoolhouse, still has the look of a relic from a lost time; the street it fronts has surrendered to modern clutter, telephone poles and squawky burger drive-thrus. Even the schoolhouse's Rockwellesque bell tower still points benignly at the sky, though the bell's long gone.

The former school houses a fabric and craft store, one with a subtle reputation for eclectic and exotic selections that stretches for hundreds of miles outside the tiny dollop of a town where it nestles. Every room brims with bolts of fabric, regimented in racks or piled in bins, from burlap plain to prismatic textures and labyrinthine patterns that dizzy the eye. In at least two former classrooms long glass cases stand sentry, crowded with glittering baubles, costume jewelry. In the cavernous basement, tall steel shelves hold rows of thick fabric meant for towels, sheets, blankets, even tents. So many rugs hang from overhead racks, den-spanning designs of tigers, elephants, dragons, griffins, Egyptian gods and even wilder beasts, that they would make for mazelike layers of concealment if your quarry tried to run and you pursued—but he doesn't try to get away, even though he must know this place by heart even in the dark.

In fact, he acts as if he's invited you in. He sits down at the desk where the lamp shines, it's more of a drawing table, tilted up, scattered with catalogs and pattern books, the kind that show a smiling woman strutting in an outfit she's supposedly sewn herself. He settles a hand down next to a small red cushion bristling with needles and pins. With his other hand, he gestures at a folding chair at the corner of the table, going through motions he's long accustomed to, have a seat here, let's look this over. Beside the desk and your chair is a long coffinlike box. You study it, wonder what's in it, why he wants you to sit next to it.

A long wooden chest of some dark wood, with what appear to be elaborate Polynesian designs carved on its side—you see a horde of faces peering out through a thicket of strange trees, their gaze aimed to the right, where a large figure is stepping out from a yoni-esque opening in a wall of reeds. The lid of the chest is open, perhaps even removed. Inside, small objects glitter like treasure in a pirate movie.

You peer more closely. The chest is filled to the brim with buttons, of just about every kind you think could exist, every conceivable size and color: sky blue, gold, oak brown, blood red, sea green, India ink, rose pink, oil swirls, crystal prisms, basalt opaque; some like grains, some larger than silver dollars, disks, cubes, knobs, triangles and stars, even crosses, moons, little grinning skulls, twining oriental dragons, snarling demon heads. The entire conglomeration shimmers as if the weak glow from the lamp transmutes to moonlight across their many surfaces.

Lenahan says, It's amazing what you can find in there. Still amazes me.

You realize your attention wandered, you aim your focus and your Glock back where they belong.

Where is she?

He leans forward, his shadowed bulk alarming, his face a gibbous moon. I just gave you a hint.

You blink. His eyes have changed. You could swear when you looked at them before they were dark, not that eerie bright green.

You emphasize the command with a wave of your pistol. Don't move. Don't do anything other than tell me where she is.

Then what?

You inhale slowly. You tell yourself it's not your plan to kill him, you just have to know.

You say, Depends on what you tell me.

He sits still, but his fingers on the desk twitch spider-like, drum softly in some random Morse code. He leans back a little, face going from gibbous to full, and you see his eyes are different, unquestionably burning bright green, like seeing your own eyes in a mirror.

He's playing games, not taking you serious.

The little cushion full of pins trembles as his fingers drum. You shoot it.

The Glock hiccups in your hand, the sound like a sledgehammer smashing concrete. The cushion is simply gone, a long second before Lenahan jerks his hand away. The moment punctuates with the clatter of the spent shell casing on the floor.

Lenahan holds up his hand, stares, his sensuous lips parted. There's a needle jutting from the tip of his ring finger. His expression makes you squirm inside.

He puts finger to mouth, grips the needle in his teeth, pulls. It protrudes from his incisors like a toothpick. Then he tosses it away.

He doesn't seem frightened, but your heart is pounding crazy against its cell of ribs.

Under the lamp, a bead of blood wells from his fingertip. I don't want to make trouble for you, he says.

A flick, the blood is gone. Why does the skin of his broad hand seem smoother, paler, the hairs between the knuckles somehow absent, reverse-werewolf?

Stop moving, you say.

He obeys, watches, waits.

You still haven't answered, you say.

Answered what?

You scream an obscenity, put the gun almost to his chin.

His eyes flick to the button bin.

Just as with his eyes and hands, the buttons in the bin have changed. It's hard to quantify what's different, but you hit upon it: they look more real, more like the things they represent. The sea blue disks look like circles of ocean, the skulls gleam like real bone, the laughing demons seem to wink, the moons and suns shine with their own light, the faces on the fake coins frown or grin or simply breathe.

He knows your name. Shaun, he says. You reach in there, you'll find her. You'll know what happened.

You aim the Glock in his face and say, You do it.

DON'T YOU REMEMBER what Billy Willett told you? So intent you were on the who and where of Mr. Lenahan, perhaps you only lent half an ear's credence to the other things he said.

You found Billy's apartment, inside a house sided with flaking paint and rotting wood in a neighborhood once proud and rich, now long abandoned to poverty, slouching among the drug lairs with cars coming and going at all hours, a rundown convenience store at the corner with crack pipes for sale by the register.

Half of the front porch has collapsed, you don't know how whoever lives in the front apartments can get to their doors, but it's not your problem because Willett lives in the basement apartment accessed from the back. A sullen pit bull watches you from a chain-link kennel as you walk past; the dog's black back is splotched with mange or scars. It has no shelter from the sun.

You walk down the short concrete steps to the door. The house has sunk into the earth over many years; the bottom step and the threshold no longer meet. You bang the door, hear a woman's voice croak inside.

A moment later she pulls the door open and squints at you, a short stick figure with tattoos flanking her withered cleavage, crowned with a shriveled apple face, dirty mop-grey hair cropped close to her head. Above her a chain stretches to its taut limit, restricting entrance.

You try to sound pleasant. I'd like to talk to Billy.

Get oughtta here, she croaks. You go.

The Glock presses cold against your skin, hidden in the waistband of your jeans beneath your baggy T-shirt. For a moment you think of simply forcing your way in. Surely, given the house's decay, the chain would pull out of the wall with just a burst of pressure. You see yourself stepping over the old woman as she flounders on the floor.

I really need to see him, you say.

Let us alone, she says, and shuts the door. You turn to go. You look at the other houses, great rambling derelicts like this one, some sporting mock towers and turrets that were no doubt gloriously gaudy in their heyday. You wonder whether those windows will be lit after dark, if anyone might be watching. There's a half-formed plan in your head, what you might do if you come back then.

But behind you, the jingling sound of the chain undone. A click, a creak, the old woman's croak: He want to talk to you.

Once you're inside, she watches you with eyes narrowed, wrinkles radiating out from the disapproving line of her mouth. The room you've stepped into is cleaner than you expected, a cramped dun sofa facing a vast widescreen TV with the sound off and the picture hopelessly blurred. She points down the hall, where a door stands ajar—this door incongruously painted with a crude scene of two kids playing on a swing set beneath a smiley-face sun.

As you head for the bedroom, she croaks behind you, Don't you hurt my son.

You want to say, No promises, but you don't.

The room is decorated in the same childish way as the door, but you don't take it all in. You're looking at Willett, what's left of him, half-tucked beneath sheets in a bed that would have been too small if he still had legs. His arms, though, are still stout through the biceps, taut and wiry. His shoulders bunch and ripple as he hears you come in, props himself up. The sheet slides down and for a queasy moment you think it will slide off, bare him completely, and you don't know what you'll see then, what horrid mass of scar tissue he must truncate in.

But you're spared, the sheet pauses at his navel, exposing tattoos that crawl up his abdomen and chest, oriental dragons coiled around naked bimbos. You think of Denise, staring at that vulgar art as she straddled Willett's hips and sank down, and it makes you sick.

Willett's thin, angular face, with the stubble-shrouded cleft in his chin, remains handsome, or would have without the fleshy puckers where his eyes once were. But it's as if those scars can see, because he turns to you.

You're finally here, he says. His voice sounds choked with grit.

Do you know where Denise is?

He laughs. It's a bark tinged with hysteria. Yes. Yes. Lenahan has her. He put us both deep under but he only kept what he wanted from me. Denise, he kept all of her. He planned to all along.

Who's Lenahan?

Maybe, maybe—and now he's struggling to speak, as though someone just told him an incredible joke and he's still gasping for breath—maybe if you ask nice he'll bring her back. He wanted me to tell you if you asked. He told me to.

Who is he?

And Willett tells you.

He tells you Lenahan lives four counties away, runs the craft store in the schoolhouse, took it over from the Confederate daughter used to own it, made it into something spectacular. The place is well known but you've never heard of it, had no reason to know about it.

But the man has a reputation in a far different circle, one where Willett scuffed at the edge. In that circle, Lenahan has a different name, and only a few know who he really is. But most of the meth makers and meth pushers call him Mr. Buttons.

Willett giggles. Funny, isn't it. Like some little pink bunny.

His puckered scar eyes crinkle with mirth.

He's the one with the money, who keeps his people in good supply. He doesn't use, doesn't sell, just expects returns on what he puts down. And you don't dare snitch on him if you get caught. The narcs don't have a thing on him, won't find a thing on him, and as soon as no one's watching, you're gone and no one will find you again.

Billy Willet tells you how eager Denise was to try crystal meth when they first got together. How he encouraged her by saying it wouldn't wreck her mind and body like the heroin did. He leers as he says it, like he wants you to shoot him, hopes you will. But you don't. You just tell him to keep talking.

And he details how he and Denise went to one of Mr. Buttons' top men, the one with the barrels of chemicals in the storage shed behind his barn, and what Denise did to pay because they had no money.

And how the next time they went, word was Mr. Buttons wanted to meet them both, and this time their fixes would be free of charge.

Willett tells you where Mr. Buttons' place was and who he turned out to be. He tells you he doesn't know how Lenahan took his eyes and legs. He says he didn't see what happened to Denise but he knows she can never come back unless Lenahan sets her free.

Maybe good ol' Uncle Shaun can just ask real sweet, he says. Maybe you ask him just the right way, he'll let you see her.

It took weeks of brooding, planning, stalking to reach the place you now sit.

He leans toward the button bin, the muzzle of your gun almost kissing the meaty curve of his ear.

His arm disappears to the elbow and he shudders like he's plunged it in ice. You don't hear the noise you expect, the clattering hiss of beads displaced. Instead a quiet wind-chime jostle, a patter of hourglass sand, a release of air like a lover's soft exhalation.

Lenahan pauses. I'm not going to try anything, he says. Could you please pull that out of my ear?

Move slow, you say, but you back off a little.

His arm comes out slowly as if he's having to extract it from tar and in fact the buttons seem to stick to it. There's a squelching noise as his hand comes free.

Whatever you're doing, stop it.

Just be calm, son.

He holds his hand up in front of his face, looks at his knuckles, looks at you between his fingers. Some of the buttons have adhered to his skin. There's a cat's-eye centered in the palm of his hand, gold suns in the crooks of his knuckles, blood drops around his wrist, black diamonds tracking in rows down his forearm, alternating with bone circlets. You realize the buttons have arranged themselves in deliberate patterns—it's as if they lined up along invisible seams in his skin. Your heart is a madman pounding at the walls.

You aim at one of his bright green eyes, just like yours, like Denise's.

You'll never know the answer if you shoot me.

His palm still toward you, he takes his other hand, grips a demon-face button centered in his wrist, just below the ball of the thumb. Then he pushes it through his skin and out again, undoes the button as if loosening a collar. A vertical seam in his wrist suddenly gapes, like a new eye opening.

What you should see through that opening is blood and meat and tendons, but instead there's something in there that wavers like heat shimmer, flutters like a moth, shines without color, and a scent wafts out of sadness and silence. It confounds your gaze, makes your stomach lurch.

Stop it! you say, but he's unbuttoning his wrist, the skin parting like a cuff, something pale and gleaming and alive revealed underneath. The entire room has become strange, still dark but the darkness somehow agitated, animate.

He says, Do you see her yet?

His face contorts, his neck bulges and suddenly you think of Apeneck Sweeney, Eliot's mindless brute, zebra stripes swelling along his jaw. Beside you the buttons in the bin crawl over each other, glittering mites that seethe at the lip of their container like spectators crowding a coliseum wall.

Lenahan's arm gapes to the elbow. He flexes the meat of his contorted forearm. This is not…easy, he grunts, and something bulges through the gap in the curtain of his flesh. It's a face pushed out as if birthed, Denise's face, her pink lips parted as if in hesitation before asking a question. Squeezed out from between his unbuttoned skin, her face bows, an empty mask, eyeholes dark. Eyeless because the eyes regarding you from Lenahan's sweat-sheened visage are not just like her eyes, they are her eyes.

Her mouth is moving, a fish drawing in water. He raises his arm, brings her lips to yours.

YOUR LIPS CLOSE with hers. She is almost fourteen. You are eighteen.

You and she are in your room downstairs. Even though your parents are traveling across the country, you have the door pulled shut, the curtains drawn. The radio chatters and croons, you don't know what's playing, you're not paying attention. She's lying on the rug, her overalls undone, pulled down to her hips, her T-shirt pushed up past her bra, looking up at you. You're a head taller, about fifty pounds heavier, poised over her like you're doing a push up. Staring into her eyes, like staring at yourself in an adoring mirror. You tell yourself that's what you see, adoration, that she could never be frightened of you, terrified of making you angry, terrified of what you're going to do.

On your bedroom wall hangs a poster of lions in the veldt. The lions are flickering, watching. The bed in your room is not a bed at all, it shimmers in a turmoil of beads and discs and suns and skulls. She stiffens as you push up her bra.

Lenahan again. He straightens his arm, withdrawing the face inside himself like a snail into a shell.

As you sit stunned he takes your gun away, sets it gingerly on the drawing table. He takes your hand, eyes full of sympathy, different eyes now, maybe his own, maybe Willett's, maybe someone else's. He whispers something soothing as he guides your hand toward the chest. You have no fight in you. Both of you know why you really came, not because you loved her so but because you feared, you feared the revelation of a secret you kept even from yourself. But there's nothing to fear now, Lenahan knows, has known, has wanted to meet you all along.

Gold rhomboids practically leap from the bin onto your fingers, but Lenahan isn't content to wait, he forces you to your knees, shoves your right arm in to the shoulder. You feel something like static, like a jet of water, like a mosquito swarm, then you feel nothing, your arm is numb. He pulls you back, and your arm, like his, sports an array of buttons. A seam runs up the inside, a row of green irises with black pupil insets. He runs a finger along them, they pop like snaps, lift apart like the eyes that line a scallop shell.

When I tried her on, he says, I saw what you did.

He's pushing his arm inside yours.

The memory. How she stayed petrified, silent, as your fingers pushed inside her.

His fingers, inside yours, wearing your hand like a glove as you relive the memory.

Your knees have jellified. There's hot pain behind your eyes, sticky tears on your cheeks. To your utter shame, there's a stirring in your groin, your cock flutters as you relive what you did to her, and are yourself violated.

Lenahan chuckles, his belly pressed against your back, his right arm inside yours, his fingers inside yours.

He used his free hand with the confidence of long practice, unfastening your tainted arm from your shoulder. He will keep what he wants of you for himself, as he did with Willett, keep the parts of you that remember Denise. The rest, he will dispose of how he pleases.

You can't allow that. You can't let Lenahan parcel you.

You go slack. He repositions himself awkwardly, reaching for the buttons on the underside of your arm to finish his theft, as you lunge for the gun on the drawing table.

He grunts and tries to pull you down, but you've twisted to your feet. You feel the sickening stretch where he's loosened your arm and stuffed his inside, but the buttons don't pull free. He's on his feet now too, pulling at you as you pull away, the two of you orbiting each other in grotesque conjoined dance.

He grabs your collar with his left hand, jerks you toward him, tries to get behind you again. You let him pull you closer, but he doesn't see you have the gun till you've jabbed it under his chin. He tries to grab your wrist but you're sweat-slick and quicker, pull the trigger one two three, sharp hammer strikes, flares that burn bright spots in your vision.

But the struggle doesn't stop. Now he has your wrist, tries to pull your fingers open.

Adrenaline clears your head, you see the holes punctured in him, frayed edges like shooting through sackcloth, no blood, something like light but not fluttering out through them, causing your balance to sway, your stomach to heave.

His eyes, green again. He's using her to look at you, using her eyes that brim with hurt and ache with questions never asked as he tries again to pry the gun from you.

You squeeze again. One of your niece's eyes goes dark. When he cries out, it's with her voice.

Rage and fear and years of pent-up shame fuel your own scream. You shove at him, push at him, but neither of you can escape the other. He stumbles, the backs of his knees hit the lip of the bin and his free arm flails. Then you throw your weight against him. He topples, you push and he sits in the carved chest. The living buttons swarm up his thighs and belly. You drop the gun into the seething shiny mass of baubles and grip him by shoving your fingers into the holes under his chin. You feel fibers tear and then your hand is inside the sack of his head.

Images gush into your brain, hundreds upon hundreds, flash memories of men, women, boys, girls captured at the moment Lenahan introduced them to his terrible buttons, shoving in their hands, their feet, their heads, to open them like boots, gloves, hats, coats and expose the twisted, vulnerable things of spirit inside. But what rises topmost is an image of Denise, and you do to him what he did to her, push him down full body until his head and shoulders are submerged, bury him in his own sick magic.

You're still entangled with him, your face just inches from the sparkling swarm. Numbness spreads along your jaw as the buttons attach.

You jerk back, then scream as Lenahan's head and shoulders re-emerge.

Every follicle of hair is now a loose thread jutting out from a buttonhole. Huge black stars have replaced his eyes, his mouth sealed shut with a ragged line of skulls, his nostrils plugged with ornate blue knobs. Tiny transparent disks line the ridges of his nose and brows and cheekbones, hooks fasten the folds of his neck. His head could be opened a thousand different ways.

His struggles cease. He smells, not of flesh but vinyl and lacquer. Slowly, painstakingly, you start to extract your hand from him and his hand from you. There's a weird pressure inside your arm that lessens and disappears as you finally pull free.

Now you see his skin is patchwork, a grid delineated by the buttons, every piece a different shade. Who could tell what skin first was his?

Hundreds of alien memories have faded from your mind before you can pinpoint a point of origin.

He pushed her in, your niece, all the way under, withdrew a button-studded mannequin and undid her from head to foot, pulled her on and possessed her in total in a way you could never do, though something dark and shriveled in you tried. And when he learned about you, what you did, how you destroyed her, he wanted that for himself too, set things in motion to lay claim on the moment of her undoing.

A noise in the darkness. You look up.

There, between rugs hanging like tapestries in a hall of nightmares. Lenahan's short, strange assistant has returned. She stares at you with wide-set amphibian eyes beneath a too-broad forehead, above a too-small mouth, as rough and patchworked as the creature you've just murdered.

Her eyes deep and wet as cavern pools meet yours for a long time. She simply nods.

And now you know how you will see your beloved niece again.

You start at Lenahan's forehead and work your way down, head to foot, prepare to try him on, see how the seams of a monster fit. You're sure they'll fit well, snug and comfortable as a tailored suit.

It's the only skin you deserve to wear.

THE BLESSED DAYS

Bryan woke that morning drenched in blood from toe to scalp, just as he had every morning for two and a half years.

But this time, scraps of images swirled in his fogged brain, a hurricane rush of faces, a sense of squirming, worms under pressure—*dreaming.* He could remember the dream. His heart started to pound. He had to tell Dr. Patel about his breakthrough.

He groped for the towel dispenser, wiped off his hands, his feet, and sat up. The plastic sheet covering his body crackled as he peeled it away from his blood-sticky skin.

Beside him, Regina stirred.

He'd almost forgotten she was there. He turned, afraid he'd woken her, but no: she was still sound asleep. She fidgeted, eyes moving under their lids, perhaps in muted reaction to a dream of her own, one she'd never remember.

She lay naked between plastic sheets just as he had, slats of moonlight groping through the blinds to stripe her contours, long curvy torso and short legs—and at that moment, the Blessings touched her. Her flesh turned ink black beneath the sheet as blood welled from every pore of her skin. When she finally woke she would be covered head to toe, just as he was.

Bryan felt no revulsion, only sorrow. Every human on the planet endured this now, whenever they slept, whenever they woke.

For the longest time, Bryan had resisted that word, Blessings, whenever he spoke of the bloody awakenings. Amazing, how fast the word caught on once it started happening, once every single human on the planet would rouse from sleep to find every inch of skin slick with blood.

Infernal logic reinforced it—*bless* derived from old English roots that meant *mark with blood*—but Bryan knew it was just euphemism, a way to render the grotesque palatable. He had resisted until prolonged exposure to the usage made him unable to define the phenomenon with any other word.

In the shower, watching the blood sluice down the drain, snippets from his dream returned, resonating with the pink swirl of water. He *had* made progress last night. He had to call Dr. Patel, as soon as the hour was reasonable.

He wiped condensation from the mirror and met his reflection's eyes. Behind his temples, the sides of his bare head bulged. He knew his skull's proportions were wrong for a shaved head, and envied other men whose looks were enhanced by baldness. But he had no choice. The Blessings rendered a full head of hair utterly impractical. Even some women had caved, though most had adopted tricks to keep their treasured coifs sanitary. Regina was one who climbed out of bed at ungodly hours to scour the blood from her roots. This was how Bryan knew it was too early to call the professor without having to glance at a clock.

He resolved to use the time for an early morning jog, donned sweats and shoes and snuck out. Halfway up the stairs to the parking lot, he stopped short. A derelict lay curled in fetal position on the landing. If it weren't for the wet rasp of the man's breathing, Bryan might have thought him dead.

Unwashed for weeks, the accumulated residue from the Blessings masked the man's features in a gruesome black crust. As Bryan stepped around him, the bum's eyes opened, twin ovals of bloodshot pink in the scab of his face.

ON THE FIRST day of the Blessings, billions woke up screaming.

Every human on the planet had emerged from sleep looking as if they'd crawled from a blood-filled tub. This happened to newborns and elderly, tribesmen and movie stars, prisoners and dictators, soldiers and presidents.

On *that* morning, two and a half years ago, Bryan jerked awake as Regina shrieked in his ear.

He and Regina first met at the fitness club downtown. He worked as a reporter for the smaller of the city's two metro papers; she worked at a bank branch only a block away. At their first conversation he had felt a fierce attraction to her—dark hair with exotic blond streaks; green almond eyes; quirky lopsided grin; a head shorter than him but not at all short on curves. He found everything she said fascinating, and she appreciated, and reciprocated.

Within two weeks they became intimate. At four weeks out—the night before the Blessings—they were still in the giddy exploratory stages. Her olive skin fascinated him; it tasted oddly sour and salty; he wasn't sure if he liked the flavor but took every opportunity to re-evaluate the taste.

They fell asleep on her sofa that night, limbs tangled together, neither the least bit concerned about personal space.

She woke first, and screamed at the sight of his blood-covered face.

He had practically leapt from the sofa, and seeing her dripping with abattoir residue, revulsion struck ahead of thought and he shoved her away, so that she fell onto the glass coffee table—which shattered beneath her.

Miraculously, she wasn't cut, although at first it had been impossible to tell. Once they were clean, once it became clear the blood came from neither of them, once the television news showed them that something had gone wrong not just in Regina's living room but all over the world, then their panic changed, and to each other they could be civil, even tender. He apologized repeatedly, and she told him she accepted.

But seeing each other, feeling each other's skin *that way* overwhelmed their fledgling attraction, almost severed it. Neither wanted to touch the other, not then, not for weeks, not for months.

THAT MORNING, BRYAN'S profession had meant that he couldn't stay home, couldn't recover from his freak-out. He had to get to his cubicle, man the phones, conduct interviews, shove aside his own confusion and despair and charge ahead, write something to help the paper's readership make sense of things, or at least understand they weren't alone. He had endured this before, when the twin towers collapsed, and closer to home, when a crazed gunman killed thirty innocent young students at Bryan's alma mater.

But this was worse, far worse.

Too agitated to stay put in his chair, he hadn't noticed the blinker for new voicemail till after he finished his first interview: an insincere message of all-is-under-control from the city's audibly frightened director of public safety.

The voicemail came from Sukhraj Patel, sleep specialist, his odd friend of more than five years.

"It happens in your sleep, Bryan. And only in your sleep. You have to come down and see what we recorded. You have to get here!" The usually imperturbable professor so rushed his Indian bass-baritone that Bryan couldn't make out many of the words. And he had no time then to replay it. His editors were determined to print a special edition by noon, and it was proving damn near impossible to reach anyone by landline.

The phenomenon started in the Americas, and news of it traveled the world with the dawn. It wasn't until a few days later that sufficient information pooled to show the Blessings truly began everywhere on the planet at once.

In San Francisco at 2 AM, a security guard woke from a forbidden nap and raised his red, glistening hands to the light above his desk. His befuddled mind gradually registered that his entire uniform had soaked dark.

In Brasília at 8 AM, a boy who had spent the night sleeping beneath cardboard under a bridge scrambled out of his refuge, holding out his blood-covered arms and crying "Murdu! Murdu!"

In Kabul at 2:30 PM, a young mother singing a lullaby over her baby's crib stopped with a shriek of horror, as red beads welled from every pore of her sleeping daughter's skin.

Five days later, in Sukhraj Patel's office, Bryan watched a video on the professor's paper-flat computer monitor. The footage was of himself, lying face up in a laboratory bed, electrodes pasted to his shaved scalp. He watched himself drift off to sleep. Watched the blood well up. Watched as he endured what everyone endured every time they slept.

Because the Blessings didn't stop with that first day. They never stopped.

BRYAN AND PATEL met over their common interest in dreams. For Patel, they were a subject of research; for Bryan, a lifelong battleground.

Cursed since infancy with an overactive imagination, Bryan's dreams spiraled into terror in the wake of a handful of Poe stories read aloud by his third-grade teacher. None of his classmates seemed fazed by "The Black Cat" or "The Tell-Tale Heart," but the stories left Bryan deeply disturbed, unlocked nightmares, even night terrors: mist leaking from the light fixture above his bed that gelled into an eyeless old man; spidery legs long as tree branches that groped from closet shadows; dark dream-alleys where he ran from people tugged by puppet strings formed from their own arteries and veins.

His ordeals didn't end for years. A night-light did no good. Some nights he became so terrified he'd pee into his Smokey Bear sheets rather than risk the walk to the bathroom. With escalating impatience, his parents told him to keep focusing his mind on Jesus. At first he lied and claimed it worked, but after yet another bed-wetting episode his enraged father shook the truth out of him.

What finally saved him at the not-so-tender age of fourteen was a book about lucid dreams he found at the community college library. He followed the recommended exercise out of desperation, repeating until he fell asleep: "I will know when I am dreaming. I will remember what I dream."

Just as his first encounters with the morbid plunged him into nightmare, his first attempt at lucid dreaming introduced him to unlimited power. He again found himself in the City of Mazes, pursued by a crowd pulled on fleshy strings. *You are all inside my head*, he thought, and knew they were. He commanded, *Stop*, and they did, collapsing to the ground as their severed strings thrashed like loose hoses.

From then on he reigned, wizard-tyrant in the kingdom of his own skull.

At fourteen, Bryan had other dreams, much more mundane. Win fame and fortune as a freelance writer. Marry a saucy redhead from Ireland, and build her a mansion with his riches. When he met Patel, he had inched toward the first of those goals.

The university in the next county had called for volunteers to participate in an experiment meant to test a therapeutic cure for recurring nightmares. On learning of this, Bryan begged the higher-education reporter to let him step in and write a feature story. Once he turned in his profile of the professor, he begged his managing editor for permission to chase a freelance article. Permission granted, Bryan signed up for the tests.

His face a wide brown square above his white lab coat, Patel approached life and subjects like the coolest of poker players. The professor's perpetually half-lidded eyes rarely hinted at anger or amusement. The rumble of his voice stayed perpetually even-toned. He was by far the most unflappable man Bryan had ever met, though he wasn't without a sense of humor.

As soon as Bryan described his lucid dreaming skills, the professor wished to observe for himself. They performed a simple verification: Patel asked Bryan to move his eyes right to left and back again twice every 10 seconds while "awake" within his dreams. Bryan found this easy. The EEG graphs recorded during Bryan's REM sleep displayed sharp spikes for the paired eye movements, over and over, making his brain waves appear regular as heartbeats.

When he woke, he heard Patel's rumble. "For what reason would you hone such a skill?" The professor tapped Bryan's forehead with a cold finger. "Do you keep a harem organized in your head, perhaps, like the crazy man in that Fellini film?"

Bryan kept his voice as flat as the professor's. "Wouldn't it be *obvious* if I did?"

Silence hung between them. Then Patel's scowl fell away, and Bryan had the pleasure of actually hearing the professor laugh, like a mirthful bellow from a bear.

As often happens with writer and source, the two pledged to keep in touch after the article's publication, but didn't—until the Blessings began, and Bryan discovered he could no longer remember dreams.

Nor could anyone else.

It wasn't as if dreams were simply gone, driving a sleep-deprived populace toward madness, but as if something else had supplanted them, an enigma that let people maintain their sanity even as it washed the world in blood.

When Bryan returned from his jog, predawn light cast the cookie-cutter houses of his neighborhood in dark silhouette. The derelict had left the stairwell.

Regina was up—he could hear the shower running when he opened his door. She'd already stripped the bloodied sheets from the bed and replaced them with clean ones. He called Sukhraj's cell and left a voice mail.

His eyes flicked to the bureau by the side of the bed Regina had claimed. Her new pendant dangled there from one of the drawer knobs, an object escaped from a bad dream, a red diadem inscribed with a gothic "G." Regina had a knack for involving herself in loopy things—she believed wholeheartedly in ghosts and nature spirits, paid to take classes in energy manipulation and chakra healing—a trait that Bryan at times found exotic, endearing, but now found alarming. Yet he'd kept his mouth shut, held back, when they met for dinner last night and he noticed the red G glittering in her cleavage.

The casual text she'd sent that started it—*how r u doin?*, then, *I want 2 c u*—caused a pang of longing in his chest that was amplified tenfold by his first glimpse of her beneath the dimmed lights at Pazzari's. She'd cut her silky brown hair short, added red highlights. The blue half-jacket adorning her shoulders was the same she'd worn on many lunch dates before the Blessings. Even with the lights turned down low, her green eyes shone.

They hugged and forced the hostess to wait before escorting them to their table. As Regina took her chair, Bryan's eyes eagerly followed her neckline down only to discover the diadem. The discovery stabbed as if he'd stepped on a nail.

The Gaians held that the blood of the so-called Blessings washed the human race each morning as a warning from the Earth spirit—or, as a sarcastic radio personality once phrased it, "Mother Earth's PMS"—in response to the many ways Modern Man had damaged the world: pollution, strip-mining, clear-cutting, bomb testing, oil spilling, on and on. They claimed the blood of the Blessings was the blood of the dead mysteriously regurgitated.

Bryan knew animal welfare was a big deal for Regina, but he couldn't imagine her associated with the dozen red-clad extremists who'd walked arm and arm toward a military oil refinery chanting, "Our blood will be on your bodies. Our blood will be on your bodies," until the guards were forced to shoot stun grenades.

She noticed his grimace. "What's wrong?"

It was hard to bite his tongue, but he managed. "Nothing." He shook with nerves as he propped open his menu. "Just thinking about Mom and Dad."

Which had in a way been true. All sorts of explanations existed for the Blessings, beliefs people wrapped around themselves for shelter against the sheer madness. A so-called psychic had once called Bryan at the office to claim the Blessings were the result of a bloodthirsty God gorged beyond its limit on those dead from modern warfare. Bryan hung up on him.

By contrast, a few Christian sects interpreted the blood-drenched mornings as God's desperate attempt to save souls before the end-time, a literal attempt to cleanse the people who refused to accept the gift of their Savior's blood. His parents had been among those, further deepening his estrangement.

And the irony: the Blessings could in fact bring disease if you didn't make the most meticulous efforts at hygiene before and after sleep. His mother and father had both fallen ill. The diagnosis: a new strain of bacterial pneumonia, allowed to thrive by a devastated immune system.

Visiting their bedsides, listening to the wheeze of their breath, how he had wanted to scream, to shake their frail bodies, to call them the fools they were. But he who could believe nothing had no right to tell others what to believe.

Gina's hand on his wrist stirred him from his reverie, brought him back to the restaurant. He told her what he'd been thinking about, but not what inspired the train of thought. She squeezed his wrist as he spoke, and just listened.

Later, in the midst of dinner—fettuccine Alfredo for him, eggplant Parmesan for her—she asked him what he believed the Blessings were. He knew he was on dangerous turf: she was idly fingering her pendant, perhaps thinking of making a point. "I don't have an opinion," he said quickly, but much to his own surprise didn't stop there. "I know what they *feel* like."

She tilted her head, a gesture that meant "go on," green eyes watchful above her wide cheekbones.

"When the trade center went down," he said, "when I stood there with my co-workers in front of the TV and watched the towers collapse, I felt like I'd been stained, like something inside me, spirit, soul, whatever—like it was the rug those deaths would never wash out of. I think that feeling was there before, when I used to have to go out to cover spot news, the things I'd see—like when the firefighters couldn't get that old woman out of the house in time, or that sorry drunk's body I saw wedged underneath a minivan. But when the towers fell, I couldn't ignore it anymore. And each new thing makes it worse. The shootings at the university made it a lot worse."

"Worse things happen all over the world," she said, gripping her pendant, twirling it. "Much worse. Much more often."

"I know. I'm not saying anyone should feel sorry for me." He spread his arms. "For us. But you asked. To me that's what the Blessings are like. Like this stain I feel, but it's real, it's on the outside. It's on everyone." He surprised himself again as his voice cracked.

Now it was Regina's turn for judicious silence. She let go her symbol to put both her hands on his.

Later, it surprised him more, how hungry she was for him, he for her. For the longest time he had avoiding staying over at her place or vice versa because of what they would see when they awoke, that terrible memory that hung between them. This time, without saying it, they both resolved to defy that memory. They strove to wear each other out, translating their hunger into action, arms clutching each other's thighs as they devoured each other to climax. And again, even later, her pinned beneath him, the sweet pressure of her hips flexing up, him grinding down on her as if he meant to obliterate them both.

Then, his miraculous awakening, with the memory of dream still fresh as the blood on his skin.

BRYAN STAYED NEAR his phone at the office, annoyed by the trite assignment he'd been saddled with (a water main break downtown), neurotically cleaning his fingernails with his pocketknife as he willed Patel to call him back. When the professor finally did call, about noon, he broke character for only the second time since Bryan had known him.

"You *dreamed?* You *remember* dreaming? That's incredible! Are you sure it's not wishful thinking?"

"I'm *certain*, Raj. But I don't remember all of it, just flashes. Like still photography."

"Well…well, maybe we can help you get clearer." If Bryan didn't know better, he would have thought the professor's voice almost sounded devilish. Then from out of the blue, Patel asked, "How much do you know about the Mayans?"

"Hmm. Didn't they throw little girls into pits? Or are they the ones that cut the hearts out of enemy warriors?"

"Both. Though more often, enemy warriors had their heads cut off."

"Well. Okay then. Why do you ask?"

"I'm trying to digest a rather exotic set of ideas. I'll tell you all about it tonight. You can come tonight?"

Of course he could. He phoned Regina at the bank, left a message to let her know. She texted back, *u have fun. luv u.*

WHEN HE MET Patel outside the university medical center, he was immediately struck by how much older the scientist seemed. His square face sagged as if the skin had loosened from within. But the doctor's gaze had not lost its intensity, nor did he bother with opening pleasantries. "I hope for both our sakes your memory is good. This is going to cost me some overtime."

"Your problem, not mine."

Patel regarded Bryan's shit-eating grin for a moment before leading him through the glass double doors. The professor didn't crack a smile. "I'd be highly skeptical if it were anyone other than you."

"Skeptical? Come on, Raj, there *must* be other people dreaming."

"I have heard from others," Patel said as they walked. "Most proved to be wastes of time and resources. A few, there may have been something to their claims, but in the labs they couldn't deliver. You give me hope."

Queasiness sluiced through Bryan's gut and bubbled in his throat. "I'm the only one."

"I can't claim that. But at this moment you're the only one I know of." He pressed the button to summon the elevator. "Pegah and Sonoko should be here in an hour. I called them in special for this. Let's go to my office."

As they ascended, Patel informed him, "We're going to try something a little unusual tonight. Before we put you to sleep, I'm going to have you take a small dose of psilocin."

"What's that?"

A devilish smile spread slowly within the bracket of Patel's block-like jaw. "Pharmacologically active extract of a certain mushroom."

Bryan coughed. "You're kidding me."

"Ordinarily, I would be, but since you're the first person I know of since the Blessings started who claims to remember a dream—whose claim might be credible, that is—the extra barrier breaker seems well warranted. Don't worry, the dosage will be small. We want to make sure you can sleep."

"You're allowed to do that?"

The smirk remained. "We have a DEA exemption. There's no scandal for you to uncover."

Nothing in Patel's office seemed different except for the background image on his flat-screen monitor. The icon-dotted screen displayed two stylized figures drawn in a fashion Bryan recognized after a beat as Central American. One figure, standing, dangled a head from one hand. The other, kneeling, had no head. From the stump of the headless warrior's neck sprang snakes, and a strange, winding, branching form that seemed to represent a flowering tree.

Patel followed Bryan's gaze. "The ceiba tree grows from the blood of the sacrifice. The Mayan tree of life."

Bryan immediately thought of his father's rants. "Sacrifice? So we all start turning into trees?"

"No. At least not anytime soon." Patel tapped the screen. "This is a souvenir from a phenomological line of inquiry I and some of the other faculty have delved into, one that wouldn't be popular in certain circles. It has to do with how the Mayans conceived of blood. Blood was the fountain of youth and life. Blood was magical. Blood was the gate used by the powers in the underworld, which in their fanciful conception housed a central river and a variety of gods, not to mention a sacrificial basketball court."

"They used blood to make gates to the underworld?"

Patel regarded him levelly. "No. Blood *was* the gateway, once it was spilled. It was blood that allowed the underworld to come through into ours."

"What are you saying?"

"You know as well as I that no one has been able to figure out where this blood comes from. Yet I'm inclined to think it's not coincidence that so much human ceremony regards the spilling of blood as essential to otherworldly transfiguration. The Mayans were especially eager for the power the underworld brought. The literature tells of ten thousand captives slain in a day." He put a hand on his throat. "They had yokes they clamped on the necks of sacrifices that cut off blood to the brain. When the sacrifice collapsed, a dagger to the heart. As efficient as any modern slaughterhouse."

A nervous laugh escaped Bryan's throat. "The Mayans understood the Blessings? How is that even possible?"

"I am not saying they understood it. I am only saying what we're dealing with perhaps isn't new to humanity. Perhaps this phenomenon has ancient roots, and some cultures were more in tune with its principles than others. Though if the Mayans were truly on to something, it's hard to glean."

Bryan contemplated the branches sprouting from the severed neck. "Great. Now I'm going to dream about all that."

The professor's smirk returned. "Assuming you do dream at all."

BRYAN FOUND THE old routine a comfort, even the acts of stripping, piling the contents of his pockets on the bedside table, tying on the ridiculous hospital gown. Dr. Patel's assistants did their work quickly: electrodes stuck with adhesive to his bare scalp, the sides of his face, under his chin, on his chest and left leg; a sensor by his nose and mouth, to monitor breathing; a belt strapped around his ribs and abdomen to register the movement of his breath; a clip lightly pinching the index finger, tracking oxygen in his blood. At Patel's request, he blinked, took deep breaths, helped calibrate the equipment.

The eye of the camera floated above him. If the drug had taken hold, he couldn't tell.

"Bryan, you remember the signals?" Patel's voice, piped in from the control room.

"Eyes right to left, twice when I'm dreaming, five times when I'm awake. I'll count seconds if I can."

"Everything's working, doctor." A woman's voice, picked up by the control-room mic. Higher pitched than the other. Her name is Pegah, Bryan thought hazily.

His room felt cozy—much like a motel room, but pristine. The black box next to the bed, the one all the electrodes led to, emitted a soothing hum. The amniotic red space behind his closed eyelids faded softly to black.

"I will know when I'm dreaming. I will remember what I dream. I will remember what I dream."

He walked the empty streets of the City of Mazes, with its towers like teeth, the ribs of its arches, doors like sphincters, eaves like cheekbones, gutters like stretched intestines, streets merging and splitting at impossible angles, the corners of buildings deadly as razor blades. His shoes splashed in dark puddles, the sound echoing from vacant storefronts.

Seeing this place, this horror from his childhood, badly rattled him. But he knew he dreamed. He counted, one two three beats, moved his eyes: right, left, right, left.

Above him, the clouded sky roiled, bruised-meat haze. One two three right left right left. He heard a heartbeat, presumably his own, though as he walked the noise grew louder. Another noise, the sound of something sliding. Snake on its belly. *I know that I am dreaming. I will remember what I dream.*

A thin cord brushed his face, a spider thread; he backed away, flailing. How could he not have seen it, this glistening red string stretched in front of him? Many of them, twitching like fishing line, reeling something in, dragged through the muck behind him. One two three right left right left. He turned.

Shapes thrashed behind him, slimy cocoons drawn forward by the glistening red wires. Were these the marionette people, pulled from the grave of his childhood by some unseen puppeteer to haunt him again? *Stop*, he thought, and the threads broke. *I know that I am dreaming.*

And then the threads reattached, and the forms slid past him, men and women crusted and scabbed, mouths open in silent shrieks. He stepped after them, called *Stop!* as they disappeared into the expanding shadow ahead, where the heartbeat grew louder, louder, louder. Right left one two three.

Something was happening that had never happened when he dreamed this before.

The buildings before him caved into a growing sinkhole. Architecture suppurated, bricks and mortar sloughed off like corpse skin as a thunderous heartbeat shook the world. The City of his childhood nightmares, consumed in a whirlpool, a hurricane pit with a devouring heart for an eye. Bryan teetered as the edge of the great hole raced at him, a reverse tsunami that sucked down all it touched. *I will remember what I dream. Stop. Stop! STOP!*

His command changed nothing. The expanding abyss had its own will. He couldn't control it. Beyond the edge a new nightmare teemed, worms under pressure at the bottom of a well, slithering over each other in suffocated madness. The hole grew and grew, as fast as he could flee, the things at the bottom boiling at him like lava. Bryan screamed in his bed of electrodes as he plummeted into the squirming maelstrom, as the underworld swallowed him.

The first living man to enter their realm, unwitting, unwilling sacrifice, found no rivers, no castles, no gods. Just the pressure. The pressure. *The pressure* that crushed his lungs, jellied his stomach, bent and squashed his limbs as the thick red worms swarmed over him.

In seconds he was airless fathoms beneath their mass, the weight of a billion slick serpents pushing against him, thrusting into him. He thrashed and spat helplessly as an eyeless snout forced its way into his mouth, burst his throat from the inside.

"Bryan!" Hands shook his shoulders, yanked the electrodes from his head. Cold water on his face. A slap. Harder.

Bryan sat up, blood drenched. The Blessings dripped from his forehead. *The pressure.* He couldn't breathe. *The pressure.*

But he could still see the great worms. Crawling behind the walls, above the ceiling tile, beneath the floor. He felt them in his veins, nightcrawlers bunching and stretching inside the cavities of his body.

He had become their dream.

And when he knew that, he knew them, a terrible knowledge that bloomed in his brain, branches of a many-tendrilled tree. They writhed within him, these primordial powers that had grown in strength since mankind first awakened to sentience, phantasmal beasts that gorged on flesh-tearing violence; mindless creatures the ignorant spilled offerings to without ever fully understanding the things they fed, misnaming them as gods, massacring thousands in order to feel just a fraction of the sensation electrifying Bryan's viscera.

The accumulated slaughters of the modern age had so swollen these beasts of blood, placed them under such crushing pressure, their residue had begun to seep out of the underworld, drip into the land of flesh. They drenched him in their cravings, eager to ride their captive completely out of dream. Their searing hunger coursed in the fluids of his heart, eyes, spine, bled from the pores of his skin…

He opened his mouth to tell Raj, to scream a warning, *They're dreaming me now*, and gurgled as blood sprayed from his throat.

"Call an ambulance," Patel barked. Sonoko ran to the booth outside, as Pegah helped the professor lower their charge back onto the bloodied mattress. Bryan had an arm around his friend's shoulders, clutching at him like a drowning man clings to driftwood.

And yet he couldn't be saved from drowning. Their desires submerged him, flooded all corners of his mind and body. He was the breach in the dam and having found him they couldn't force their way through fast enough. No reason motivated them other than the overpowering urge to be born, and he would widen the fracture. He would be the first vessel ruptured open to relieve the pressure but not the last.

Could Patel see how he cried tears of blood, how he was nothing but stigmata from head to toe? "I'm sorry, my friend," Patel said. "I could not have imagined this would happen."

Bryan bubbled back, "I'm sorry, sorry, sorry," as the worms that ruled his flesh guided his hand, found the pocketknife on the bedside table, brought it to the professor's neck.

As Patel stumbled away, life spurting through his fingers, Bryan subdued the Iranian assistant, clamped his free hand around Pegah's windpipe, squeezed away any possible noise.

He didn't know what made Sonoko drop the receiver; the sight of him as he dashed into the lab, compelled by his puppeteers, or the view into the sleep room through the one-way glass, where a dark hydra rose from the spreading blood like a monstrous tree and stretched a dozen hungry necks.

Bryan dragged her into the room by the black cords of her hair, pulled her under the shadow of the beast with many heads and no face, offspring of consciousness and bloodlust, and opened her to it. The reward of the serpent's pleasure rushed through him as it drank. He shuddered, moaned: millions had died for just a sliver of *this.*

The hydra swelled to fill the room, and he fell to his knees before it, for the first time in his life awestruck, for the first time in his life a true believer.

THE DERELICT LAY curled in the stairwell again, filthy beneath the merciless fluorescent light. Bryan showed the man a mercy, watched in mute rapture as the black fluid escaped its shabby house of flesh. It swam upward from the exit he had made, a tentacle of blood spiraling through the air to join its new master.

He had called Regina and left a message as he departed the lab. "Stay with me again tonight. I need you. You still have the key?"

Her answer, *yes i'll be there.*

Regina, his love, who could believe without evidence or proof, would surely become his first convert. The first to understand the lesson: that the bloodstained feeling he had foolishly agonized over for so long was not a stain at all, but the wondrous sprouting of a long-gestated seed, the birth of a true Tree of Life, a Lord whose existence could not be doubted.

The door was unlocked. Eager red tendrils coiled around and around his hand as he turned the knob. His master followed him inside.

She watched his approach, wide-eyed and tremulous. Her silence could have been reverence.

HUMPTY

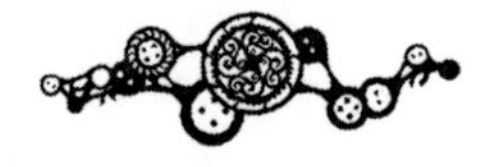

"Michael. Michael, wake up."

Soft-paw caresses gently shook me awake. I crawled from the sludge of dream-sleep, my body still soaked through with the movement-suppressing drugs of slumber. I only vaguely sensed the weight upon my chest.

A long snake-like limb jabbed at my face. I jerked my head up from the pillow.

Humpty smiled, his ragged teeth like shards of broken glass. One of his serpentine arms twisted forward to scratch me under the chin. "Rise and shine," he tittered. A sickly green glow burned in place of his missing eye, blinking shut in time with his laughter.

It's my oldest childhood memory:

The bars of my crib slice a cage of shadow out of the moonlight shining through my window. The air feels thick as a pillow, wet and hot, all sound muffled, a wall of silence sealing me from my father, who's sleeping in the room across the hall; the night congealed so dense not even an insect could scuttle through its murk.

Humpty crouches over me, his button eyes and felt smile an idiot mask, his blue-striped arms coiling slowly around my throat.

I pull him off and throw him out of the crib. He makes no noise when he strikes the hardwood floor. I stand up, my hands clamping around the comforting solidity of the crib rail, and watch my new enemy right himself.

He gets up on all fours, his spindly tubular limbs arched around his egg-shaped body like spider's legs. His face tips up to look at me, then he scurries underneath the crib. When I turn around he's climbing up the bars, his limbs coiling and uncoiling like monkeys' tails, his idiotic grin unchanged.

When he reaches the top of the rail I tear him from the bars and toss him away. Immediately he rights himself again, spidery limbs splayed around him, and ascends the bars of the crib. He's fast, but neither heavy nor strong. I throw him down, over and over and over again, each time watching as he recovers his balance and scurries back.

I don't remember how the conflict ended. I'd always assumed I was recalling a nightmare.

"IT TOOK ME ages to find you."

His voice was deep, gravelly, but fused with a oddly whiny desperation, and it sounded as if it came from around a corner somewhere, not from the toothy grin sparkling before me. "You should thank the Creator I've come in time," he said.

My own voice came out a croak. "What are you going to do?"

"You didn't understand then. Why would you now?" The red glare from my alarm clock glinted off his teeth. How dangerous was he, in this new form? Could I just toss him away?

"I'm glad you came to help," I said, scanning the room. No bars etched in moonlight entrapped me. The clutter of familiar objects served to further convince me this was no dream: My guitar with both E-strings unstrung, sprawled on top of the clutter of my desk, awaiting my attention. The picture of Melissa on my bedside table, trapped behind cracked glass I hadn't yet gotten around to replacing. The grinning-skull poster she gave me just last week, taped to the door that leads onto the balcony. The dirty uniform of my dreaded burger-flipping employment, strewn limp across the foot of my bed.

"Then maybe you'll listen to me?" His green eye-cavity kindled bright.

"Yes," I said, and grabbed for him. His teeth closed around my wrist.

THE MORNING AFTER that endless nightmare in my crib, I begged my father to get rid of the doll.

"You love that doll. You've had it since before your mother died." He glared down at me, the corners of his jaw flexing. When I grew older I would learn to recognize that tensing of his jawline as an involuntary warning, an outward sign that his annoyance had reached a dangerous edge. "You'll be whining for it back as soon as I throw it in the trash."

"No, Dad. It tried to hurt me."

"What?" He hunched toward me, his teeth showing as he spoke.

"It came to life. It wanted to hurt me."

"What? What did you say?" His face twisted in a rictus. He lunged. He'd boiled over so suddenly I had no chance to react, but instead of reaching for me he pulled the Humpty doll out of my crib. "You don't want this any more?" He tore an arm off the doll. It made a meek thread-popping sound as it was mutilated.

I started to wail; I hadn't yet learned not to. This only egged my father on. He was panting through his teeth, the rush of the kill taking over.

Humpty's oval body split at the seams, and I thought I saw a yellow vapor pour out from the wound, pour into my father through his mouth, eyes, ears. A final roar of effort from my father's throat, and Humpty's white innards sprayed everywhere. I screamed.

"Won't hurt you now, will he?"

I looked up into my father's lunatic eyes. This time, he reached for me.

HUMPTY'S TEETH SHATTERED against my skin. As wicked as they looked, they were fragile as eggshells. My hand closed on *something*, stuffing, intestines, a tongue. I sprang from the bed and pushed open the sliding doors. He'd been able to climb back over the rails of my crib; but a fall from a fifth-story balcony into the traffic of Salem Boulevard, still busy even at this time of night, would present a more formidable challenge. Not to mention the wind that blows so cold and hard at this height, a wind that would sweep my tiny friend into God-knew-what predicament.

But only silence and darkness greeted me beyond the balcony. Empty heat stifled the air. No half-shaded windows ogled me sleepily from across the street, no bloodstream flow of headlights washed the boulevard. I'd walked out onto a perch offering a view of a vast, empty stage. What was worse, the structure housing my apartment continued down into darkness, a featureless pillar, no other balconies or lights adorning it.

The piece of Humpty in my grip squirmed. I tossed him aside with a yell. He propped himself up on all fours in his spiderlike manner, his face oriented topside. His mouth opened and closed, his gums flexing like a shark's, new teeth popping in to replace the broken ones.

"Explain this," I demanded, grateful my voice didn't shake.

"I was trying to when you attacked me." He used the balcony grillwork to pull himself upright. "You are in metareality. The auxiliary macrocosm of the timestream you inhabit. Connected events that you would normally experience as single points along the long straight line of your existence are directly linked here, grouped into wholes through the grace of a higher dimension. We're at the heart of everything, here. And everything here, is *you*."

I barely heard him. A pall of familiarity had settled over this strange new landscape. The mottled plain I perceived far below might be nothing more than a mite's-eye view of carpet. The pillar we looked out from, and the identical ones looming to either side, nothing more than bars of a crib.

An evil shape, unimaginably huge, approached through the greater darkness, its titanic footfalls muffled by the stagnant air. Amorphous, mottled with shifting light and shadow, it towered into the gray sky. I backed away, meaning to hide, but Humpty whispered, "No! Stay. Watch."

From behind us, a burst of blue light suddenly cast the shifting form into full relief—my father, his broad bare chest, his thin sinewy arms, bulbous belly, the malformed moon of his face. He opened his mouth and an orange jack-o'-lantern glow gushed in a stream from his throat. Behind us, a horrible scream rose, as my father's ectoplasmic vomitus bored through a sudden blue light, and I screamed too, in recognition.

It felt like a tongue, a sandpapery cat's tongue, scouring me out from the inside.

Hollowing me out…

My father's demon visage hovered over me, his skull outlined in flame beneath his skin, a monstrous sun over the well of my crib. That stream of yellow spiraling out of his mouth, burrowing into me. I knew the blue shining out of me was my defense, my only way to fend him off, but I didn't know how to use it. I didn't know how.

"Good," Humpty whispered. "You remember. But do you understand?"

The stage was empty again; my father had vanished.

"Understand what? What was he doing to me?"

"You don't know, Michael? After all *you've* done?"

The temptation to hurl my tormentor off the balcony returned. I thought about how his strange flesh would feel, tearing apart underneath my grip. "You're on thin ice. I don't care what kind of little god you might be here. Don't talk in circles. Tell me what this is about."

Humpty curled his limbs into the grillwork of the rail. His smoldering eye-socket winked at me. "I should have known. Here inside your macrocosm, you're insulated from who you are. Here, you're what you want to be."

"You're full of shit."

"No, foam." He grinned. All his teeth were restored. "So who are you, really? And whose apartment are we in?"

I knelt down to glare at this demon from my past, eyes to eye. "My name is Michael Carver. And this is my apartment. If you weren't in my head, I'd be looking down on Salem Boulevard right now."

"Wrong. This is Melissa's apartment. Or at least that's the name she gave you. If you weren't outside space-time, the view you'd see from here would be the view you had when you tipped her body out over the street."

A worm slithered inside me. Humpty casually unwound one of his arms, held out a hand as if offering change to a beggar. "Would you like me to tell you what you did to her before you pitched her into the dark?"

My fingers crooked into claws. "This is a dream, and this is a lie."

"The T-shirt you're wearing." His free hand tugged at my collar. "It belongs to Jerry Coolidge. You remember him?"

"My name is Michael Carver. I live here above Salem Boulevard. I fucking flip burgers for a living, stay home at night and try to write music. I've even sold jingles to a local auto dealership."

"You met Jerry at...the kind of establishment you frequent, and invited him back to your domicile, which looks nothing like this. He even agreed to the handcuffs. Then you strangled him."

I grabbed for himm—his teeth gnashed, even more of them shattering—but my fingers were suddenly on fire. When I held my hand up, the slashes across my knuckles were outlined in radioactive green. They faded as I watched, the sting that accompanied them lingering a few seconds more.

"See," he said, "I'm more dangerous then you think. Just hear me out."

"No. My name is Michael Carver. These calluses on my hands come from plucking guitar strings, thinking notes out loud. I would never do what you're accusing me of."

"But you do, all the time. You don't flip burgers, Michael. You work in a slaughter house. You line up the necks of turkeys so that the spinning blades cut their throats. The little peeping sound they make when they die drives you absolutely ape. You couldn't even finger the first chord on a guitar neck. Carver isn't even your last name. It's what you *do*."

My insides writhed. "That's not true."

Humpty's fiery eye-socket narrowed. "Would you like it not to be true?"

What if it wasn't a dream? What if it wasn't? "Yes. Okay. How?"

"We have to leave this place."

Whether I was dreaming or truly in another universe, it made sense to me to follow this homunculus from my childhood and bring this nightmare to a quick end. And wake up to what? Fingering guitar strings above a flow of headlights, or dried blood, sweat, and a stink of death in my pores?

Strutting like a majorette, he lead me out into a featureless hallway that terminated in stairs. "They're steep," he remarked. "Be careful."

The stairs plunged in a tight spiral. Their texture gradually changed, from the rugged carpeting of my apartment complex to the warped and creaking boards of my grandfather's house, that conglomeration of peeling plaster and rotting wood where my father raised me. Humpty scurried before me on all fours.

I called down to him, "Why are you helping me? I made my father shred you into pieces."

The glint of green that was his eye-socket paused in shadow. "There's no more time. Even using the shortcut of your macrocosm, I nearly found you too late." He continued his descent. "Right now, within the bounds of normal space-time, the police are on their way to your flat. And they're going to find the things you have stuffed under your bed. And they'll find what you have soaking in your bathtub."

"I told you I haven't done anything."

"Once they find those things, once you're caught, it's all over. Too many other time-streams mingled with yours. It won't be possible to fix what your father did."

We emerged from a portal, began a hike across the convoluted terrain of sheets and blankets. Cresting a fold, I beheld the remains of my childhood. The body I wore in infancy, a boneless shell, a shriveled egg case. Empty eyeholes stared in wildly different directions from my collapsed, deflated face.

"He's in there," Humpty said. Your father."

We ascended the spongy slope of a boneless cheek, lowered ourselves into the fleshy cavern of an empty eye. "He lives here now," said Humpty. "If you want to save yourself, you'll have to evict him."

"How?" No answer came. Humpty had vanished, swallowed up, it seemed, in the folds of my childhood's hollowed-out husk. This abandonment brought only a moment's panic, quickly replaced by relief. That creature was no source of nostalgia; I was glad he'd left me.

I continued the descent, intent on bringing this ordeal to its conclusion. I clambered down through the optic nerve channel, through a heavy wooden trapdoor, into a space I assumed to be my own skull cavity. But it was my father's cluttered study, a room I'd only seen via forbidden glimpses through a keyhole while my father was still alive. The same room where he'd finally had his heart attack.

He was seated at his desk, digging a fountain pen into a cut on his hand, using the blood to write in a book. All at once he started, looked up at me and bellowed, "What the *hell* are you doing in here?"

"This is my universe," I said. "You don't belong in it."

"The hell I don't. I created everything here, including you." He stood up.

"You scooped this out of me. You stole the life that belonged to me." I could feel the blue aura building inside me that I'd been helpless to use as a child, that I never had learned to use.

"Shut up!" Fire erupted from his mouth. Suddenly I was blind. I stumbled over something and fell, my face a mask of pain. My vision returned, blurred with agony. He stood over me, smoke streaming from his eyes, mouth radiating red from the magma heat inside him.

Blue light reflected from the polished floor, that glow coming out of me, and I was helpless, unable to strike with it, unable to comprehend how. My frustration imploded into the purest rage I've ever felt. I came roaring up, seizing the leg of the lamp table as I rose. The lamp shattered on the floor as I swung the table at my father's head. The blow connected, the impact jarring my elbow, wrenching my shoulder; then the table exploded in a burst of fire.

The force threw me against a wall. I felt a hundred splinters embed themselves. I screamed. A stack of storage crates collapsed on top of me, their weight crushing the air out of my lungs. Humpty's idiot smile leered at me, his torn-up remains spilled from one of the boxes.

I grasped one of his long cloth arms.

My father loomed over me, grinning, gloating. He opened his mouth to breathe. I hooked his ankle with mine, and sent him sprawling. He grunted like a boar when he landed. I sprang on him before he could recover, and wrapped Humpty's arm around his throat.

He drew in breath to blast me, but I twisted my arm-tourniquet tighter. He thrashed, his face purpling. The smoke from his eyes fizzled to nothing, leaving empty sockets.

Humpty's arm twitched in my grip.

I cried out, jumped back. Instead of releasing, the arm began to tighten of its own accord.

My father's face withered like paper set aflame. First smoke rose from his chest, then flickers of combustion, then a roaring fire. I scrambled to find a door, but I couldn't see for the smoke. The soot from my father's pyre filled my lungs, and the chaos of the scene drifted away.

* * *

"WELL, BROTHER, I have to thank you." Humpty sat on my chest, whole again, his ruptured stitches repaired with shimmering threads of ethereal yellow, that essence I'd seen my father swallow so long ago. "You're free now. We're both free now."

We were back in my bedroom—or was it Melissa's? Mine, I decided. "You. You were my father's familiar. His magic totem. His power source." A vast shape squatted on the bed, something hunched and multilimbed and only vaguely humanoid, formed of nothing more than pinpricks of darkness. Its convoluted anatomy corresponded with the doll's in only one place—the wide, glass-filled mouth.

"So you can see me. What I really am. You could never do that before." I felt the combined weight of his two forms squeezing out my breath. "I never enjoyed being owned. Your father was strong, as you are strong. You would not believe what I went through, to sneak a way out of your private hell, to bring you in. Now we can both leave."

"Get off me. Please."

"Your innocence has always been so delectable. I've always known that if I could claim your strength I could escape. But under your father's iron fist I was too weak. No more. No weakness now."

He began his four-limbed spider crawl toward me. The vast black shape shifted above me. I tried to throw him off, but he was too heavy.

His teeth closed around my face.

I AWAKEN IN Melissa's apartment. Mine, as well—we live together. I hear her breath rasping beside me. Her face, round and beautiful, is rendered ghoulish in the green illumination. The greenish glow is emanating from me.

I get up, go to the sliding doors that lead to the balcony, stare at my reflection in the glass. Green embers smolder in one hollow eye-socket. My own idiot smile flashes back at me.

A great form composed of darkness looms behind me, the pitch black of its presence matched only by the abyss of hunger that yawns inside me, that causes me to turn to my sleeping partner with a new appreciation for her innocence.

HER ACRES OF PASTORAL PLAYGROUND

Lynda chews her peas. Her husband watches, his wary gaze fixed on the beauty mark beneath her left eye, no bigger than a felt-tip stipple, fetching accent to the delicate sweep of her cheekbone.

When Delmar first placed her plate in front of her, that mark wasn't there.

"Your pork chop okay?" he asks. "Not too dry?"

She nods, mutters "It's fine" through a mouthful. The muscles at her temples flex as she chews, drawing his attention to the lovely streaks of gray that flare above her ears, so exotic, so witchy—the angles of her project into his mind just so and a sleepy flutter of lust stirs deep within him. And a flutter of alarm, too, though why that is, he doesn't understand.

Then the black spot on her face moves. It's larger now, no longer a beauty mark, a lumpy mole with a thick black hair sprouting from its center. The hair twitches again, like a bug's antenna.

A whippoorwill starts its saw-motion song outside as a warm breeze stirs the kitchen curtains. Through the window Delmar notes two of the Appaloosas grazing in the pasture closest to the barn. Despite the brooding, overcast sky, sunlight washes the farm in soft watercolor hues.

Lynda picks up her ear of corn, peers out the window just as a faint spatter of rain belies the filtered sunlight.

"The Devil's beating his wife," she says. "Meaghan would love this. I hope she's better soon."

"She will be," Delmar replies. He says it automatic, like it's a programmed response, a catechism. The growth on the side of his wife's face thickens into an articulated tentacle, long as a tablespoon, and like one of those it flares and bulges at its end. The growth waves up and down as if it's sniffing the air. Lynda brings the cob to her mouth, paying no attention to her new deformity.

Delmar goes to the stove, where he has set a wooden-handled butcher knife so that the top half of its blade rests on a red hot coil. He picks up the knife. "Honey, I'm sorry, but I need you to hold still a second."

What he does next he does with the impassive face of the parent who must every day hold his daughter with cystic fibrosis upside down and beat her to make sure she can breathe another day. Lynda holds still, closes her eyes, seems to *shut down*, almost. When he finishes, there's a raw circle on her cheek, like a cross-section of severed sausage, bloodless, and in seconds it's stretched over with new skin, pink and healthy. She starts again as if nothing has happened, picks up her ear of corn and starts to gnaw.

The black thing squirming in Delmar's hands screams when he drops it in the pot, but he clamps the lid over the boiling water before it can crawl out. Before it can speak. He knows he can't let it speak. *Why* he knows this, he can't really say; it's as if someone is whispering in his ear, whispering frantically, *don't let it, don't let it, don't let it*, but there's no one else in the room, just him and Lynda.

Outside, the rain-sound stops, and the landscape brightens, though the clouds stay gray as ever.

"Sweetie," calls Lynda, "could you bring me the butter?"

"You bet," he says, keeping the pot lid pressed down hard. "In a minute. Just a minute." He eyes her sidelong. "Just don't forget who loves you."

She smiles wide over the decimated contents of her plate. "I haven't. Ever."

AFTER LUNCH, HE trudges out to the vegetable garden, not a trouble on his mind. Though there's no break in the clouds, the light that so kindly warms his land makes its gentle presence known on his face. Most of his farm is given over to pastureland—he likes to joke to Lynda that he's renting from the horses—but he keeps a half-acre tilled, and the animals, with preternatural discretion, leave it alone. He's never even had to put a fence around it.

He's imagining a sweaty but productive day spent plucking hungry bugs off the potato leaves, pulling weeds from between the beanstalks, harvesting the ripest ears of corn. How easy the work comes to him, a lifestyle he once knew only from the half-listened-to tales—more like shaggy-dog complaints, really, long growly rants with no real point—from his grouchy father, God rest his soul. Delmar agrees now with his father, that he really was born to this work. He can hardly remember his life before he brought Lynda and Meaghan here.

The corn rows tower at the edge of the tilled square furthest from the house. He gets to that task last of all, and once he's there something in him grows uneasy, and a sensation crawls through his shoulders—like the prick, prick, prick when a wasp alights and starts to scurry across exposed flesh—but he feels this on the inside of his skin, not the outside.

And at once his mind fills with the sight of the black limb twitching on his wife's face. The texture of her flesh when he cut into it, spongy and yielding not a speck of blood. He doubles over, his insides pricking, but that voice is back, soothing in his ear, *Don't think about it, just don't think about it, don't let yourself think about it.*

And though his heart is racing, he can stand up straight. The pricking sensation is gone. He breathes deep, his eyes take in the beauty that surrounds him, the grass-green slopes, the fecund garden, thriving as a result of his proud handiwork. Yet he's still not at ease.

Beyond the corn lounges a long stretch of pasture that the animals hardly ever visit. Beyond that rises a gray haze of fog. He thinks nothing of it—this wall of fog is always there, misting up in a thick curtain to join with the low-hanging clouds overhead.

Instead, a spark of light in the pasture catches his eye, orange and pulsing like fireplace embers. A brush fire? Couldn't be. Something pricks in his belly, once, sharp, and stops.

His boots whisk softly through the grass.

For as long as he can remember, there's been an oddity present in this particular pasture, a blackened spot, perfectly circular, about the size of a manhole, where nothing grows. *It's a lightning strike*, that internal voice always tells him, whenever he gets close. *Nothing special. Not important.*

But now the burnt circle in the ground has rekindled. He comes upon it to find it alive with curling lines of pulsating orange and yellow light. Stranger still, the lines etched by the glow form patterns, some of which he recognizes, though it's as if a brick barrier stands in his mind between recognition and understanding. The patterns throb.

A sound from the fog bank. A sob.

The pricking beneath his skin returns. Delmar takes a step toward the foggy veil, despite the voice whispering, *Stay away. Stay far away.*

"Who's out there?" he means to shout, but the sound barely leaves his throat.

The sobbing within the fog continues. It's unquestionably the sound of a man, weeping.

Delmar goes pale. It's been months at least since he's heard another human voice out here. There's been no one save him and his wife and his daughter, safe from the rest of the world, the way he's wanted it to be. Confusion and anger and that hideous pricking fear all slither inside him.

Worse, he thinks he recognizes the voice, but he can't place it. The man's sobs grow louder, the sound of someone unhinged with grief, a father finding a child's murdered body in the trunk of a car.

Delmar takes another step toward the gray wall. "Get out of here," he says, louder, but still not with the strength he'd like. "You're trespassing. Go back where you came."

The man in the fog starts to scream. It's a sound ripped from the belly, and the screams keep coming, like the man is being shredded inside by something small and burrowing. And Delmar has heard this agony before, this man screaming in torture, and he covers his ears, because he can almost make out words. He reels and steps back—

No, no, no! hisses the voice in his ear.

He looks down. He nearly stepped into the black circle, which is no longer burning, no longer glowing. And he shudders. He doesn't know why, but he knows he should never step in the circle. Never cross its edge.

The screams in the fog have gone silent. He feels no desire to know who it was, whose voice shrieked from the fog, no more than he feels desire to know why that fog never moves, why the sky never clears.

Go to your family. Love them. Let them love you.

And he goes back to the garden, not a trouble on his mind. Before the light starts to fade, he's filled a big wooden basket full of fresh-picked ears of corn. He'll shuck them so Lynda can slice off the kernels and can them. They like to do this together, let their smiles do all the speaking. They'll do it tomorrow. He so looks forward to it.

BUT THINGS IN the house take a turn for the worse. His heart won't settle. His mind won't stay quiet.

Dinner goes wonderfully enough, built around two thick steaks he set out to thaw early that morning. He even speaks to Meaghan for a little while once the rich meal lulls her mom into an evening doze. While Lynda slumps comatose at her end of the sofa he settles comfortably at the other end and listens to his daughter's high, sweet voice sing the alphabet, or mouth nonsense syllables to the same calliope tune, and he feels consciousness drifting off.

An electric hum accompanies a constant, steady rattling. It takes him a moment to place what he's hearing: the rapid-fire click-click-click of a home movie projector. Delmar hasn't heard that noise since his twelfth birthday, when his father dug out that seemingly ancient machine to show the gathering of school chums embarrassing footage of the family dog wrapping her leash around a younger Delmar's stumpy legs.

It's now Delmar's father who sits with him, hunched at the other end of the couch. His father's head turns on a neck mutated by swelling cancer lumps. *You asked me to dig out this one,* his father says, the sound coming through the surgery hole in his throat. *Don't whine to me. This is all your cross to bear.*

The beam from the heard-but-not-seen projector shines on a wall of fog that conceals the other side of the room. Distorted on the fog, Meaghan's face flickers in close-up, framed by straight dark hair just like her mother's. The footage is black and white, rendering her bright green eyes a moist gray. He recognizes her unicorn pajamas.

A large hairy arm, a man's arm, reaches into frame, takes her wrist. Her eyes bug, her face contorts. Delmar feels the prickling inside as the huge hand turns her wrist palm up, as another hand, the right to match the left, stabs a butcher blade into her forearm, slices a long black line.

All this has unfolded free of all sound save the rattling projector, but when Meaghan's mouth stretches open to scream it's loud and piercing and absolutely real.

Delmar starts awake. Lynda is beside him on the couch, still comatose. Meaghan screams again, somewhere in the house. Lynda doesn't stir.

Delmar can't bring himself to move, paralyzed by a gut-dragging-and-twisting spin of disorientation. He can't remember a time when he's heard Meaghan's voice without Lynda close by, and he knows something is wrong with that, really wrong, and the voice that protects him is saying that too, that something's wrong, he can't really be hearing that. Yet upstairs—she has to be upstairs—she cries again, "Dadd-eeeeeeee!"

The noise as raw and loaded with pain as if she's fallen on a bed of nails.

He runs for the stairs pell-mell. His daughter screams again, the sound like pins stabbed into his eardrums. When he reaches her bedroom door, her shrieks hardly sound human.

But he throws the door open, and she isn't there. There's nothing there. The room is empty, even of furniture.

Meaghan shrieks again. Now, the noise comes from downstairs.

The voice in his ear is whispering, *It's gotten out of control. You need the book. You need to get it* now.

Delmar doesn't understand what the voice wants. Or something in him doesn't want to understand.

At Meaghan's next howl, he plunges back down the stairs. But stops halfway.

On the couch, in Lynda's place, a monster writhes, a black sunburst of ropy worms. The shrieks he hears are coming from somewhere in its center. It lurches to the floor, dozens of snaky limbs flopping blind, turning over lamps and end tables, capsizing the tv.

The book, hisses the voice in his ear. This time, he understands, and knows he has to obey.

He dashes through the den, toward the hall and the utility room at its end, but one of the black ropes twines his ankles, and then the thing is pulling itself on top of him, wailing in Meaghan's voice. Keening syllables that are almost words.

His bare hands tear at the cables of black flesh sliding against his skin, but it's as if two tendrils replace each one he breaks, lashing around his forearms and thighs and belly, struggling to hold him still. The thing is still screaming, now with Lynda's voice. A snake-smooth band of contracting muscle coils around his neck, starts to tighten.

But he is stronger. He shoves to his knees, rips out the boneless limbs by their roots, hurls the thrashing tangle across the room.

Lynda screams, screams, screams.

He returns from the utility room with a huge book, its leather binding on the verge of crumbling, its pages flopping as he holds it open. The symbols in dark brown ink mean nothing to him, though they radiate a head-spinning wrongness. If these scribblings form words, he doesn't know what they say—and yet he does. It's as if another person inside him uses his eyes to see, his mouth to speak, knows the precise rhythms and pauses. And as this happens the squealing black thing in the den begins to foam, to buck, to lengthen and thicken and lighten in hue. Delmar's vision blurs, with tears that he understands no more than he does the incantation.

His voice rises in crescendo, and all the space around him seems to ripple, in a way that can't be seen physically—yet his mind still senses it. The ripple starts where he's standing and spreads through the room, the house, even the land beyond, and he knows that the power in that subtle wave is setting things to right. The voice tells him so.

The black thing is gone. There's only Lynda, resting peaceful on the couch, her only motion the soft rise and fall of her breath. There is no sign of Meaghan, but the voice is telling him not to worry about that. He might not see her, yet whenever he asks, she'll speak, and he'll know she still loves him.

Lynda's limp as a bag of straw, but he's strong enough to lift her. He carries her to bed.

Using the book always makes him uneasy—vaguely, he recalls he's had to before—but now all is restored. Outside, there are no stars, but neither is there darkness. Just as with the sunlight, an unseen moon bathes his farmland in its shine. He can make out the shapes of the horses, straight-legged and still, possibly sleeping.

He snuggles in beside his lovely, witchy wife, no troubles on his mind, and settles his head in the pillows.

He's back on the sofa, and behind him the projector rattles. Meaghan sits next to him, kicking her legs, which don't quite touch the hardwood floor. *I asked grandpa to get this out again,* she says. *We haven't watched it since forever.*

The film unspools in grainy black and white, just like before. But now it resembles hidden camera footage, the view angled down from a corner of the ceiling. From this vantage the disembodied observer peers into a large room with cinder block walls, its carpet and other objects, mostly large plastic toys—a playhouse, a hobby horse, a Sit 'N Spin—shoved hastily against the far wall to bare the cement floor. Three figures huddle at the center of the bare floor, a man, a woman, a girl maybe seven years old. And the man has a book, a huge ominous tome. There is a small window in the far wall, placed high, indicating a basement room. The window is just out of the camera's range of clear focus. Beyond it, through dingy glass, shadows move with chaotic fury. Sometimes blinding light flares there. Sometimes the window goes completely dark.

The man is drawing frantically on the ground. The film speeds, somehow recorded in time lapse, an effect that drastically accelerates the chaos seen in silhouette through the high window. The man completes a huge circle inscribed along its entire circumference with headache-inducing sigils. The circle encloses him and the woman and child.

"You were always so good at drawing when you worked at that school," Meaghan says beside him.

"University," he corrects out of reflex.

She giggles. "I remember how you came home all the time with those weird drawings in your coloring book."

"Sketchpad, darling. It was a sketchpad."

"How you said you got 'em from some book you were studying and you never let me look at 'em. Never."

He turns to tell her to stop sounding mad, it was all for her own good, but she's gone. Yet he's not alone: he's looking at a copy of himself, but with bruises on his face, a cut down one cheek, dressed in an Oxford shirt with a deeply stained collar, a torn sweater vest, fancy slacks ruined by more flowing stains. He looks like an academic who just escaped from the mouth of Hell. He's dressed just like the man in the movie. He *is* the man in the movie.

I try to stop you from remembering, this new self says, *but you fight me. Some part of you is always warring with me, trying to remember everything. And when you do, you'll understand why you have to forget again. Understanding means madness.* The man's voice, the voice of this other self, is the voice he always hears whispering in times of terrible stress.

His guardian self keeps talking, but Delmar stops listening, because a new voice distracts him, murmuring right in his ear. It's Meaghan again; he can practically feel her lips against his skin. "Don't listen, Daddy. He can't stop you from knowing."

Delmar watches himself in the film, scrambling to draw a second, smaller circle, about the size of a manhole, at the center of the larger one. It's an agonizing, slow process, taking time even in time lapse, with the activity seen in shadow at the far window getting more and more frenzied, impossible to comprehend. Oftentimes the mother, who his mind admits is Lynda, must be Lynda, seems like she's having an exasperating time keeping the little girl inside the circle.

As Delmar watches, his immediate surroundings fade. Soon's there's nothing left but the picture show flickering on the fog and Meaghan's voice in his ear.

"Sweet Daddy. Don't you worry 'cause I still love you. I understand it all. You tried to use evil to do a good, good thing, but you had to be evil to use evil. But you did it 'cause you love us and love can be evil and good together."

The time lapse reverts to normal speed. In black and white, Delmar and Lynda are arguing. She turns hysterical, terrified as his gestures grow more frantic. In the background, unnoticed by either of them, the little window rattles. Darkens. Bizarrely, it looks like hair is growing around the frame.

The voice changes oh-so-subtly, still with the timbre of a child, but more adult, more knowing. "What you did was so powerful it could never work, never, without the blood of an innocent. I know, Daddy, I know."

In the film he screams, the contortion of his face grotesque in total silence, and his wife pushes his daughter toward him. He takes her wrist, produces the knife. Still unnoticed, the window pushes open, just a crack, and the hair-tendrils that have worked their way into the room begin to thicken and lengthen into streams, into ropes. Something huge is oozing through the gap around the glass, pouring down the wall as if made from soft clay.

"I should have been smarter, Daddy. I shouldn't have been so scared."

The image goes out of focus, becomes a crazy split screen, left and right visions going out of sync. In one lobe, Delmar, weeping as he chants, holds his daughter's bleeding arm over the inner circle, its black designs coming to life, shining, burning as the blood strikes it. In the other lobe, the window pane bows and shatters as a slimy mass of dense hairy jelly shoves its way through, unfurls in an explosion of sucking lamprey mouths and clusters of lidless human eyes.

Staring down from the corner again as the insanely hideous thing lands on the debris and springs—and it is as if the creature strikes a wall where the outer circle is drawn, as if it crashes straight into curved aquarium glass. The creature is not repelled by the barrier, but hangs there in the air, sticking to the invisible wall like a tarantula hugged against a fishbowl, its dozens of limbs splayed out radially from its squirming core, like a spider escaped from a deranged hallucination.

Delmar has released his daughter's arm. He's kneeling by the circle, the book beside him, cords standing out against his neck as he chants. And the little girl sees the horrid thing hanging in the air. And she screams. And she runs. Away from the center of the circle. She runs out of view of the disembodied ceiling observer, and the thing crawls so fast around and across the surface of the invisible barrier, scuttling spider-fast, as Lynda lurches too late to catch her daughter.

All through this, Meaghan's whisper has never stopped.

"Don't you want to know really why we love you so? Because you're just like us, just one of us, all part of us and us part of you. We ate you all up, we did. You made the spell work, you made the monster back into mommy and me with that magic from my blood, but we're still it and it's still in you, it's always been in you, changing you inside, one slow cell at a time, because your spell can't protect you that small."

The dream camera coldly documents what follows. The burst of dark fluid that sprays into the circle. A woman's severed arm lands on the floor, a foot lands another place, snakelike black limbs greedily snatch them up, gulp them down. The man's face a mask of horror, but he doesn't stop his chant, even as the multi-limbed thing joins him within the invisible aquarium, squeezing in through the opening made when the outer circle was fatally crossed. The dream-Delmar doesn't stop his chant, even when the creature sends long hooked limbs around the burning inner circle to hook into his vulnerable belly, punch in and drag out the gray ropes coiled inside. The man's face contorts in unspeakable agony and mystic ecstasy as he howls his final syllables. And it's at that moment that the inner circle surges in a pillar of blinding fire, and the film changes to color, *Wizard of Oz* technicolor.

"But Daddy, the part of us inside you is going to wake up. And then we'll be together like we should be and you'll never be alone again. You'll never, ever, ever be left alone. When you hear my voice, I'm saying other words too, words that you can't hear, but the sleeping part of me that's inside you can. It hears me and it wants to wake up. And when it does, that voice you always hear won't really be yours. It'll be ours. And we'll trick you, and you'll ruin the spell. We'll trick you, Daddy, when we wake up."

The burning circle, now a blackened spot in a beautiful pasture. And the man, his body whole, his clothes changed to suit his surroundings, picks himself up as he watches a black mass shrink and thicken and transform into a new, familiar shape. But only one shape. Never two.

And behind them, at the edge of the pasture, the fog. And above them, the grey clouds that will never, ever lift.

A tickling at his ear, a whisper.

"Wake up. Wake up. Wake up."

He springs awake and gropes for the lamp. The bulb casts its light across the comfortable contours of his bedroom.

His wife lies on her side, sleeping peacefully, her back to him, the cartoon cat on her favorite nightshirt flashing its inane grin.

From under her collar a dark tendril stretches, no thicker than a strand of yarn. Its end rests on his pillow, bulging out into a plush-lipped mouth that nestles beside the indentation where his head had rested. It continues to mouth words as if it doesn't know he's not there anymore.

Delmar trembles, staring at the tiny mutant mouth that murmurs in his daughter's voice. His eyes bulge. Tears smear his cheeks. All the barriers he's built inside his own mind to survive day to day in this world he created for his family, for what remains of them, have crumbled. He comprehends everything.

He only ever hears Meaghan's voice when it speaks from Lynda's body. Confronting this truth isn't what causes him such disgust and dismay. What rips deep inside him, aggravates once again that pricking beneath his skin: never before has that voice turned against him, said things that Meaghan herself would never have said.

He leaves the bedroom, comes back with the book. Sets it down. Sits on the edge of the bed beside Lynda, sets to work with a blow torch and knife. His tears never stop.

He returns to the book, starts to read aloud.

IT'S DARK BENEATH the ever-present clouds, but he knows the way. He walks across the verdant pastures that always stay green and thick with grass no matter how long the animals graze. He walks past the burnt circle, its ember glow patterns pulsating brighter than he's ever seen, a silent blare of strident warning. He leaves the circle behind, strides into the fog, consumed by the message he needs to deliver.

The rustling of his feet through the damp grass grows muffled in the dense mist, then fades altogether. It's as if his steps alight on the fog itself.

He takes ten strides, twenty, thirty, and then abrupt as a bird striking glass the fog ends. His land ends. The entire world ends.

Beyond the edge: an ocean of inhuman flesh, seen from undersea.

Just as the protective circle he drew in his horribly failed attempt to save his wife and daughter gave rise to a clear fishbowl barrier against the things it was intended to keep out; so does this island of sanity built from his daughter's blood and his father's rambling stories terminate at a barrier, one that shuts out the madness that swallowed the Earth whole. He and what's left of his family—that disgusting black thing, forced to take the form of his wife when the spell touched her piecemeal remains, but not enough of his daughter left to take form too, only a voice—he and his family dwell now in this single pocket of peace, a bubble in the belly of the all-consuming beast.

On the other side of that barrier, pressed hard against it, pink translucent ropes thick as tanker trucks pulse and swell as rivers of ichor flow through their veiny channels. These titanic kraken tentacles move, slowly, like slugs on glass, and plasma churns and boils in the spaces between them. Sometimes the bubbles look like faces. Sometimes smaller things squeeze in between the vast squirming limbs, enormous urchins with eyes lining and crowning the spines, or amoebic creatures that spontaneously form mouths or multi-jointed arms as they flow bonelessly through the cramped liquid spaces. Sometimes gray skinless beings, sculpted crudely humanoid, emerge and scrabble desperately against the invisible barricade before the currents sweep them back into the sickening organic soup.

Delmar understands all now. If the clouds ever parted above and around his farm, these sights would form his heaven and his horizon.

He stares into the nausea-inducing chaos, unblinking, and speaks. "I'll keep them alive, as long as I can." He spreads his arms. "I'll keep this alive, as long as I can. I'll never, ever give you what you want."

Behind the sliding pink tentacles, a vast eye peels open. Even through the layers of wormy flesh, he can see it.

And when it opens, pores gape all along the massed coils of pink, translucent flesh. They gape and flex like octopus siphons sucking water. Perhaps it's these that make the noise Delmar hears as countless whispers speaking in one voice. *Inside your shell, time still flows forward, but that time will end. Outside, time is still. Outside, your future is now. Outside, you are with us and have been forever and will be forever. Your future is our now.*

While the orifices whisper, an immense mouth yaws apart above the eye. Things crawl inside its lips. And somewhere inside the crawling darkness, a man screams. He howls in such a magnitude of pain that Delmar can't begin to imagine what's being done to him. The man screams, and screams, over and over—then perhaps there comes a fraction of respite, for the howls crumble into high-pitched and pathetic sobs. Maybe there are words, repeated pleas, but Delmar can't make them out before the screams start again, and the mouth closes, sealing them away.

The voice of the screaming, sobbing man—it is his own voice. The voice of his future self, once his safe haven has perished.

Delmar's eyes are wet and bright and knowing. But his voice doesn't waver. "I'll keep them alive. As long as I can."

As he retreats into the fog, the million-strong voice whispers back. *We wait.*

LIGHT STREAMS THROUGH the open kitchen window as Delmar slices onions for the omelets. The soothing breeze accepts his invitation to drift inside.

Delmar has the vaguest memory of an upsetting night, but a voice whispers in his ear, his own voice, telling him he has to forget for now, compartmentalize, or the weight of knowledge will keep him from what happiness he has left, with what's left of his family, in the time he has left.

Whatever it was, it hardly seems to matter now. He breathes in the warm, sweet air that mingles with the smell of his own cooking and knows he can handle whatever life has to throw at him.

The sizzle of the bacon in the skillet doesn't completely drown out water rushing onto tile as Lynda showers. He can do this almost without thinking: the bacon first, then eggs to soak up the flavor. Lynda always tsked him for that vice, frying eggs in bacon grease, but she can't stop herself from wolfing down the results. *Just an evil way to show my love*, he likes to tell her.

He raises the knife above a helpless onion, then stops short. There's singing, coming from the shower. He freezes, listening, because it's Meaghan's voice that sings, and that doesn't seem right, and part of him knows the many, many reasons it's not right, but that part of him refuses to share its concerns aloud. And so he shrugs it off. It's not important.

Back to his task. He realigns the onion and steadies it for the killing stroke. Then something catches his eye. He lifts his hand to his face. His heart starts to pound.

A black growth shivers on the back of his ring finger, just below his wedding band. It extends as he watches, reaches out with twin protrusions akin to a snail's eyes. They twitch toward him. He feels a painful, pricking sensation, but *under* his skin, and for a brief flicker another vision imposes over his own, a vision of his own face, monumental in size and monstrous. The inner voice he always hears, the one that comforts and warns him, speaks again, but only says, *We wait.*

His wife's singing has stopped. The bathroom door opens.

"Sweetie," Lynda calls from the shower, "can you bring me a towel?"

"Sure," he answers, as he positions his hand on the cutting board. "In a minute."

AN INVITATION VIA E-MAIL

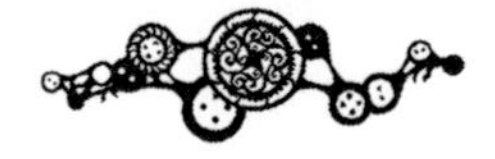

From: Giles Milko <gjmilko@va.fairleigh.edu>
To: Miranda Statzler <mastatzler@va.fairleigh.edu>
Subject: Excellent piece in the Critic!
Date: Wed, 5 Nov 2003 11:12:03 -0500
X-Mailer: Internet Mail Service (4.4.1545.48)

Hello, Ms. Statzler, Giles Milko here. Hopefully you remember me from the conversation we had last Thursday at the after-hours faculty party.

I have to say, I really enjoyed your essay in the newest Fairleigh Critic on the subjective nature of fear. I'm very much in agreement with your contention that the most extreme phobia or paranoia, no matter how crippling, can be overcome through the gradual building up of confidence. I must say that aside from being informative, I found your piece also to be quite entertaining, especially the self-deprecating wit you used in describing your efforts through therapy to overcome your fear of spiders. In my head I could hear the mental squeals of horror as Dr. Sherrill placed the tarantula in your hand; then feel the overwhelming burst of triumph as you set the spider gently on the table and realized: I did it! I did it!

Some of the asides in your article made me realize (Gods, can I be dense sometimes) that when you spoke of concerns about "arcane rites" in response to the invite to my Halloween party the next evening, that you possibly weren't kidding and perhaps had some genuine anxieties. I really should stress that my wife and I had planned for the Halloween party to be occult-free—no spirits other than the liquid sort!

I realize I've gained a facetious reputation among students over the years, usually for little more than addressing poor Giordano Bruno's attempt to understand the world through sorcery in a History of Science class! (I must say though, Bruno did have a knack for concocting ominous-looking magical symbols—it's no wonder the Church made kindling out of him.) Obviously some such rumor reached you long before our first encounter in the flesh—so as soon as I finished your essay I felt compelled to write you and set things to rights.

The thaumaturgical ceremonies conducted in my home are not fearful, black-robed affairs reserved for special nights. They're actually very casual things, held Sunday mornings or the occasional Saturday if someone wants to see a football game instead. They're not geared toward any more sinister a purpose than furthering the careers of the participants. (I, for one, need the boost. Consider that I teach nine credits a week, write a column for the town paper and complete a new book every two years. Do you really think I could do all that without "outside" help?)

A few faculty members take part, as well as one freelance writer from town who needs to combat his "day job brain drain." Sometimes writers or artists from out of town make "guest" appearances. It's all quite open and friendly. No one dresses up—T-shirts and sweats, in fact, are perfectly acceptable attire.

Of course, there has to be a sacrifice. Our ideal choice is one of those horribly misguided individuals (sadly, almost always a parent) who goes to the school board wanting to ban this book or that book, or goes whining to town council to cancel Halloween as a Satanic holiday. Unfortunately for the world, but good for us, there seems to be no shortage of them (though we've done our best, I swear). And if we can't get our hands on an adult, one of their children will do the trick—those sorts of genes don't need to spread.

The sacrifice doesn't need to be conscious, but he or she does need to be alive, so that each of us can take a small bite of their still-beating heart. Making the proper cuts to remove a heart this way is frankly rather tricky, though we've all gotten well-practiced. Of course we have to pass a "chalice" around—a coffee cup will do, really—for that token chaser of blood. Then we summon the "outerdimensional persona" (that's the politically correct term these entities seem to prefer nowadays.) Now at this point you might experience some of that anxiety you discussed in your essay, but there's no need to worry. We've drawn the right symbols and circles so that the persona (our favorite is a fellow with a pleasantly dry wit named Mephisto) can't do anything other than talk. Once we see his (its? Gender is never clear with these things) disembodied head hovering over the remains of the sacrifice, we pepper him with questions about the status of his labors with regard to our projects (in the ears of which editors or agents has he whispered, what bargains has he struck, did he give an appropriate nightmare to the woman who wrote that rude rejection, etc.)

After we get our update, he heads back to New York. Really, that's it. He (it?) takes most of the sacrifice for sustenance until next weekend. We knock on my study door so my wife knows we're done, and she'll usually bring in something like sweet rolls and hot chocolate, so we dig into those while we sit around talking shop. What's left over of the sacrifice we give to the new puppies, who love their weekend meal (it's usually cooked a bit as a result of the persona's presence.) Of course, the cat doesn't want to be left out, but her teeth have gone bad, so she just gets a little saucer of blood.

You're probably wondering why the authorities have never barged in on us. Well, as a condition of this arrangement, Mephisto or whichever persona we happen to dial up, erases the memory of the sacrifice from the minds of everyone who ever knew them (except for us.) So if no one remembers their existence, no one misses them. (And we've managed to improve the gene pool a tad in the process.) Of course, if there's a lot of physical evidence left behind, like, say, wedding albums or newspaper articles, the entity will have to work a bit harder to make sure everyone's curiosity is sufficiently dulled. But overall it's a very efficient system.

I'm not sure how close the lot of us has gotten to achieving our ultimate goals, but these weekend get-togethers do seem to help. You're certainly welcome to come by this weekend (or any weekend of your choosing, there's no hurry) and join in. Perhaps we could help you to produce more wonderful essays like the one I just read. Or maybe there are some *solidly grounded* fears (I hear rumors of a troublesome ex-husband?) that we can help put to rest for good.

I hope all of this helps to reassure you.

Yr obt. servnt.,

Milko

* * *

From: Giles Milko <gjmilko@va.fairleigh.edu>
To: ScienceFaculty@fairleigh.edu, EnglishFaculty@fairleigh.edu, ligotti@morbid.net
Subject: Apology Date: Mon, 11 Nov 2003 7:48:03 -0600
X-Mailer: Internet Mail Service (4.4.1545.48)

To all,

My sincerest apologies!

Ms. Statzler seemed like an intelligent, inquisitive woman who would understand the benefits of our arrangement. How could I have predicted she would interpret my explanatory e-mail as a joke? Henceforth I promise to be more careful when screening new members.

I'm still not precisely a master of this new e-mail system, so if you received this message in error and have not a clue to whom I'm referring—well, just take comfort that things are exactly as they should be. :-)

All best,
Milko

LACING OVER HIDDEN WOUNDS

THE HIKER'S TALE

Help me! yelled the boy.

No noise disturbed the steep wooded incline where I froze, my heart dancing a crazy flatfoot. A distant catbird screeched above the flying saucer whine of the cicadas; that was all.

Yet the boy's voice shrilled again in my head, loud as a rifle shot. *Please help me!*

I dropped my aluminum hiking staffs. One of them tumbled down the bank, right through the place where the boy crouched, right through *him.*

Nothing more than an outline sketched in the furrows of bark, the cross-hatching of pine needles, yet clearly *there*, cowering amid the trees about ten yards below the trail. A slender boy, maybe ten or eleven, muddy face streaked with tears, his sweatshirt ripped, one jean pocket torn open.

Through him, the late summer sun dappled knotted branches, twisted ropes of creeper, glistening pine.

His lips parted, and in my head I heard his voice: *Don't let it get me.*

I felt as if someone dropped a boulder in my backpack. I staggered—*swooned*, my grandmother would have put it—and grabbed at a birch sapling to keep myself from tumbling down the slope.

A commotion erupted below the pines, in the brambles at the bottom of the gully. It sounded like a deer, like a herd of deer, trying to fight a path through the tangled thorns.

The boy ran at me.

I raised my arms to block him, but he ran through them, through *me.* I howled as a cold electric jolt galvanized me from inside.

When I screamed, it wasn't just from the sensation, but from a burst of impossible recognition. I'd felt this before, this ice lightning. Suddenly I was terrified as a five-year-old shut in a cabin full of ghosts. My sinuses seared with the reek of copper. Static blasted in my ears. My skin curdled in goose pimples.

Then the hallucination vanished, quick as it had struck.

Whatever made the commotion in the brambles then crashed away through the brush, out of earshot in seconds. A stench of rotten eggs drifted past me like seeds on the wind.

Then all was calm. No sign of a boy. No sound of running footsteps. A distant cicada changed its pitch from whine to buzz.

To my right, the slope descended to the impassable brambles where I'd heard the deer moving. To my left, the ground rose even steeper in a mad, rocky quest to reach the mountaintop. I stood on a wide hump in the trail, gasping as if I'd sprinted the last quarter-mile. My mouth felt desert dry. I thought of sipping from my canteen, then decided otherwise, realizing that the sulfurous taint still lingered in the air. My stomach twinged.

I denied that shock of recognition with every fiber of my being. I told myself that my imagination had run haywire, that I'd never encountered anything like that in my twenty years of life. I took a step, then bent over and dry heaved.

As I squatted there, eyes shut, a phrase repeated in my head. *Leave it alone, little panther.* At first the voice was unfamiliar: old, dry and crackly as fallen leaves just before the first snow. But then, like twin muted beacons, I pictured my grandmother's eyes, her sky-blue stare clouded by cataracts. The voice was hers. When had I heard her say that?

She had died thirteen years before, when I was only seven. It was a miracle I remembered the sound of her voice at all, and so strange that I remembered it *then*.

The rustling continued—at first I thought her voice had somehow escaped my skull, but as I recovered from this odd spell I noticed motion at the edge of the path. A large, grey spider, a wolf spider, its leg span as wide as my palm. Tiny brown young clustered on her back. She was so large that as she crawled across years of shed leaves they whispered beneath her weight.

Leave it alone, little panther.

I told myself that nothing had happened, that maybe I just needed fresh water. It was easy to buy into my own sales pitch. *All in your head. Thirst and exhaustion. Just need to find a good resting spot.*

I picked up one of my aluminum walking staffs, then clambered carefully down the bank to retrieve the other, avoiding the mother spider and the thorns of a honey locust sapling.

The trail wound uphill past a row of scrub pine, around a bank of cherries. Beyond their long, drooping leaves stood a wooden sign which read CRABBES SUPPLIES in carved block letters. Directly across from the sign stood one of those wooden boxes mounted on a pole you see all along the Appalachian Trail, containing a notebook hikers can use to leave each other comments.

The arrow on the sign pointed to a narrow side path that climbed straight uphill, forging through dense clusters of laurel.

At that moment I realized I couldn't think of anything I wanted more than the company of another human being. I made a mental list of things I could stand to restock and started up the hill.

CRABBES SUPPLIES TURNED out to be a 1850s-era log home about the size of a storage shed, perched atop the mountain ridge. Tan chinking filled the gaps between wooden slats aged mildew black. The roof's blocky, gray shingles had been hand-cut with a hatchet.

An ancient jeep as dirty as the slats sat behind the shop, parked on an old logging road that wound its muddy way down the other side of the mountain. The jeep's fenders were caked with enough layers of mud to justify an archeological dig. Somewhere nearby, a generator hummed.

Through the window's dusty glass I could see a heavyset woman, her back to me, her silver hair pulled up in an elaborate bun. The painful pink and green print of her flowered skirt made her disproportionately wide hips seem even wider.

I leaned my staffs against the wall and set foot on the single front step. It creaked under my weight.

Then I drew up short. Viscous strands of cobweb crisscrossed the open door. I'd almost stepped through them.

I checked for spiders—there were none—then brushed the webs aside. Except I didn't. My hand passed through the webbing without breaking a strand. An electric tingle numbed my forearm, the same cold jolt I felt when the boy ran through me, though not as strong.

The old woman spun around as if yanked on a string. At the same moment, a rail-thin and stunningly ugly old man stood up from behind the cash register.

My hand shook as I passed it again through the cobwebs. Again, the cold, the shock.

That happened.

The boy's terrified face, etched in shadow, flickered before my mind's eye. As I stood paralyzed, the old couple watched me, both their heads cocked at precisely the same angle. I grew conscious of their gaze, and embarrassment compounded my fear.

Leave it alone, little panther.

The old man finally broke the detente by displaying a smile full of long, crooked teeth. "Well, son," he drawled pleasantly, "are you coming in or not?"

His tone made up my mind for me. I hopped through the door with an apologetic "Hi!"—but the syllable was strangled by full-body shock as I passed through the cobwebs.

"Whoa, there, tiger, you all right?" He came around the counter, a spindly arm extended to brace me. His wife put a fretful hand to her mouth.

Something in me squirmed as the old man took my arm, but I didn't resist as he helped me out of my backpack and steered me to a wooden chair. I was all too grateful for the chance to sit down.

He must have been acclimated to decades of hikers stomping through, because I was a fright myself. Cheeks hollowed from day after day of dining on raisins, peanuts, jerky, granola and the occasional nasty but edible meal plucked and boiled directly from what the trail offered. Those sunken cheeks almost completely hidden in a scraggly shrub of black, curly, untrimmed beard, with my densely curly hair grown out three times that length. Even without my Nine Inch Nails t-shirt sticking to my body, I stunk from four weeks away from air conditioning and plumbing. Not to mention I was freakishly piebald, my sun-exposed forearms and face dark as hickory, the rest of me pale as cream. And people with my complexion don't normally have green eyes. That alone has earned me many double-takes through the years, but none of it phased him.

"Check him for a fever," his wife said.

I tried to wave him away. "I'm fine, really. Just need a little break."

"Don't usually see a man this young in such a state," my host said. He had to press his hand to my forehead before he was satisfied. His touch felt so strangely cool that I wondered if I did have a fever. But finally he nodded and backed away. "No problem with letting you sit for a spell. I think you need it."

Next, as I recuperated, came the small talk. Their names, they told me, were Herman and Gertrude Crabbe, the kind of names no sane parent would ever give their kid nowadays.

As Gertrude approached and I shook her flaccid hand, I wondered how a woman so wide through the hips could have such a pinched, hungry face. Yet her voice had an earthy, soothing cadence.

"Welcome to our little oasis," she said. "You want something while you're here? Bottled water? Crackers? Maybe a pillow?"

My panic faded, though a nagging sense of unease never left. Something still bothered me about the Crabbes, though they acted as pleasant as you please. During the give and take, they told me they'd lived for the past fifty years in a cabin nestled in a hollow on the east side of the mountain, so secluded they never saw hikers there. Both had been born and raised in the Blue Ridge Mountains and didn't much care to live anywhere else. Gertrude told me she and Herman had both been born to large families, back in the days when *everyone's* family was large, and each had been the family "eccentric," the lone introverts marooned among their gregarious kin.

Their serendipitous first meeting took place at a saloon in the tiny town of Warm Springs, where both had been reluctantly dragged by cousins with wild streaks. "I couldn't believe how perfect we were for each other," Mrs. Crabbe said. "I just looked at him, and I knew, and I could tell he knew. We hardly had to say anything."

I had no trouble believing in that instant attraction. These were two of the homeliest people I had ever met. Her with her hunched shoulders, beady eyes and crooked jaw, her head configured as if God had gripped her cheeks with thumb and forefinger and squeezed; him with those eyes set too far apart in his narrow face, the spiny hairs protruding from his ears and nostrils, that lipless mouth. They belonged together.

Under normal circumstances I would never have revealed so much about myself in return, but every tidbit they offered seemed bent to draw something out of me, and even as I recognized the game I couldn't stop myself from playing it.

I'd not been the happiest boy, growing up in the coal-shaft riddled mountains outside Kingsport. A bookish waif is nothing to be among the sons of miners, who see you as something to piss on for sport. The only bookstore was at the Kingsport Mall, half a day away by a switchbacking road that made me throw up in the back seat more than once.

My father taught at a high school in Sullivan County while my mother quietly seethed at home, a college educated woman bound to cooking, cleaning, and chasing after an awkward, oversensitive and insolent brat. My dad would build up ferocious squalls of temper in the gray-bricked classrooms and release them at home in full glory once they were seeded by my mom's resentful needling. Was it any wonder I spent so much of my childhood alone in the wood,s exploring the endless web of well-worn footpaths, a mite scaling the surface of our country's oldest mountains?

Nothing had delighted me more than landing that art scholarship at UNC in Asheville. That, folks, was my great escape. And a setup for complete failure. I loved dabbling in art, but not living it under a professor's dictatorship. Even the grace of the brush between the fingers, the high-inducing turpentine stench, changed into something sickening. After my terrible grades wrecked my scholarship, I managed to stick around a semester and a half, reinvented as an English major supported by a student loan. If anything, I performed even worse, and quit before midterms with most of my spring loan still in the bank—and that became the funding for my trek out of civilization.

"You're starting out pretty late for a thru-hiker," Mr. Crabbe said. "By the time you hit Massachusetts, you'll be knee-deep in snow, boy."

I told him that a good friend from my recently left-behind school and his lovely wife awaited me in Pennsylvania—though this was half-truth. I'd winter with them, I said, then finish the journey once the world thawed. In fact, I planned to look up my friends, but had no idea if they'd take me in, or what I'd do after that. I was lost.

The Crabbes listened to my tale of loserdom with the rapt attention due a death-defying war story. Whenever I stole glances at the doorway I still saw the ethereal webbing.

"But you seem like such a smart boy," Gertrude said, pursing her lips. "Why're you even struggling in school?"

I couldn't believe what came out of my mouth next.

"I kept having nightmares after I left home. Just about every night. I couldn't remember what happened in them, but I know they were bad because of the way I kept waking up. My heart would be pounding. Sometimes I'd scream. I burned through four roommates my freshman year. I started to…well, I dabbled in substances, to try to get it under control. But that wiped out the focus I had left."

"That's a shame," Mrs. Crabbe tsked. "A good woman would've taken care of that."

"Nightmares," Mr. Crabbe said dreamily. Unbidden, I saw the ghost-boy's face scream.

There had been a woman, named Yolanda, whom I'd lived with up to and after my academic implosion. She was a candle-burning new-agey type who loved weed, and she started calling me Panther, like my grandmother had, though I couldn't remember telling her about that, and finally I asked her to stop. Our cohabitation was the last thing to go sour before I took to the trail, the thing that made me decide I had to leave for the forest. I wanted to return to my roots, but not, absolutely not, to go home.

I was trying to explain this, without indulging in too much uncomfortable detail, when Herman Crabbe floored me.

"You got some Melungeon in you, I think," he said.

It took long seconds for my startled brain to even form a response. "Wow, that's…I don't think anyone's ever…I've had people ask me if I'm Turkish. Or Arab. Or Greek. Or Indian. Even mulatto. No one gets it on sight."

Mr. Crabbe snickered. "You ain't no Arab."

"My grandmother," I said. "She was full Melungeon, if you can really properly apply such a term." Both of them nodded as if I was confirming facts they already well knew.

"Sure is a shame about that boy," Mrs. Crabbe said, with no transition, as if it were the topic we'd been addressing all along. "I hope they at least find his body before the animals get it."

I nearly fell right out of rickety chair.

Herman sighed and shook his head as he straightened the assortments of candy, crackers and trail mix next to the cash register. "Probably too late."

When I recovered my balance, I asked, "What boy?"

Herman stood and licked his crooked teeth. The couple exchanged glances. Gertrude asked her husband, "You bring the paper?"

"Yep, sure did." The old man ducked behind the counter and started rummaging. "Here somewhere."

"Sad, very sad," Mrs. Crabbe tsked, picking up her duster again. "A city boy from east of here, I think. The paper might've even had his name. Fell off the top of Angel's Leap, about fifteen miles north of here. Surely you've heard of Angel's Leap?"

When I said I hadn't, she was all too ready to explain it to me. Its real name was McGlothlin's Knob—that, I'd heard of—but everyone referred to it as Angel's Leap: a craggy outcrop of rock with a popular but strenuous path winding to its peak and a 100-foot fall off one side waiting for the careless, of which there were no shortage. It was the biggest attraction on this part of the AT, in part because of its evil reputation. Bad things happened in the woods beneath its shadow, Mrs. Crabbe told me.

Her husband reappeared, spread newspaper pages on the counter and crooked a finger to invite me closer. Gertrude stayed at my side, filling me in on the lore of Angel's Leap as Herman guided my attention to a block of type.

I spotted a name, Thomas "Tommy" Wayne Saunders, 9, of Hillcrest.

Seven years ago, Mrs. Crabbe told me, a couple from Montana had been found dead inside their tents, their throats cut. Five years ago, a boy who wandered away from his family's campsite escaped with his life, barely, from a man wearing a white mask. A year later, baffled police made a public appeal for help catching the suspect, and revealed the boy had been molested before he got loose. Two years ago, a missing college student turned up dead. An anonymous source quoted in the paper said his body was naked and impaled on a crudely carved pole.

Gertrude counted off the horrors on her bony fingers as I tried to read. "They've never caught whoever did these things, whoever did any of it," she said.

The boy had vanished two nights before. His parents told the rescue workers they last saw him standing at the wooden railing at the top of McGlothlin's Knob. No one saw him climb over or fall. A team of two dozen searchers still hadn't found him.

"Those parents should never have taken him up there," Gertrude said. "They should know better. It's a bad place."

"I keep telling you, woman, it ain't the place that's evil." Herman had kept his hand on the page to hold it flat. Now he moved his fingers, uncovering the black and white school photo above the story's headline.

I had guessed what I was going to see. But it still chilled me to the marrow to see his face smiling up at me. His unmistakable face.

I fought to keep calm but didn't quite make it. "That poor kid," I said. "I bet his parents are devastated."

I became acutely aware of how close their faces were to mine, how they'd boxed me in on either side. They couldn't have missed the way my eyes widened, the goose bumps that stood the hair on my arms on end.

There are some things I just never wanted to believe. But I'm not stupid. They knew about the boy. They knew I'd seen him, seen his ghost. I didn't understand how they'd read my mind, but I was sure they had.

Abrupt as a warning, I noticed empty eye sockets staring at me from the shelf behind and below the counter. An astonishing number of deer skulls, something like forty, sans their antlers, sat in regimented stacks down there. Quite a few of the eye sockets were occupied with dusty cobwebs, like leprous cotton.

How long had I been talking with them? I had to get out. But an instinct I couldn't explain told me that a hasty exit would be a bad move, a very dangerous move.

"You know," I said, "I think I do need some more water. And some dried fruit would be good. Do you have anything freeze dried?"

The old man gathered my order while his wife went back to dusting.

As Mr. Crabbe manned the cash register I noticed an acrid, unwashed smell that undermined the comforting scent of old wood. It originated from *him*. I hadn't noticed it before.

One last surprise lay in store, when the old man handed me the bag. Two of the fingers on his right hand were malformed. They were oddly bent, insect-like—plastic substitutions for a missing pinky and ring finger. Skin had been grafted over these prosthetics.

He grinned when he noticed the grimace I failed to suppress, and waggled his grotesque appendages in front of my nose. "That's what happens," he said, "when you don't put food on the table quick enough for the missus."

Gertrude Crabbe cackled hard enough to trigger a coughing fit. While she was recovering, I quickly thanked them both and left, suppressing another cringe as I passed through the ethereal webbing across the door.

I set off at a brisk pace, just shy of a trot, my mind and stomach churning all the way down. The sun had lowered considerably, its light sparkling faintly through the trees.

When I reached the main trail I opened the box containing the notebook for hikers' messages. A ratty, spiral-bound pad lay inside, nearly filled with pen scrawls. Nothing that I skimmed help to enlighten me, though the final message read: "The Crabbes are creepy."

Beneath that, I wrote "Amen!" and signed my trail name, a concession to my long-gone grandma: Panther.

Two hours later, with the sun banished beneath the mountains, my reason overcame the urge to put as much distance as I could between myself and the Crabbes, I sought a place to camp for the night. I came upon a wooden shelter that had once been used as a smokehouse. Inside, the crusty smell of salt mingled with a fruity hint of tobacco.

I should have been laying out my sleeping bag, donning an extra shirt and calculating how much of my crackers and jerky and dried fruit I could afford to eat that night. Instead I sat on the bench inside the shelter, my pack on the floor beside me, opening and closing my Buck knife, listening to my own heartbeat, thinking.

Crickets and peepers provided an eerie soundtrack to the film spliced together in my head. The ghost-boy. The webbing.

Herman licking his teeth. Then I broke the spell by swearing. In my preoccupation I had managed to slice the pad of my thumb.

I held my hand up to the light of dusk drifting through the doorway and watched my blood form a bead. It threatened to drip.

That happened. It all happened.

A memory welled in that drop as it fell. A small boy exploring the collapsed shell of a mountain cabin, feet crunching on rotten boards. A noise rising in my ears like the plaintive dial tone after a hangup. Darkness congealed into a face. The freezing fire of a ghost's touch.

I remembered: my tiny foot settling on a board that snapped even beneath the slender weight of a five-year-old. The sudden noise froze my heart. Inside the cabin, that hollow moss-caked husk that squatted in the woods above the ancient cottage of my mother's mother.

Even in my childhood my grandma's house creaked with disrepair, central crumbling landmark on the farm gone to seed since my grandfather died, years before I was born. Her house fascinated me with its unending supply of nooks and crannies, with its leaning outhouse, with its chickens behind frayed wire, with its covered well.

But nothing fascinated me more than that dark relic in the woods, its shadow always drawing my eye from beneath the elm trees whenever I slipped out the back door to play.

Grandma was a tiny woman, her waves of grey and black hair always tied back in a frayed ponytail, face chestnut brown with wrinkled webs around her eyes and mouth, eyes a startling blue beneath thick black eyebrows. She frightened me; I didn't like to be alone with her, though she was always kind. There was a tension between her and my mother, who took after her late, lighter-skinned, taller husband; a cold barrier that I sensed in some instinctual way but did not catalogue consciously until I was much older and noticed how mom fell quiet on the rare occasions someone spoke of *her* mother. Not so dearly departed, I could see. I came to believe it was all about skin color.

But, when grandma was alive, she had insisted on visits, insisted on every opportunity to see her grandson, and my parents had dutifully obeyed, making the long trek on those horrible rutted roads in the rusted VW Beetle that was all they could afford when they were young.

I asked Grandma many times about the caved-in cabin in her woods, and when she answered it was always the same. "Leave it alone, little panther."

I never asked her permission, but decided I would see for myself all the same. Toward the end of one week-long stay I snuck away from my cot in the middle of the night. I had no flashlight, but the moon was bright enough to let me find a way in.

I barked my knee crawling in through that hole in the wall.

What was I hunting there?

I remembered: a face formed from darkness. That terrible touch, cold lightning through every inch of me.

I couldn't recall what happened after. More blood dripped as my hand trembled.

A snatch of an image: my grandmother's eyes, practically glowing in the moonlight, her nose inches from mine. She had pulled me from the ruined cabin. Inside it, something whimpered.

I clenched my bleeding thumb in my fingers, once again aware of the fruity tobacco scent, the *reep reep reep* of the peeper frogs.

I was a fool on a fool's mission. The old man was right—by the time I reached Massachusetts the trail would be smothered in snow. The world I was trying to escape into would flush me out without a sliver of sympathy.

That creepy storekeeper had the better of me in more ways than one.

I've always felt alone, been aware of a boundary that cordoned me off from others, evoked awkward silences and downcast eyes when I've tried to bridge the gap. I once chalked that up to skin color, my mother's shame.

I didn't learn what a Melungeon was until my senior year in high school. My blood was mixed, yes, but not in the way I'd come to believe.

Melungeon was once an insult, now defanged by virtue of being mostly forgotten. They called themselves Black Dutch or Black Irish, but people believed they were a mix of Indian and Negro, and in some towns in eighteenth-century Tennessee the government took away their property rights. The Melungeons did intermarry with blacks, because of the societal forces that throw outcasts together, but their origins weren't solely African.

Some claimed them to be descendants of Moorish sailors from a marooned Portuguese vessel, taking Cherokee and Powhatan wives. Others sources point to the lost Roanoke colony, with its cryptic CROATOAN; some fancifully go even further back, much further, to Carthaginians fleeing the Roman tyranny, to the Phoenicians, even to a certain lost Biblical tribe. And there are tales that supposedly originate among the Cherokee of a tribe from under the hills, a tribe with features that could be called a combination of white and black and Asian, who walked without fear among the beasts of the spirit world, and did not know death until they came to live above ground.

My grandmother was unmistakably Melungeon, and she met death when I was little and didn't come back. I knew nothing of a spirit world or any beasts within it.

But I thought about that webbing in the shop door, and the way the Crabbes had known *what* I was without asking, and it frightened me.

Then a shadow flickered beyond the doorway to the shelter, and I knew a different kind of fear. My gasp of surprise caught in my throat.

I saw nothing through that opening but the jumbled blur of trees in deep twilight, but at the same time I saw, unmistakably, the scrawny figure of a boy, etched out of the darkness.

He stared at me, wide-eyed.

I started to say his name, but he had vanished. A breeze shifted the branches.

I heard a rhythmic rustling of leaves, somebody walking through the brush. A stench of rotten eggs assailed me.

My bleeding thumb forgotten, I opened the Buck knife and crept to the door.

On the crest of the hill high above me, in a gap between trees, a figure stood in silhouette against the bruised twilight. The figure—a man, I thought—turned and walked below the line of the hill.

It was a strange thing to think at that moment, strange especially for a twenty-year-old man facing the unknown with his heart in his throat, but it's what I thought: *Grandma would know what to do.* A woman who was little more to me than scraps of eerie memory, yet there was strength in those memories. A tiny old woman who had ventured out in the middle of the night to pull a frightened little boy from a place he didn't belong.

I stepped outside, avoiding leaves and brush as I stalked up the hill. As a child I'd had a gift for padding silently that drove my mother crazy. This gift did not fail me now.

On the hilltop I peered down into a long, narrow gully, dug by uncounted centuries of converging water runoff. The bottom of the gully widened into a clearing, shrouded by encroaching night. Though my vision reduced most everything to mottled black and white, somehow without squinting I could see Herman Crabbe in the clearing. Gaunt, an animated skeleton, he spread his arms, and a ring of what appeared to be blue smoke stretched open in front of him.

It was as if his hands had pierced a membrane, and he was forcing the hole to gape large enough to pass through.

A bewildering double image confronted me. Though I saw Crabbe using both hands to hold the opening, other limbs were reaching through, spiny arachnid limbs.

Then he stepped completely through, and changed. What crawled out the other side of that smoky opening was not human at all.

The monster ascended the far side of the gully on legs like arched lightning, climbing into the murk at heart-stopping speed. The vast spider I beheld was formed of shadow and movement, like my ghost-boy.

Once the Crabbe-thing crawled out of sight, my heart didn't slow its pounding. But the opening he made, the blue smoky ring, still hung in mid-air, slowly shrinking.

Knife held before me, every nerve screaming at me to run the other way, I descended into the gully, stepping as light and catlike as I think I've ever managed. I expected the Crabbe-spider to lunge from the shadows any moment. But nothing like that happened.

When I reached the opening it was little more than an wispy curl of blue light, dangling before like bait in the deep woods abyss. I poked my finger in it, and felt a mild jolt, that nerve-chilling shock that was starting to become familiar.

I shoved in two fingers, then both hands. The substance yielded to my touch. I spread my arms, as I'd seen the storekeeper do, and opened the hole in reality.

Through the hole, the trees, the gully, the shadows all looked the same, but another world was superimposed over them in double-exposure: a landscape of sourceless silver light, of odd refractions that twisted objects into shapes that hurt my eyes if I stared too long.

I put one foot in the opening and stretched it to the ground, then paused. If I passed all the way through, would the opening still be there when I returned? Would I be stuck on the other side, in the spirit world, like poor Tommy Saunders?

For now I was certain what had happened to this poor boy. Not all the pieces fit, not yet. But I was sure that Tommy Saunders, against all odds, was still alive.

The Crabbes had brought him into this shadow world, somehow, for who-knew-what horrible purpose, but he'd escaped them. Maybe they'd believed him dead, but from my meeting with them they'd gleaned in some arcane fashion that their prey still lived. And now Mr. Crabbe had returned to the shadow world, to hunt the boy. Tracking in his true form.

I didn't dare leave the opening to search in that unfamiliar space. But I'd seen the boy just minutes ago. He couldn't be far away.

Holding out my knife in the direction Crabbe had crawled, I yelled Tommy's name.

The woods fell silent. I threw away all caution, shouting, "Tommy? Can you hear me? Tommy?"

"Here!" A boy's voice.

Something stirred nearby, something large. The sound made my guts flip-flop.

"Run to my voice!" I screamed. "Run! Run! Now!"

I couldn't tell if Tommy heard me, the commotion in the woods became so loud. I clutched the knife in a white-knuckle grip and kept shouting. Then the boy appeared, stumbling pell-mell out of a tangle of silvery gloom. He pitched himself headlong into the gully. Behind him the tops of trees whipped back and forth, as something giant shoved its way between them.

But the thing that emerged from the shadows a moment later wasn't the gigantic spider I'd braced myself for. It stood upright on two thick legs. Thorns covered its body.

The gully flooded with a rotten egg reek.

Tommy tripped and landed on all fours. I yelled for him to get up. Then the thing chasing him stepped down into the gully, and I lost all coherent thought.

Wicked hooks of bone protruded at every joint from a hide like layers upon layers of burn scars. The pulpy mound of its head spilled over its chest and shoulders in a cascade of sucking mouths and writhing eyestalks. Spined organs that had to be genitalia jutted from its abdomen like tusks.

A spike of nausea and terror hammered me between the eyes. I shrieked something, I don't remember what. Tommy shrieked too, and scrambled to his feet.

Repulsive as the demon was, something rang false about it, a hint that what I was seeing wasn't real, that it wasn't a monster so much as a costume, or a suit of armor. Somehow I knew this, and the thought held me fast, as did Tommy's wide, terrified eyes. But whatever hid inside it, the thing was a murder machine, and I was just flesh.

I screamed for Tommy to move. Then they were both running toward me, the creature just yards behind its prey.

Tommy bowled into me as the demon's spike-studded fist descended. I stuck my arm out through the hole in the world and slashed blindly with the knife.

A sledgehammer kissed me.

A howl split the night.

Then I landed on my back in the wet earth, panting, with Tommy's warm weight on top of me. Nearby, a muffled voice groaned in pain.

I put an arm around Tommy's shoulders and hauled us both to our feet. As I did so, someone put a hand to my back and helped me up. With a cry I turned, holding out the knife, and found myself face to face with Herman Crabbe. The shadows and highlights cast by the flashlight he carried amplified his ugliness tenfold.

"Whoa, there, tiger," he said, as his flashlight beam found the blade.

I backed away, keeping the knife between myself and Crabbe, my other arm cradled protectively around the shivering boy. Tommy pressed his face against my stomach. His clothes were wet, and he reeked of sweat and urine.

The muffled voice groaned again, then coughed. Crabbe turned his flashlight in the direction of the noise. "You did quite a number on him, tiger," Crabbe said. "I'm impressed."

The hole in reality still remained, but had thinned to a wispy blue outline. Beyond it, a man lay on the ground, wearing jeans and a torn flannel shirt. At first I thought he had the palest face I'd ever seen, but then I realized he wore a papier mâché mask, painted white.

Gertrude Crabbe stood over him, pressing the business end of a shotgun against his chest.

The man's shirt was shredded down one side. The flesh revealed there bled from a series of deep, parallel gouges. Claw marks.

I held up my knife in wonder. The blade was clean. Despite that little boy cuddled against me, I said a few choice words, several in a string.

Panther, my grandmother always called me.

And then, as if not focusing on it somehow made it easier to see, a scene unfolding in shadow-forms edged onto my awareness.

Before me, the thorned demon lay twitching. Huge though it was, it was dwarfed by the tremendous spider crouched over it. Clearly female, its grotesquely swollen abdomen blurred the moon. With its forelegs, it was winding, winding, binding the monster beneath it in a tight cocoon.

"It's like she says," said Gertrude's husband. "It's amazing, how perfect we are for each other."

He aimed his flashlight at me again. "Looks like you took his prey away, and a good thing, too." He laughed, a harsh, alien sound. "You get that boy back up to the store. Clean him up, put some blankets on him. Give him some water, make sure it's in small sips, maybe a candy bar if he can hold it down. When we catch up to you, we'll drive you both into town."

Had the Crabbes been watching as my face-off with Tommy's abductor went down? They must have. What would have happened had I lost the face-off? The balance of events seemed too delicate to disturb. I didn't dare ask. Instead I tilted my head toward the man on the ground. "What about him? He's bleeding pretty bad."

Herman's lips peeled back in a toothy grin. "We'll take care of him. You go on."

I was still trembling with revelation. "How am I going to find my way in the dark?"

Though his face was hidden, I'm sure he kept onsmiling. "I think you'll find that you can see just fine."

I didn't see fit to argue. I glanced back once as I carried Tommy up the trail. The demon, still twitching, was almost completely encased in Gertrude's webbing.

I'M STILL AMAZED I made it up that hill, carrying that child. My mind reeling the whole way.

The pieces fit now, at least as well as I would ever understand them. The man who I had...*slashed*...was something like yet unlike the Crabbes, a self-made monster who had turned Angel's Leap into his stalking grounds. He had stolen Tommy into shadow with the worst of intentions, but his quarry had escaped. A terrified boy, snatched out of the world, but still resourceful enough to stay out of this demon's clutches for what time he had left to him.

I was both chilled and completely unsurprised when the Crabbes arrived at the shop without their captive in tow. They made no mention of him, and I chose not to ask as to his whereabouts. They had retrieved my gear from the shelter, though. I thanked them. Gertrude Crabbe fussed over Tommy while Herman readied the Jeep. He indicated I should follow him.

As the engine warmed up, he put a hand on my shoulder and leaned close, so that I was staring right at his crooked teeth, ghoulishly lit by the Jeep's headlights. His acrid breath assaulted me as he spoke.

"We're going to drop you off a block down from the dispatch center. You go in, tell them you found the boy wandering in the woods. Don't mention us, and don't mention anyone else. Tommy won't remember anything different than what you say. Gertrude's made sure of that."

Given everything I had been through that day, I had no problem swallowing the idea that Gertrude Crabbe could hoodoo a boy's memory.

A question burned in the back of my mind and it escaped before I could stop it. "Why didn't you stop this? You could have ended all these terrible things a long time ago."

He stared at me, his face a horror mask. "You know that ain't our nature. We don't seek. We wait." He shuffled closer, raised his hand with the malformed fingers to make a pinching gesture. "A little lasts us a long time."

Then he patted me on the shoulder. "The old blood's gotten thinned out, but it still shows itself in all sorts of strange ways. Some of us know from the moment we come out of the womb, what we've got, what it means." His too wide eyes caught mine, as he grinned in a manner that I can only describe as mischievous. "Some of us have to learn all that the hard way."

All four of us rode down the logging trail, Herman driving, me in the passenger seat, Gertrude in the back with Tommy, who, amazingly, was asleep. Herman's eyes never left the patch of light cut out of the darkness by the jeep's headlamps, but when he spoke it was as if he was looking at me, his bulbous eyes staring into mine.

"You know, tiger," Mr. Crabbe said, "you're all right. When you come back down the this way, feel free to stop in. We'd love to have you by, for a bit of supper."

"I'll keep that in mind," I said with a shudder. Of course I had no plans to take the Crabbes up on their offer.

But I did keep my word. I followed instructions and kept my mouth shut. I didn't stay around to witness Tommy's reunion with his family. The accolades that could have been mine, plaques, newspaper stories, television crews, would have drawn too much attention. I wanted nothing to do with that.

By the afternoon of the next day, I'd abandoned my hike. Showered, shaved, gotten a haircut. I was nestled uncomfortably in the back of a bus, heading Pennsylvania way, intending to drop in on my friends a little sooner than expected—but maybe not *too* soon. From there, I didn't know. I just knew, I still didn't want to go home.

As the road rumbled past and the world rolled into night, I saw things moving in the twilight, and in the dark. Creatures in the fields, or clinging to branches or sheer rock walls, lumbering or scuttling through the midnight streets of the scattered towns that clung for their lives to the highway.

But I didn't pay near enough attention as I should, because I peered at them through the memory of my grandmother's eyes, the night she jerked me by the collar of my pajama top from the haunted cabin that she allowed to linger on in the woods above her farm. I still didn't know what was in there, what shades she lived with in that lonely valley.

But now I could remember: how I turned at the sound of whimpers between the rotted wooden slats, and she took my chin in her hand, and made me look at her, at her dark face and her startling blue eyes that practically glowed in the moonlight. The shadows formed a shape about her, something massive and terrifying and full of flowing, feline grace.

You leave those ghosts alone, little cub, she said. *You come away. You've hurt them enough.*

THE MUSIC OF BREMEN FARM

But for a flat tire, no one would have ever known that Old Hag Bremen was dead.

Her forebears, like other settlers from Germany, staked out plots in the shadows of the Blue Ridge Mountains even before the white colonies declared themselves a nation. Throughout the rolling hills, where houses regard each other across wide vales, and narrow roads still ford streams with wooden bridges held together by iron spikes, the Anglicized names speak from rusting mailboxes: Anselm. Flohr. Krone. Newman. Schrader.

Yet even in this place of isolation, with cornfields blanketing the land for miles before giving way to defiant oaks on ancient mountain, the Bremens stayed a world apart. They sent no sons to fight in the War of Northern Aggression. They did not come to the whitewashed A-frame churches. They did not grow crops, or ask for work in others' cattle farms or dairies or tobacco fields. Those few who knew the business of the Bremen family left them to it, and spoke of it at most in late-night whispers that by morning seemed like half-forgotten dreams.

By the time the single-lane dirt ruts finally gave way to asphalt, only one Bremen remained, a sad, solitary heir rattling alone inside a rambling home more than three hundred years old: still with an outhouse, still with a kitchen standing separate from the building where she made her bed. Only the squirrels and wasps that took shelter in the walls kept her company.

The rotten roof of the family barn, which only ever held what animals the family needed for themselves, had partially collapsed under a heavy snow around the time of the Korean War. She had never tried to have it fixed, and no one had ever offered to fix it for her.

No one was even certain of her name, but the children who on dares spied through her windows called her "Old Hag" and that seemed fitting enough.

Folks in the nearest semblance of a town, about five miles away, rarely saw her, and on the few occasions she ventured in to buy simple things like bread or grapefruit juice, she never spoke. The fact is, the cashiers who found this pale, smelly, shriveled woman with grey eyes and long unkempt hair staring at them from across the counter were grateful for her silence.

Only the children had any inkling how Old Hag Bremen spent her hours, and those inklings came from short, frightened glimpses after dark. They returned whispering of how she lurked in deep shadow through what was once one of her ancestors' bedrooms, tinkering with tubes spouting strange colored flames and glassware filled with bubbling fluid.

Those whispers protected her as well as any fence, until things began to change in the county where she lived. The people there elected a new prosecutor, an aggressive, agitated young man from the North named Edward Jacobs. Echoes of those whispers reached his ears, and he took the scene they described to mean something rather different from what the native folk believed.

The sheriff, a tall, lean, leathery man born and bred in those hills, argued to Jacobs that he should leave well enough alone, that the old lady hurt no one, but at last deferred to the prosecutor's wishes, as the law required, and sent two men in the dead of night to spy. They came back talking of a laboratory, and chemicals, and Old Hag Bremen downing the liquids brewed in her beakers. The next night, six more men went, with rifles and a search warrant. They brought the old woman back to the jail, seized her glass equipment and destroyed it.

She spent a month in the city jail to the south, as the county jail had no place to house women. But after that month, she was free, as the state's lab tests found no evidence a crime. No chemical that she had kept in her possession, nothing she had brewed, was against the law.

An innocent passerby, a stout laborer from a neighboring county, discovered her death a mere three months after her return to her family's farm. He'd spent a day sawing down trees on the slopes adjoining her property, and as he drove his pickup down the unpaved logging trail he blew a tire. Discovering his spare was no good, he hiked to the sprawling old house he could see through the trees in hopes of using a phone.

The second thing he noticed when he neared the old log house was the smell: the overpowering stench of a decayed body. The third thing he noticed, the flies swarming on the inside of the windows.

He had first noticed something else: a thin strain of music, tinny notes that conformed to no melody but still made him catch his breath and strain to hear, as if someone were singing and he couldn't quite make out the words. But the second and third things made him forget the music, made him run down the overgrown path from the house to the nearest paved road and frantically wave down a logging truck as it groaned around a curve.

The volunteer ambulance workers found the old woman in an indescribable state. Her pale, shriveled hands clutched a music box, an ancient heirloom from the Old Country, so tarnished and corroded that whatever song it held must have been silent for centuries.

WHEN JACOBS LEARNED of the old woman's death, he felt a trickle of sadness, a fleeting twinge of guilt, but no regret, no lasting sorrow. Mostly what moved behind his close-set brown eyes was a sense of relief. He didn't celebrate her death, but her passing, to his mind, made the world a simpler, safer place.

He did experience a different kind of regret, as proving this reviled woman a criminal would certainly have boosted his standing, politically and socially, in this community where he otherwise might always remain an outsider. He believed that if he had had a close watch kept on her, that opportunity would have come sure as sunrise. His one meeting with Old Hag Bremen (whose real name, he knew, was Adelia) convinced him of it. A week after her release from jail, she had come to his office to demand compensation for the destruction of her lab.

No one who lived in the county seat, nearly thirty miles from her land, had ever seen her there before. Jacobs' elderly secretary, inherited from the previous top lawman, cut short a scream when she saw the hag sitting in the lobby in a tattered dress the color of ash, her brittle cobweb hair draped past her waist. Her pale face peered from between the tangles of her locks, grey eyes cold and unblinking as she stared at the quailing woman and rasped two words: "Edward Jacobs."

Jacobs had seen many unpleasant things, even in his short career, but he grew queasy at the sight of this nightmare woman, terrible and pathetic at once, sitting across the desk from him, utterly out of place amidst the crisp law books on the shelves, degrees and paintings of sailing ships on the walls, the photographs of smiling wife and baby that watched over his drumming fingertips. He had held the leathery visitor's chair for her, then taken his seat and waited for her to speak.

When she did, it was like ice cracking. "You owe me."

Poker-faced, Jacobs replied, "I don't think so."

"You destroyed my dignity," she said. "How can I ever get that back? The least you can do is give me the money to replace the physical things you destroyed."

"I don't think so," Jacobs replied.

She stood, slammed both hands on his desk, and he flinched despite himself. "You ruined any chance I had to restore my family's fortune!"

Jacobs cocked his head, folded his arms and smirked.

"So much of what my ancestors had is gone. What they owned. What they knew. There was still one way I could bring back glory to my family's name, and you took it from me!"

"Lead into gold?" the prosecutor sneered. Old Hag Bremen trembled with rage, but Jacobs interrupted when she tried to speak.

"Woman," he said—he couldn't bring himself to call her "lady"—"I don't know how you did it. How you fooled the lab tests. But I don't believe this story you're spinning, not for a minute. Your house is not made of gingerbread. You're not a witch, or an alchemist, or whatever it is you pretend to be. If I have my say, you won't have your lab back, and mine is the only say that matters."

She snarled. "You think you understand, but you don't, not one bit."

"I don't need to understand." He stood up, and glared down at her. He wasn't a tall man, but for all his visitor's fearsomeness, he loomed over her by a head. "Get out."

But she wasn't looking at him. Eyes focused somewhere distant, she muttered his name, then repeated it.

"Don't do that," he said.

"I'll call the musicians. They were with my family in the Old Country. They're in the other Old Country now. But there's still a way that they can hear me. It may be the death of me, but they'll come."

"Get out."

"The story they tell about the musicians is all fiction, Mr. Jacobs. The real robbers never left our house alive."

"Get out!"

Jacobs had taken to wearing a shoulder-holstered pistol beneath his jacket as soon as he'd learned of that particular affectation of Southern prosecutors. He pushed back the flap of the blue suitcoat he wore and put his hand on the pistol's cold grip, making sure the old hag could see it. "Go!"

The hag stared, long enough that he prepared to shout again, his agitation and, yes, fear, building as each second passed. But when he opened his mouth, she turned and left without another word.

He heard no more from her, until the discovery of her death.

Jacobs sat in the passenger seat, and another deputy rode in the back, as the sheriff drove over steepening hills and through switchback turns toward the Bremen farm.

The old hag's body had been removed, and still lay in the city morgue an hour south, unclaimed by any family, as she had none. Now that the house could be endured without wearing a mask, two deputies had gone to inspect the place with gloved hands in search of any evidence of foul play.

Jacobs had ordered the sheriff not to send any more men than those two, not even to secure the scene with yellow tape. "If we do that someone's sure to notice, and then they'll call the press. We don't need any reporters asking about this right now."

Most of the ride unfolded in awkward silence. As he turned onto the final stretch of road before the house, the sheriff looked at Jacobs sidelong. "What if it's a murder, son? You can't sit on that. You can't keep people from finding out."

Jacobs clenched his jaw. "Then we control what they find out. Every word of it."

Besides, murder seemed unlikely. From the descriptions of the condition of the old woman's body, it sounded as if she had been savaged by animals, perhaps wild dogs, or a bear. Bears were such a common problem that one had actually wandered down the main street of the county seat and through the automatic doors into the hospital, where a game warden had to put it out of its beastly misery.

The sheriff barked into his radio as they pulled off the road and parked, asking the men for their locations. No answer came, causing the sheriff to grumble about outdated equipment. It wasn't at all uncommon for firefighters or deputies to respond to calls in the county's far corners and discover their radios no longer worked over long ranges.

The trio hiked toward the house through the woods, but as they came within short range, the sheriff still couldn't raise a response from his men—not even as the log buildings came in view. The sheriff drew his revolver, and the deputy cocked his rifle.

Jacobs drew the pistol from beneath his coat. The sheriff glanced at him sidelong again, his voice shaded with contempt. "You sure you know how to use that?"

"Yes," Jacobs snapped.

"I just don't want you to shoot me by mistake," the sheriff said, with an emphasis on "mistake" that Jacobs didn't like at all. Before he could reply, the sheriff walked to the main part of the house, the building that held the bedrooms, where the old woman's body had lain. He shouted the names of his men, but again, no answer. He gestured to his deputy, who circled around to the back. The sheriff stepped onto the front stoop and tried the door, which opened with a loud wooden groan. Silent as a puma, the sheriff slipped into the darkness within. Jacobs followed, not so silently.

Though the foyer was dark, beams of light sliced through the rooms beyond, piercing through holes in the chinking and gaps between the roof boards. The foyer let out into a sitting room where chairs stood sentry that had once been ornate and grandiose, but now were splintered and mildewed, feather down bleeding out through rips in the stained cushions. The sheriff stood at the door to a different room, sweeping the floor with a small flashlight. He gave a sharp intake of breath, and ducked inside.

Jacobs came in behind, and stopped short. But for the nameplate and badge that glinted in the flashlight beam, there would have been no easy way to recognize the torn body on the floor. Dark stains spattered the walls. There was no doubt what the stains were.

"Animals," Jacobs said.

The sheriff aimed his flashlight in Jacobs' face. "More men here, and this wouldn't have happened," he said, his voice like red hot iron. "We'll have to get at least a mile away before we're in range to call for backup." When the prosecutor didn't answer, the sheriff pushed past him, shouting the name of the other missing man.

"Sheriff!" called the deputy from outside. "There's blood. Leads up to the barn!"

THE UGLIEST ROOSTER Jacobs had ever seen squawked and scurried from the barn door as the men swung it open. It had no comb and no feathers on its head and neck, and bare pins jutted out here and there like spines from the salt-and-pepper plumage along its flanks. It squawked a second time as the men came inside, and flapped up to land on a beam above the door.

The sheriff asked, "You see any livestock when you came here last?"

The deputy shook his head.

The inside of the barn was in ruins, though apparently, incredibly, still in use. Much of the roof had collapsed, leaving old, rotten timbers strewn everywhere. The far end of the barn was a pile of rubble, but the near end still held its shape, though it looked as if a push with a finger could send it tumbling. A trough lay capsized in the straw on the ground, its wood splintered. To either side, stalls that once housed horses leaned askew.

But one was occupied. A wiry-haired old donkey stood in one of the stalls, its hindquarters to the men. It turned its long head to watch the strangers with one black-pearl eye.

"Well look at you," the deputy said, stepping toward the donkey. "Handsome feller. That crazy old woman was really off her rocker to keep you in this place."

The sheriff shushed him, whispering, "You hear that?"

Jacobs listened, and realized he heard music, thin notes that conformed to no melody. At first, given how they overlapped without rhythm, he thought they might be from a wind chime, but the sound was too continuous, too full of purpose, and somehow beautiful despite its chaos. And the sound, inside the decades-decayed barn, was also somehow frightening.

The trio advanced with the sheriff in the lead. The deputy edged toward the donkey, intending to approach it gently and lead it out. The rooster squawked again, startling them all. For a moment, Jacobs pondered shooting it. It held its ugly head sideways to glare down at them all with one baleful round eye.

The music didn't get any louder. Jacobs looked right and left, up and down, but couldn't pinpoint its source.

"There, there. Easy," said the deputy as he put a hand on the donkey's flank, running his palm across fur bristly as a wire brush.

Standing before a precariously balanced pile of timbers, the sheriff shined his flashlight over a suspicious-looking mound of straw packed underneath the boards.

The donkey shifted on its hooves at the deputy's touch, but made no noise. Puzzled, the deputy squinted into the stall, and noticed something lying by the beast's front hooves, clothed in dun and dark brown, the same colors as his own uniform. As the deputy realized what the shape on the floor must be, the donkey kicked him with bone-breaking force.

Neither Jacobs nor the sheriff saw what happened, though both heard a crunch, then a loud crash. They turned to see the deputy lying on his back atop a pile of broken wood, across the barn from the donkey's stall. Then a deafening rumble filled the barn that resolved into a deepest-basso growl. The straw pile under the strewn timber erupted.

A jet black mastiff lunged at the sheriff, its mouth distended to reveal teeth like white daggers, its shoulders higher than the lawman's waist.

But Jacobs was distracted by the rooster flapping past him, its talons nearly tangling in his hair. He stared at it in amazement, for its flight was no longer ungainly. Its long wings swooped in a manner impossible for such a bird. As Jacobs stared, he thought for a moment that he saw a completely different form flicker through the air, long sleek legs drawing up, muscled back rippling, a flash of something celestial and malevolent.

The rooster alighted, and the deputy screamed as it pecked his face.

The sheriff shouted too, firing his revolver point blank into the mastiff's muzzle, the gunpowder flashes leaving spots in Jacobs' eyes.

The prosecutor held out his pistol, wavering back and forth between the other two men, stymied as to what to do. Then he noticed the donkey. During the distractions, it had silently sidled up next to him, its huge shaggy head longer than one of his shins.

It was smiling at him. Its lips were stretched along its heavy muzzle in a manner that seemed impossible, showing teeth that seemed too large and too numerous, as if a human smile had been carved in some atrocious way into its countenance. The single black eye that met Jacobs' wide-eyed stare sparkled with mirth.

The beast stretched its neck as if it intended to nuzzle. Then it bit down on his arm, and bit through it. The hand holding the gun dropped away to land in the straw.

As Jacobs reeled backward in pain and shock, a piercing yowl shredded the air, and a dark shape sprang from the rafters. The last thing the prosecutor saw was the blood-flecked donkey's face, still regarding him with one mirthful eye, mouth still stretched in an unnatural, elongated grin. Then a hissing black thing with green eyes and needle claws landed on his shoulders, and the claws took his sight away forever.

With a wail, Jacobs fell.

As his life ebbed away, the bird stopped its attack on the prone deputy, and leapt, wings flapping in great sweeps, to the rafters where the cat had hidden. It opened its beak, and the sheriff distinctly heard words, bellowed loud as a vengeful angel's trumpet:

BRING THE ROGUE TO ME.

The dog stopped growling and stood on its hind legs, as did the donkey, as did the cat.

The sheriff saw four figures, like men, but still beast-like—creatures out of Faerie, or Hell—each baring teeth in unnaturally elongated smiles. The strange music that had tickled the ear so maddeningly when he first came into the barn grew louder, and the air grew darker around the beings as they began to dance. The dance could have been a simple folk jig, but the smiles of the things performing it charged each motion with stomach-churning menace. Each raised their arms and turned, and as they did so, they vanished, taking the music with them.

The sheriff, heart pounding, rushed to the stall where the donkey had stood, to discover the musicians had also taken Edward Jacobs' body.

AFTER THAT, THE *robbers never dared approach the house again. But the house suited the four musicians of Bremen so well that they did not care to leave it anymore.*

THE LEAD BETWEEN THE PANES

1.

With his tenth birthday only a week away, Rodney Muse hated to admit to his younger brother that he was too scared to go out the back door.

Why? The spiders. Seven of them, bodies round as dimes, legs striped like witch stockings, had stretched webs over the back porch light, from the porch rails to the tin roof, nets in every corner.

Little elfin Paul stood in the doorway, the overcast day beckoning over his shoulder, yelling,"C'mon!" and tugging the screen door so its hinges creaked. Rodney blurted, "Watch out for the spiders!" and instantly regretted it. Paul, only eight, had no fear of spiders.

He laughed. "Chicken!" He jumped, tore at a fistful of web. A big brown body landed in his hair.

Paul screamed, swatted the wriggling thing to the boards and crushed it under his sneaker. Then he started bawling.

Of course Mama blamed Rodney, her cold iron stare and pale scowl all for him, her smiles and coos for sniffling Paul and the red bite on his scalp. Mama doctored the wound at the kitchen table. She's always told Rodney never to go into the horse barn that used to be grandpa's, or the old chapel further up the mountainside, because they were infested with spiders. Rodney had never been bitten by one, and seeing the results made him that much more terrified. He stared until Mama noticed and smacked him.

The next morning all the webs were gone from the back porch. Rodney waited till after dinner, when Mama had curled on the couch with her knitting, herself thin and straight as her needles, and thanked her for banishing the spiders. Her smile held ice. "I didn't do that. Could have been bats. Or owls. They eat spiders."

Rodney lay awake that night, thinking of mouths that arrive suddenly in the dark to tear you out of the world. Beneath him in the lower bunk Paul breathed soft and easy.

2.

Light shone bruised through the stained glass window, which shouldn't have existed at all.

It had of course been Paul who broke Mama's edict and set foot inside the rotting church. He returned to recruit Rodney, eyes bright with what he'd found. "You won't believe what's in there. I bet it's worth something."

If a shark made of decaying wood had swallowed them, its gullet would have looked exactly like the inside of this old church, its floor strewn with the broken skeletons of chairs, the ribs of its ceiling beams skewed. The space reeked of mud and mildew. With each step Rodney feared his foot would plunge through the floorboards into the black hollow visible between them. Paul rushed past the leaning block of the altar after grabbing up a long flat board that had a few small sections of two-by-four nailed to it crosswise at irregular intervals. He propped up it against the back wall. It almost reached the base of the window.

"Hold this," he said.

Rodney stared at the figure of Christ formed in panes of colored glass and lines of lead. Ablaze with the noonday sun, his gaze tracked Rodney as he approached. Blood trickled from his crown of thorns, the holes in his hands, the rip in his side. Though no cross was visible, he stood in the crucifixion pose, shedding blood-red tears. A horde of smaller figures swarmed at his feet. Almost all pointed up. Most appeared to be screaming.

Rodney shook his head, mute. His brother laughed. "You are so chicken. I want to see. Up close."

Rodney stood under the board and gripped as Paul climbed, his arms and legs trembling either from the strain of the ascent or despite his bravado. Later, Rodney remembered the red light that bathed Paul's face as he craned his neck to peer into the window. He remembered, too, a revelation that the pointing figures weren't screaming. They were laughing, the corners of their mouths curled up. Even later, when he was old enough, he'd question this memory. He was at the wrong angle, he couldn't really see them. Paul could.

Rodney tried and tried, when his mama shook him and raged with questions, when the doctors and police investigators worried politely at him for hours, but he could never remember what happened after Paul looked in the window. Or where his brother went. His mama blamed him. She wouldn't accept that he couldn't control his younger brother.

In his heart of hearts he knew she was justified.

The historical preservation society removed the window. Mama called him a liar, said it didn't look at all like what he described. He fantasized about finding the place where they stored that window, breaking in with a bag full of rocks so he could smash out every pane. He never did track it down.

When he married Anne, Mama didn't come—nor did she come to the hospital when Chris was born, the ceremony when he earned his GED, his community college graduation.

He and Anne and Chris attended Mama's funeral. They were the only ones there.

3.

I see it now, Paul said.

But Rodney didn't. He saw nothing. He hung in the dark, the rhythmic chirping in the far distance his only sensory anchor. That and a wind that iced his flesh.

He tried crawling away from the cold, yet as his back legs clung to the thread that was his only link to safety, his forelegs found nothing. The breath that buffeted him grew warmer.

Stay away, Roddy. It's full of spiders.

Not Mama's voice—that was Anne's voice. He called out. "Sweetheart?"

Teeth closed around him. The unyielding edges split his flesh, crushed his bones, squeezed his neck shut as he tried to scream.

The scream he woke to wasn't a human sound. The pulse of Anne's heart monitor switched to a steady drone, the rasp of her labored breathing replaced by silence, breast cancer's final statement.

He did scream then, and if he'd had any real power, that scream would have cracked the earth.

Anne's body, nothing but bones in his embrace. Rotted wood strung into a mannequin. Gentle hands pried him away, levered him out of her hospital bed.

Chris, all of nine, watched silent from the door. Rodney blinked at the stains under his son's eyes, saw they were just tears, filtered through his own blurred sight. Chris in a button-down and slacks, that Gwaltney boy beside him in jeans and a black T-shirt, a heavy metal devil on his chest. Rodney didn't much like or trust Jimmy Gwaltney but at that moment he was grateful to see his son's shifty friend sticking by him, because dear old dad was going to be useless for a little while.

For a long while.

4.

The storm pounded the office window glass. As Rodney's cell phone buzzed in his trouser pocket, all the eighth floor lights went out. He fumbled for the device as lightning roped beneath the sky. The flare revealed one of the city's decorative pear trees toppling into the street as the wind ripped it from its moorings. A van screeched to a halt just short of striking it.

The phone's display flashed Chris's name. He flipped it open. "Everything okay?" Crackling on the other end, a transmission from the Arctic.

He sought a stronger connection. By the time he reached the office tower's roof garden, panting from the stair climb, he could actually see the shadow of the freak storm's hindmost bulk retreating up the slopes of Bent Mountain, fleeing the valley, with smaller clouds overhead milling confused like cast-off ballast.

He opened the phone, saw he had a voice mail message. Within the shrinking darkness on the mountain slope something blinked bright.

Chris's recorded voice faded in and out. "Dad, Jimmy just came by...blew over the old church on Granma's...says we won't believe..."

And then Paul's voice whispered, "I want to see. Up close."

Rodney looked up, following the whisper. He staggered as his head went light. The morsel of the sun hung muted in the post-storm haze as the remnants of cloud poured together into a silhouette, its wingspan stretching from horizon to horizon. Half-formed jaws closed around the sickly orb and blotted it. For an instant the city returned to darkness.

The clouds dispersed into blue.

Bent Mountain was released from shadow. The light shining from its slope remained. Rodney recognized the place where this light hung in the air. He squinted. A distinct outline: the Gothic arch of a stained glass window, an unanchored portal where the chapel stood. Had stood.

He pressed "Call." His son's phone rang, rang, rang. He pictured his boy arriving in the clearing on the back of Jimmy's ATV, trundling toward the wet rubble, face bathed in light from Christ's blood-rimmed gaze.

None of Rodney's warnings, reservations or affections had ever saved anyone he loved.

Paul laughed. *Chicken.* And added, *It's dark and lonely, bro, once you've been eaten.*

Rodney sprinted down the stairs three at a time.

STONE FLOWERS

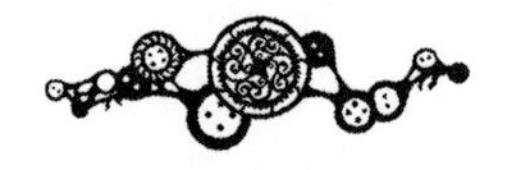

Prologue

An elderly woman smiles wanly from a tiny photo on the newspaper's front page, above the fold, off to one side.

The accompanying article describes how, inside 87-year-old Galina Brodsky's body, doctors found and removed an object with the alien-sounding name "lithopedion"—more readily known by its romanticized common name, a stone baby. A fetus that starts its development in a place outside the uterus and then dies. The mother's body protects her by calcifying the baby's corpse, rendering it harmless, an undetected passenger. A woman could go on to birth other children—as Brodsky had—and never know she still carried a child inside.

No more than three hundred cases have been recorded in the last four hundred years, the story states. A Muslim woman in Casablanca was believed to have carried her unborn baby inside her for almost fifty years. That had been the longest documented case until last week. Galina's doctor told the paper that he believes the lithopedion he removed could have been in her body as long as seventy years.

If so, the reporter writes, Mrs. Brodsky has made medical history.

Galina granted a brief interview only because the reporter was an old friend, the story says. She told the reporter she was embarrassed by the attention and that she'd be glad when she was out of her hospital room. Given her husband's accident and stroke, providing a new answer to a medical trivia question seems completely unimportant.

She calls it freakish coincidence that the pain inflicted by what turned out to be the lithopedion overcame her when she discovered her husband lying injured in the basement.

The article sketches Brodsky's extraordinary life in quick brushstrokes. How she and her husband Danilo escaped from three dictators—Stalin, Hitler, Perón—before coming to Virginia and building their dream house and art school atop Tinker Mountain. How, going by the name Daniel Broadsky, her husband became for a time the most sought-after sculptor in the nation. How they had raised three children, who all now have children of their own. How, after so many miracles, he'd been felled by that most mundane of misfortunes, a stroke, which sent him tumbling down the basement steps.

Astonishing, really, that he had even survived the fall.

Odessa, 1921

The skeleton-thin boy, his head a great thatched melon above scrawny neck and jutting ribs, played his crudely-cut reed in the prison yard. A man had given him this plaything, though he did not remember the man's face or name. He believed the man had been a prison guard, though he could not remember a uniform.

Each day he woke with the sad women, in the cell with the stinking bucket and the blankets that crawled with lice. Then the feed hole slid up in the bottom of the door, and after the bowls slid through and the women gathered around them, scooping the scraps of bread from the water with their fingers, a jailor's gruff voice would call to him. "Danilo," the guard would say, "You may come out." And he crawled through the feed hole, the gritty floor rough on his knees. They let him play in the prison yard, a child alone, surrounded by stone walls and forbidding doors.

It was a miracle, perhaps, that he could even produce a note from the reed. No one had taught him how—he seemed to simply have a knack for it, as some do. He knew few songs, so often the notes he chose were random. He once played a song he remembered in his mother's voice, and after he repeated it a few times, from one of the cells a woman's voice joined in: *bayu bayushki bayu, bayu detushku moyu*, she sang, *chto na gorke, na gorye, o vesyennei, o pore.* He kept playing, wanting the voice never to stop, but it finally did, and he never learned who it was who sang that day.

One of the four walls of the prison yard held no doors. The stones and mortar were pocked and stained. He liked to run his fingers in the dirt before the wall because of what he sometimes found there, shining buried treasures. He remembered from the days outside, when the warm winds from the sea heralded the great battleships, and the men on horseback would greet them, their swords at their sides, their coats glinting with shiny medals. That's what he found in the dirt: officers' medals, badges, pins, a trove of them.

He hid them in the yard now; he didn't bring them back to the cell. The only time he did, he showed them off to the one who took it upon herself to make sure he ate, the one who wiped his face afterward, who let him call her aunt; and she began to weep. Others, too, saw the shining metal things in his hands, began to cry, started to scream at him. Soon he was crying himself. He didn't understand what he'd done to upset them.

So now he kept them to himself in the yard, unburied them and laid them out, moved them around. He tried to use their shapes and colors to create things in the dirt, letters or images. He arranged them in a face, his father's face. He did not know where his father was. The landlady's dog had tried to bite him, and when Danilo told his father, his meaty face grew dark, and he took a knife and left the flat. Later Danilo heard the landlady screeching in anger. He half-heard phrases: *You shouldn't have dared* and *I can prove* and *kontr-revolutsiya.* Only two days later the prison men came.

Danilo played in the dirt, arranging the medals in circles that radiated out like the petals of a flower.

Ural Mountains, 1932

Galina knew the truth.

Her father insisted that Danilo's carvings could never measure up to his own, not without the blessing of the Queen of the Copper

Mountain. They had no heart, he said. Pretty as they were, they would never breathe, never live, he said.

But any untrained eye could see that Danilo's work in stone and wood and paint was at least the equal of her father's, if not better. He had carved and painted a likeness of their cat so real in its tabby-striped softness she absentmindedly began to pet it one day, only to jerk her hand back in surprise—and then spotted the real tom under the big table playing with a rat's tail.

She thought Danilo already the better artisan at fifteen than her bitter sire at forty-one, tainted green with envy that when he made the monthly wagon trips to the village market the boy's creations sold better then his own.

So Sergei Prokovich lorded this pathetic superstition of the mountain queen over his ward to deny his approval, ensuring the boy always fell short of an invented standard. She had voiced this opinion exactly once, making sure Danilo saw, and heard. Her father rewarded her with a drunken backhand, then slumped with a sob into his creaky wooden chair. She continued to glare until he screamed at her to leave. She had then dashed off into the twilit field, mosquitoes swarming to drink from her flesh when she finally collapsed in the grass.

Snow-capped even in summer, the mountains pushed against the sky, weary giants slouching their rounded shoulders. Would that one could reach out its fist now and crush her.

Danilo, who had stayed silent, shaking, through the exchange, found her in the encroaching dark, perhaps guided by the cloud of insects. A year her junior, he was so fragilely thin, though so was she, so was father. Danilo had been lean when he came, after his own parents died in Odessa, and exhausted by the endless miles in the cart. Danilo's mother and Galina's father were distant cousins, he had agreed to take Danilo on as a favor to his aunts, who thought it a good fit as the boy showed an artistic spark. She had thought so many times about the sad story of the boy's imprisonment that it had become, in a way, her own memory—

"You should not fight with him," Danilo said, appearing next to her with no warning. "Not over me."

She sat up from the weeds, defiant. "He should never speak to you like that. He has no right."

Danilo would tell her later, how, despite the puffiness around her eyes, his breath caught at the sight of her face in the moonlight, and how his head swam, surrounded by the buzz of mosquitoes. But she thought he gasped at the bruise on her cheek, and when he reached with a trembling hand to brush a tear away, the touch surprised her, warmth spreading from the contact. She caught his wrist before he could pull his fingers away.

Later they lay in the grass, oblivious to the stings that welted their skin. The night grew colder, but neither wished to return to the house.

Something rustled in the grass, and Danilo sprang up. She heard him whisper, come back.

"What is it?"

His voice came in nervous starts and stops as he answered in the dark. "Sometimes when I come out here to be by myself, to play the pipes I made to please my mothers, a tiny dragon comes to listen. It has gold eyes. Scales like tarnished copper. It stays until I stop playing."

Galina snorted. "You play pipes for a lizard?" She felt strange. At times she had heard him play, and wherever she was she would stop and listen, but not go to him.

He peered long into the grass. Then he stood. His voice sounded odd. "You should not talk back to your father. What he says about me, he is right."

She watched in stunned silence as he walked away.

Ural Mountains, 1933

Galina's boots would never hold up to a hike into the unforgiving mountains, so she navigated her tiny bedroom in the dark, relying on touch and familiarity until she pulled aside the faded sheet hanging in the door. In the main room her father snored on a pallet beside the remains of the fire. Grateful that the few embers still dying in the hearth had lasted long enough to gift her with their light, she waited for her eyes to adjust. Then, stepping with care, she searched through the room for every rag she could find.

Her father stirred in his sleep, moaned words she could not make out. She held her breath until his returned to a steady rasp.

Back in her room, she grew bolder, lighting a lamp so she could accomplish the task at hand. By the little flame's illumination she wrapped the rags around her booted feet, and bound the wrappings in place with heavy twine. She pulled three plain dresses on over her leggings, and over all of that her hooded fur cloak, the one that had been her mother's.

No longer so concerned for secrecy, she took the lamp out into the main room. Horrible as the cold would be, she needed to leave while the stars still shone. She wanted the sun to be as high in the sky as it could go once she reached the mountain, because she knew that was where she would find Danilo.

In the village, the laughing women with faces like plump apples had shaken their heads in mock shame, while their thick-bearded husbands chuckled and joked about the rooster who fled the coop. A boy skilled with his hands, for certain, but without the stomach to right a wrong and endure a wedding. Hardly the first time the villagers had observed such a disgrace unfold, but perhaps, truly, she was better off.

Yet she knew Danilo: no matter how his craft consumed him, no matter how his jaw clenched at her father's taunts, he had wanted their child to have a father, she absolutely knew it in her heart. She could not believe he intended to run away from her. No, her father's lies had driven him to do something insane. And wherever he was, he wanted to come back. She knew it.

But how could he be alive after so many days on the mountain? It did not matter. In some manner not unlike the way she felt the life that was theirs to sculpt thriving warm in her belly, she knew with certainty he was alive, and trapped. She did not want to think about what the journey she was about to undertake could mean for their baby. Her faith in herself was all she could trust.

She did not notice till she was almost to the door that her father had sat up to watch her—his face, turned away from the firelight, a black oval fringed by the wisps of gray that clung to his temples.

"Your lies brought this," she said.

He began to shake. She could not tell whether he was laughing or crying.

At last he spoke, a flat whisper. "She wouldn't take me, but she wanted him." His own words seemed to choke him. "You will never get him back."

"Are you going to stop me, then?"

The coward didn't answer.

Her rage carried her outside, kept her heart pounding, a source of heat to fight the terrible cold.

The dawn found her trudging into the foothills, a black flea atop an endless snow-covered hide, slogging through drifts at times deeper than her hips. A breeze clawed her face with fingers so cold they burned, and it strove to worm those terrible fingers through the layers of her clothes. A quavering voice in her head grew louder with every cloudy breath, telling her she had already doomed herself, her baby, one suicidal fool chasing another.

But then the way became easier—because she found tracks in the snowdrifts. Tracks like she'd never seen before in winter, something with clawed feet and a belly that slid across the top of the snow as a snake's or lizard's would—though if it was such a creature, it was larger than any variety she'd ever laid eyes on. She followed the trail, and her trek ceased to be such an ordeal.

The path led her onto the stony shoulders of fallen giants, and higher still.

By the time the sun blazed overhead, she found the first of the flowers, a carving of concentric petals half-hidden in snow. She brushed the flakes away and uncovered a rose bloom, larger than her head, every petal sculpted out of the mountainside in detail that astonished.

That find was just the first of many. Not long after, still following the path drawn for her in the snow, she arrived at the cave mouth.

When she called out in that dark space, the words that echoed back to her no longer sounded like her voice.

Denmark, 1939

They fled from yet another tyrant.

Danilo's silver tongue had acquired them a second horse to drag their cart through the icy muck that snowfall had made of the road. "What do you need it for now?" he had cajoled the farmer they'd fallen in with two nights ago, as the bent and browned old man made his own plans to flee over the border. "Too many will slow you. Take no more than you need."

Around them barren trees scratched at the grey sky. They struggled on alone—once they had been part of a great caravan of covered wagons, rolling carts, even automobiles pulled by horses. A few refugees pedaled their bicycles through the sleet. The caravan was beset with storms, once assaulted with machine gun fire and artillery. To stop and help the wounded or the dying meant offering yourself to Death.

They had slipped again and again past that bony grasp.

Had Danilo not bluffed his way past a *Schutzstaffel* officer, using fake orders typed on stolen stationary marked with an official seal, they would have been forced like all the others to turn south instead of north at Hamburg—the wrong direction.

Despite the cold, she couldn't bear to stay under the stifling canvas covering. She insisted, despite Danilo's protests, on managing the reins. She would forever be the first to acknowledge her husband's genius, but his astonishing talents did not extend to horsemanship.

Eons had passed, it seemed, since the terrible winter when they left her father's farm—but she felt certain that winter and its malevolent Queen had pursued them, had found them here.

Danilo walked beside the wagon and sometimes pushed. He had grown thick as a tree, and strong. It was a wonder his hands could still be so gentle.

He hurried to the head of the cart, keeping pace beside her now, his head level with her knee, and tried to lighten the mood. "When we have our son, we should call him Sergei. Would you like that?" She stiffened, but he didn't seem to notice. "It's your father's name. Of course you'd like that."

"How could you know what I like?" she said. "But I suppose you'll do whatever *you* like."

He laughed. "What is this now? I want what you want."

She knew better, but she said it nonetheless: "I want you to play the pipes."

"What?" He laughed again, even more incredulous.

"You heard me."

"How silly. You know I can't play pipes." Yet, improbably, on this horrific day, one of many they'd endured, many more still ahead, his smile brightened. "But for you, if it is what you want, I will learn. Now, our baby—"

But she did not know, not then, if she could ever have another child.

"If it is a girl," he went on, "I like the name Tamara."

Then his sky-wide grin faltered, for she had begun to shake her head, no, no, no, no. "You cannot call her that," she said. "You cannot!"

He touched her knee, frightened. "What's wrong?"

Furious, she turned to him. "I could tell you, and tell you, and tell you," she said. "But you will never remember."

Then she spoke, and no matter how many times he asked her to repeat herself, he could not hear the words.

Virginia, 1985

A warm wind wafted through the screen door into the den, ruffled sensuous fingers through Daniel's beard. As he held up the eagerly anticipated letter—the page practically burned in his fingers—the caress of the breeze felt like Fate herself offering congratulations.

Had he sculpted a mountain and built a watchtower at its top, he could have stood no higher than he felt at that moment. Though in a way, he had done exactly that, choosing this site in the Appalachians after they arrived in New York; carving this home out of the earth; building the school through word of mouth, then advertising in print and broadcast; building a career to heights that sometimes dizzied him. And here, in his trembling hand, fluttered the ultimate reward.

As soon as the lump in his throat loosened, he pulled the screen door open, strode out onto the freshly varnished deck and bellowed to be heard in every corner of his wife's garden terraces. Students and their easels were scattered throughout the trellises and beds. He called them all inside, his order evoking frantic protests from the silly teenagers and even sillier grown-ups. "It's not time yet! I'm not finished!" whined the freckled girl perched beside the snapdragons—Jackie, not quite fourteen, with just enough talent that she could perhaps get somewhere if she ever took her lessons seriously.

He wasn't unsympathetic to her complaint. Only twenty minutes ago he had ordered all the little chickadees out into Galina's fantastic flowered landscapes with instructions to complete an oil painting from life in exactly an hour, merciless instructor that he was.

"Don't worry about that. Put your brushes down and leave your easels. I have news!"

Once certain they were coming, he turned—to find Galina leaning on the back of the couch, wearing a paint-stained smock of her own, eyeing him with a twinkle of coy suspicion. He offered her a smile bright and broad as the sky.

When everyone assembled, he read the letter aloud.

In Daniel's newest series of sculptures—the most attention-getting of his career—he molded busts of great world leaders: Winston Churchill. Gandhi. Martin Luther King. John F. Kennedy. He had chosen to include in the series the current president, whom he admired with fervor, whom he saw as Kennedy's heir. Kennedy had paved the way for civil reform here in the land that Daniel now thought of as home. But Kennedy had also understood the threat posed by the monster that consumed the land Daniel could never return to, the Russia of his childhood, a monster grown from medals sown in the dirt.

Kennedy's party lost its way in the Vietnam quagmire, lost its courage, began to act as if they no longer perceived the bear slavering inches from their exposed throats. The man who was now president, who never lost his nerve or his humor even when wounded by a would-be assassin's bullet—he understood the world would never sleep in safety so long as the monster lived.

So Daniel had sculpted him, and the great man had somehow gotten word of it. His staff had asked a price and Daniel had named one. And in the letter he read to his enraptured students, the White House chief of staff informed him that his price would be honored: the statue given freely in exchange for a private audience with the president.

They clapped for him and hugged him, and after a few minutes of that nonsense he wrenched the smile from his face and ordered them back outside.

Only once they were gone from the room did he notice his wife wasn't smiling. She asked, "What will you tell him, Danilo?"

He frowned. "You need to ask? I will tell him, with emphasis, not to waver. I will tell him not to listen to these new liberals in the media who speak of anyone who opposes communism as if they are raving reactionaries. They are no better than the revolutionaries who hated the Czar more than they loved their own country. I will tell him that while he fights to contain the spread of communism, he must remember he is in the right, whatever the outcry."

Galina's own frown deepened. "Have you forgotten that a government is not its people? Yes, the Soviet Union is not Russia, but our Russia is still there. Our families are still there, what's left of them." She fixed his gaze with hers, then looked away. "Have you forgotten even *that* now? There is so *much* you have forgotten."

An awkward silence followed. "Of course I haven't forgotten," Daniel said. "Why would you think that?"

But as he asked the question, she left.

He didn't try to follow her, nor did he let anger crease his brow for long. Galina had her moods. After all the terrors they'd endured together, a difference of opinion seemed too insignificant a thing to fret over.

He ventured out to check on his pupils' progress, acting on the well-tested principle that his hulking presence would make them work twice as fast. He found Jackie again beside the snapdragons and lavender, with reasonably competent facsimiles of those blooms taking shape on her too-tiny canvas. He jabbed a thick finger at her painting. "Those shadows should be umber, not black."

"Oh!" She started and turned around. But when he saw her face, something startled him: her eyes had flashed green, he thought, or for an instant reflected that shade.

The surprised look didn't leave her face, but she wasn't looking at her teacher. "Who's that girl? I haven't seen her before."

Indeed, a girl Daniel had never before seen on the grounds regarded them from the gazebo. A slight breeze stirred her pale hair, made it flow like soft snowfall. She was younger than most of his students, perhaps eleven, in a dress of simple gray, face a graceful oval. He could not make out the color of her eyes.

Something about her caused a stir in the pit of his stomach, a fluttering anxiety the likes of which he had not felt in decades. He started to tell Jackie he did not recognize the girl either, but his throat and teeth and tongue couldn't form the sounds.

When he looked back, the gazebo was empty. He forgot all about it soon after.

Virginia, 1987

Galina and her grandson Sam sat side by side on the loveseat in the den, their backs to a wall of river stone and a circular window framed with yellowed masonry, arranged by Daniel in a pattern like a sunburst or a daisy bloom.

Sam seemed to enjoy these moments much more than his older, more surly siblings ever had. Rather than fidgeting through the folktales she shared, he sat unabashedly spellbound. In the kitchen at the other end of the house, Irene—Sam's mother, Galina's youngest daughter—sang as she sliced carrots and cucumbers for dinner, a chore she'd taken upon herself during this afternoon's visit.

Sam listened, and Galina told: "Everyone in the village believed the boy had run away, but she knew where he had gone. Because the Queen of the Copper Mountain loved him too. She loved to hear him play the pipes, and wanted him to only play for her.

"She lured him to her lair with promises that she would make him the greatest maker of beautiful things that the village had ever seen. And because of his master's lies, he believed he needed the Queen's help, and he went to her, and she named her price, that he would spend the rest of his days with her under the mountain, and never come back."

"Did he come back?" The boy asked.

Galina answered with a thin smile and kept speaking. "But the girl he had vowed to marry did not believe he had run from their wedding. She knew where he had gone, and who he must be with. She wrapped herself in every warm thing she could find, she tied layers of old wool rags tight around her feet, and she marched to the mountain through a day darker than night."

"Did she find him?" her grandson asked.

"Not at first. But she found the cave of flowers, beautiful flowers made from stone, made by men who the Queen took. And she shouted, and shouted, and shouted that she wanted the boy she loved back."

Almost, almost, she felt no pang of regret. She ached so much to tell, to unburden, and this was the only way she knew to safely vent that terrible pressure. And so she went on.

"And finally the Queen appeared. She was like a woman and a dragon both, tall with eyes bright as fire and robes that gleamed. She was fiery too, like a dragon, because she was angry, because the boy wanted to be set free, wanted to break his promise.

"The Queen told the girl that she could have her betrothed back, but he would forget all he had learned from her. The girl begged her not to do this, because she feared he would be so unhappy at losing his skills that he would seek the Queen again. And the Queen told her for this to be so she must have something else in exchange. She knew the girl was with child, and she said she had always wanted a child of her very own.

"The girl cried and cried, but agreed to the bargain, and this made the Queen angrier, because she wanted the girl to refuse. She taunted the girl mercilessly. She told the girl her daughter's name and said that some day, when it was too late, she would give her daughter back—"

"Mom!" Irene stood in the hall, arms akimbo. "How awful! You know that's not how the story goes."

Galina regarded her daughter coolly. "Must I bind myself to those ridiculous translations you read him?"

Irene rolled her eyes. "You don't have to make it so *dismal*. I just don't want you scaring Sam."

"I'm not scared!" her son protested.

Then Daniel opened the patio door and stumbled into the room. His dark eyes scanned the walls, never settling, never finding a focal point.

He clutched a small painting in both hands—an impressionistic rendition of a pale-haired girl standing before a trellis of hyacinth bean. The paint was still wet. Some of it had smeared across the front of his sweatshirt.

"Mr. Brodsky?" called a voice. A worried-looking mouse of a girl came in behind him, a bewildered student no older than fourteen.

Danilo held the portrait toward Galina, mouth working, sound fighting to come out.

"What's going on?" blurted Irene. She had to shout again before the girl spoke.

"My assignment. That girl out in the garden. She posed for me and I painted her. When I brought it to him ...." There were tears on her cheeks. "I don't know what's wrong."

"What girl?" demanded Irene, as Galina regarded the oval face, the dun dress, the hair like snow. Her own face turned pale before her eyes narrowed.

"He'll be all right," she snapped. Then, to her daughter, "Take her to the kitchen phone so she can call her parents to pick her up. Lessons are over."

The student started to protest, but Irene had already moved to intercept. She shot Galina a troubled glance as she pushed the sputtering girl ahead of her through the hallway. Sam began to cry, no doubt from seeing his beloved grandfather in such a state, but tending to him had to wait. Galina closed the distance to her husband, took the painting away from him without a word. She followed her daughter down the hall, turned to descend the basement stairs.

Daniel shook and rubbed at his arms as if he had just come in from a blizzard. Then noticed his grandson sitting alone, sobbing.

He didn't understand how he'd gotten from the garden to the den, but what good would it do to let Sam see his fear? A graying giant, he lumbered to the boy, patted his shoulder with a huge but gentle hand. "There now," he said. "No need for worries. There's nothing to cry about. Nothing at all."

Virginia, 2003

On a night when clouds hung low enough to shroud the mountaintop, Daniel stumbled naked and wet down the central hallway of the home built by his own hands.

He moved at a speed unsafe for his sagging weight and softened bones. He skidded and caromed against a river stone wall—every stone in it arranged to suit his will—and barked his elbow. He took no notice, didn't stop until he reached the basement door, his hand gripping the knob as if it were an extension of the power that gripped him.

Behind him a snail trail of water led backward to the bathroom, where the overhead light still shone, the hot tub jets still bubbled.

In the condensation on the mirror, the frantic streaks made by his fingers still remained, not yet filled in by the steam, the space he'd wiped clear to stare goggle-eyed at a figure with hair like snow.

He opened the door to the stairwell and groped for the light switch. Right as he found it, his wet feet slipped and he fell. His shadow thrashed before him, crazy partner in a dance of pain. The cement floor that broke his fall offered no other mercy.

He lay for some time on that surface that he had troweled smooth so many years ago. What he at first took to be the rattle of his own breath sharpened into a different sound, a creature scuttling toward him across the hard floor. He looked up, did a double take to see a young girl standing at the top of the stairs, peering down at him through a snow-white cascade of hair.

The apparition distracted him from the creature's approach, until it flicked its tongue against his ear.

He cried out and turned his head, raised a pain-wracked arm to ward off whatever attack was coming, but the creature had scurried away. He caught a glint off shiny green scales as it sidewound into the darkness.

His eyes stayed fixed on the point where the creature had vanished. He didn't move, his body an archipelago of pains small and large.

The thing had gone into the storage room, that tomb for hundreds of cast-off children born of pastels and pigment and clays and canvas and stone. His unfinished, imperfect offspring.

If he shouted, if he could manage even a scream, perhaps Galina would hear him, even in this house he'd built on the mountaintop with its sturdy stone walls.

Instead, after a long silence broken only by the voices that clamored in his head, he started to pull himself in the direction the creature had gone, dragging his broken body into the dark.

no place, no year

Dreaming, Galina shivers feverish on a metal floor, in the filthy cargo hold of a ship bound for South America, while her young husband holds her wrapped in blankets. He cries quietly, leaving only once to beg the hard-faced crewmen for a damp cloth.

She shivers naked on the stone in a freezing cold cave, hearing her sweet love call her name from a place she cannot see, the warmth of his arms denied her.

The abyss gapes hungry above her and the Queen slithers across it in her finery, scales of glittering emerald, eyes like lakes set afire. Talons flex, the curving gold weapons of a monster that listened to a boy's piping in a mosquito-swarmed field, and longed.

Would that Galina had gone to him when he played, would that she had taken a rock and crushed the entranced lizard when it was small and distracted—when she was vulnerable, far away from her kingdom, green scales speckled by the sun.

Dreaming, Galina shouts, "Leave me alone!"

I give back what I took. I take back what I gave.

Then she's no longer dreaming. Beside her the bedside clock flashes the witching hour. She knows immediately that Daniel's not in the room, has never gotten into bed with her.

She pads from the bedroom, heart laboring faster as she calls his name and hears no reply. She peers down the lighted basement stairs, sees the blood at the bottom, and where that leads, hurries to the storage room as panic thrashes in her chest.

With long rows of metal-framed wooden storage bins to either side of her, she gropes in the center of the room for the pull chain that will throw on the light. She calls Daniel's name again, hears nothing.

She finds the chain, pulls, and the first blinding arc of light reveals a girl with head haloed in white, standing just inches away.

Galina screams.

But the girl is gone—and her husband lies sprawled in an aisle between two of the bins, bone jutting from a torn and bleeding knee, naked flesh blackened with bruises. He raises his head, face frozen in an agonized scowl.

He found them: the paintings made by the students who saw the white-haired girl in the garden, who painted her portrait—always the same age, the same dress, the same oval face and snow-blond hair, no matter what the year. Twenty-one in all that Galina took from his confused hands. They're strewn around him, some smeared with his blood.

She'd always known who it was who smiled shyly from the canvases, wanting so badly to be seen, to know she wasn't forgotten. At first Galina had thought it cruel, how the Queen used their daughter's ghost to taunt them. But she determined to never show rage, never weep. Why should she ever give her tormentor such gifts?

She had kept every portrait, stacked them on their sides on a bottom shelf It never mattered that they were in plain view. Daniel couldn't see them, or if he did, he would forget they were there the moment his gaze wandered

How did he find them in the dark?

Running is beyond her at her age, but at the children's insistence they had a phone installed downstairs, and that's what she steps toward when the sudden pain in her belly doubles her over, forces her to her knees.

A flicker in the corner of her vision, a sinuous strand of green.

A superheated stone burns inside her. The pain surges, brings her to the floor.

The ceiling fades. Above it space shines black. She looks up at the figure unfolding its limbs in that space, and even in her agony she snarls defiance. She addresses the Queen in Russian, her voice that of a woman pierced by a spear. "I cannot fight your power. I never could. Whatever it is that your heart demands you do to me—do it. Then, please, trouble us no more."

Like a flag the vision furls and slides away.

Despite the pebble burning white hot in her abdomen, she makes the journey to the phone, an ordeal of just a few feet that feels like hours, days, the remainder of a lifetime.

Epilogue

He lies in his bed, kept alive by tubes and tenderly held spoonfuls. Other hands move him, keep him free of bedsores. When he speaks, he hears the words in his head, but the sounds that come from his mouth are the unsculpted squawks of a baby.

He remembers now—he remembers Tamara, the stone baby, the girl with hair of snow. When Galina sits beside him, keeping him company, reading to him from the paper or from a long Russian novel, the girl is there too, resting her head on her mother's shoulder, listening.

He wants to tell his wife that the long-delayed birth did not banish their first child, it freed her, and now wherever Galina goes she follows. She is waiting for the end, when her mother will see her, and at last they will embrace.

But he cannot tell her. There is a wall between them, a barrier of stone and cold silence. There is a wall between his mind and his useless tongue, between his anger and his limp hands. He cannot carve the wall, cannot shape it in any way.

He remembers now—he remembers that he played the reeds. He could play again, if his body would move. He is frozen as he was in the cave, unable to speak as his beautiful and beloved Galina lowered her hood to reveal her wind-burned face and made her impossible demands of his pitiless, envious jailor.

But now, in his fugue of memory and delusion, her eyes find his in the cave wall, and she says without speaking, *It was a terrible sacrifice I made for you, my Danilo, but in the end it was just one of many, so, so many.*

GUTTER

Without letting up on the gas, Kyle held the box of business cards out the window and shook it open, dumping his name in the gutter a thousand times over.

He circled the entire block, drawing a line around the abandoned office buildings, a regiment of eyesores built in the 1930s and left to decay as industry shifted to the suburbs. Cornices grinned ragged, the bricks of their teeth fallen away. Crumbling gargoyles made for sad guardians, jutting lumps long divested of wings and heads. Below columns of broken windows, along the fissured sidewalks, the gaping doors whispered darkness, the plywood that once hushed them rotted to tatters.

Circuit completed, box emptied, Kyle parked in the middle of the street. He left the engine idling as he stepped out of the pickup. Its headlights provided the sole illumination—clouds smothered the stars, and city hall had allowed the corner streetlamps to die.

He marveled at how evenly he'd distributed the cards, how by wondrous accident they formed something akin to a dotted line demarcating the curb, staking out this entire godforsaken block as *his*. Fine, then—no one else wanted to admit what goes on here. He'd lay claim and shout its truth so it couldn't be ignored.

A cops reporter knows a city in a way few others do. Whenever Kyle drove through the slums, he marked his progress not by landmarks but by crime scenes. Here's where the city worker, bent over with his torso half inside the freestanding electric box, got crushed by a drunk driver in the middle of the day. Here's the duplex where a gang tortured and strangled two middle-aged sisters for their payout in a disability settlement. Here's the vacant lot where once stood a three-story home, that burned to the ground with the wheelchair-bound family matriarch trapped inside.

And now Kyle stood before the spot where the city prosecutor insisted that sixteen-year-old Jeremy Sellars had bled to death.

Kyle called to the shadows behind the broken glass. "I'm back! Where are you?"

He'd imagined this moment over and over, what he might do when an answer came, and his scrambled brain replayed options, unable to decide between them. In one scenario, he ran. In others he dashed to the truck for the pipe wrench hanging in the gun rack, or the three full cans of gasoline waiting on the passenger side floorboards. In another he stayed put and tried to talk the boy into coming out into the light.

No sound. No shapes emerged. Nothing moved.

Spikes of pain pricked behind his eyes. A bad thing he'd done to himself, mixing booze and blow to screw up the courage to come here. Booze was an ex-lover he'd begun to court again as his marriage went south, but the cocaine—he'd stayed clean so long, but after everything that happened this day…it had been so easy for him to find a street corner dealer, as if the city itself wanted him to backslide.

For a blink, a hallucination assailed him: as if he spied on himself from one of those high windows, a shaggy string bean with wild eyes, staring up from a bruised face at the derelict floors. Another blink, the vision vanished.

Sober thoughts trickled in. Suppose one of the cops he knew pulled up right now? Made him walk heel-to-toe, smelled the whiskey sours on his breath, noticed his bloodshot eyes, the way he couldn't stop fidgeting. Worse, what if it was Detective Roache? He couldn't trust Roache anymore. Kyle's face still bore the marks of their encounter at the diner.

And once Penny got wind of the police report…well, what the hell else could she do to him? She already had full custody of Aaron.

When Kyle was a kid, a brash bespectacled geek daring enough to push the big swing to the highest it would reach and let go, whether the ground below was turf or asphalt, he had thought a newspaper reporter would be a damn cool thing to be. Dammit, it *was* a cool thing to be. Whatever Kyle's other problems were, he always had his job. What he did *mattered*. It bewildered him that doing his job the way it *had* to be done could set him at odds with so many people who should have been on his side.

He took a couple more steps, winced at the vise clamping his temples. "Jeremy?"

The soft thump came from his left, around the corner of the cross street. Had there been any other sound, a distant car engine or even a slight wind, he would have missed it.

He started for the corner, following the trail of his own discarded identity. In the morning, he could imagine some angry busybody, a scowling city elder with face elongated to Puritan dimensions, scooping one of the stray cards from the walk and glaring at the name and number there.

Let the bastard try to call—he'd find no Kyle D. Friedrich answering at that extension, not anymore.

The buildings loomed closer along the side street, weaving shadows into one darkness. About fifty yards down that street lurked the alley that led to that graffiti-defiled inner courtyard, known in the history books as Century Plaza, known to the cops who had to clean up after every crime that splattered there as the Boneyard. They said it with a laugh: "Got another one in the Boneyard." A stadium audience of birds usually congregated there, pigeons and crows, their noise deafening. Yet silent now.

Past a broken telephone pole, Kyle spotted it, what Roache would call "the bait." A black buckle-strap high-top, Jeremy Sellars' missing left shoe, waiting beside a storm drain. Kyle's brain screened an unpleasant short film of an arm reaching out from the black pit of the drain, setting down the shoe.

They never found Jeremy's body. Only the mate to that shoe, so drenched in blood it dripped when the evidence technician scooped it up.

He took another step and his headache surged, to the point he actually clutched his temples and doubled over, collapsed onto the asphalt and curled in on himself.

Hallucinations flickered: his own memories squeezed to the surface, as if fingers made of unbearable pressure sifted through them. He'd been through bad trips before, but never entwined with this level of agony, like worms of fire squirming through his skull. A freak smell of oil filled his sinuses. A voice in his brain: *I can't talk to you anymore. I shouldn't even be here.*

* * *

HE AND ROACHE sat in their customary booth in the back corner of R.W. Brews. Gary Roache had become his best source for goings-on at the police department, gave him the edge that meant he wasn't stuck writing stories from the official press releases. A bunch of guys from a construction crew played pool near the front door while Roache's pint of Bud went untouched.

[Shuddering in the road, Kyle rode shotgun within the memory, a time-travelling ghost.] "Demetrius Penn. Face down in the door of the old Holmes Clothiers building, bullet in the back of his head." Kyle used his fingers to mark off each death on his list. "Dorothy Hodges. Breaks a utility pole in half with her Toyota. Everybody thinks she's drunk, then the M.E. finds the stab wound in her ribs." Another finger. "Her drug addict boyfriend goes to the Boneyard not five hours later and slits his own wrists with the same knife. All in that same block. *That same block.* In just two days."

Roache ran a hand through nonexistent hair. "You don't have to go into all these details. I know 'em better than you ever will."

"But that's just a scratch. Only a year since I moved here, Gary, and I could swear nine out of ten crimes I cover happen in that one block in Old Southeast. The Boneyard block."

Roache chuckled, shook his head. "Ain't so."

"Yes it is. You know, it's weird how you boys are never there when it happens, only after. If you guys kept a patrol there every hour of the day, you'd cut the murder rate down to one or two a year."

"I'm not over patrol. I don't make those calls."

"I asked the Chief."

The detective's eyebrows rose. "And?"

"He just laughed at me. Wouldn't give me an answer."

Roache picked up his beer, took a long sip. "How's Penny doing?"

Kyle blinked. What did Penny have to do with it? "I think she's starting to like it here. Aaron's doing well now that we have him paired with that remedial teacher. That's helping out her mood. Why?"

[Outside this so-real flashback, Kyle whimpered, the fire worm writhing in his brain as the setting changed.] Roache's next words came from a conversation that took place two years later. He now

sat facing the front door, watching it warily, hunched forward so his meaty shoulders strained against his polo shirt. "Tell me you didn't just say that."

"I did. Audie Long is innocent."

Roache's face reddened. "Like hell. He had the blood of that Sellars kid all over him. Damn it, you know we found him curled up in the Boneyard, not ten seconds away at a good run from where they found the shoe. What's *wrong* with you?"

"He's a diagnosed schizophrenic, Gary. Doesn't mean he's homicidal."

"There's plenty of violence in his history—"

"It does mean he can't stick to one notion of reality. And that makes him easy to set up."

Roache glared at Kyle from under lowered brows, his jaw flexing at the corners. "I think you and I are done talking."

Kyle swallowed. He had nothing to lose. "I know Jeremy Sellars isn't dead."

Gary sat upright. "What?"

"He's not dead. I've seen him."

He expected his bull-necked sometimes-ally to call him a liar. Or punch him. Instead, Roache fixed his gaze on his half-eaten burger. "Where?"

"I went back to the Boneyard yesterday."

Roache paled and clenched his fists. "You shouldn't be going there by yourself."

"I had no choice. There's too many things that don't make sense. And I know Audie Long's no killer." Roache tried to interrupt. Kyle didn't let him. "When I stood outside the alley to the Boneyard, I saw somebody move, up on the third floor of that building that used to be a PR office."

"Bond's?"

"Yeah. And Jeremy Sellars was staring down at me from the window."

"How much did you have to drink before you drove down there?"

"Nothing," Kyle lied.

"Did you get into anything *else* before you went?"

At that moment Kyle regretted more than ever that he had opened up to Roache about the problems that cost him his previous newspaper job. "It was *him*, Gary. I yelled his name. He put his hands around the bars in the window frame. Then he drew back and wouldn't come out again."

"So where is he now? You go in and get him?"

Kyle had stared for many minutes at the black maw of that building's front entrance, but he hadn't dared to set foot inside.

"I thought not," Roache said.

Kyle felt his temper slip. "You sound just like Tom."

"That your editor there at the Herald?"

"Yeah. I told him about this, and he just stands there by my desk like a scarecrow, and he acts all grandfatherly and puts a hand on my shoulder and tells, me, 'Son, I know things are bad at home, but you have to get a grip. You start talking all crazy, it'll get around. Our city's too small for secrets.' And I tell him they're holding a innocent man in jail, charged with a crime that never happened. And then he says I need some time off…and damn, he sounded just like Penny. I try talking to her about this, and she keeps telling me I shouldn't rock the boat. She's never talked to me like that before."

"Your editor's a wise man. And your wife is right."

[Pain jabbed behind his temples. Fingers made from agony, searching.] They weren't in the bar anymore, but in its back lot, behind the dumpster, out of sight of the main road. "What are you doing?" Kyle said, tongue clumsy with liquor. "You gonna break my kneecaps?"

Roache grabbed him by the shoulders and shook him once, hard, then set him on his feet. "You need to snap out of it. The whole damn department's talking about you. They think the divorce broke your mind. You keep it up, they'll search your house."

"They won't find anything."

"That so? Then why are you so jittery?"

Kyle wasn't about to give his law enforcement friend the complete answer to that question. "What I need to know is, what are *you* on? What kind of psycho trip is this whole goddamn city on?" He spoke rapid-fire, words tumbling over one another. "This morning, there's Tom at my desk. And he gives me a speech. 'Kyle, I'm getting calls. City Hall's calling me. The Chief's office is calling me. The judge's office is calling me. One of our biggest advertisers called me at home. At home, Kyle. They all said you're asking too many questions about the Boneyard. Talking crazy, like that Sellars kid is still alive. Yelling in their faces that Long is innocent. They're all telling me you're wrong.'

"And I tell Tom it's our job to print the truth. And then he says, 'Penny's called me too. I hear it's not just whiskey anymore. That prosecutor over there, he likes you, likes the way you write about the job he's doing. He doesn't know how long he can keep looking the other way.' And I said, 'You want me to take part in a cover-up. You all do.' And he said, 'I want you to clean out your desk.' Is that a good enough reason for me to be agitated, Gary?"

Still and silent, Roache could have been a megalith.

"So what are you gonna do to me?"

"Jeremy Sellars is dead, Kyle. Let it go."

"Fuck you." And Kyle took a swing. He missed. Roache swung back, and didn't.

[He wanted to break his skull open on the asphalt, just to make the pain stop. He heard gasps, his own.]

Roache held down a hand, and with misgivings Kyle took it. His lips were shredded from the inside. His right eye socket throbbed. Blood trickled down his face. More of his blood stained Gary's shirt. They stood now behind the warehouse next to the bar, where their fight had taken them.

"Goddamn you," Roache said. "I never wanted it to come to this. This is my fault."

"Then fix it," Kyle said. "Help me go public."

Roache's huge hands covered his face, then balled into fists. "You still don't get it. Kyle, Jeremy Sellars *is dead.* That face you keep seeing. That's not him." He went on as if muttering to himself. "It's because you keep asking questions. It's bait. Laid out for you."

"What are you talking about?"

"You're messing with the deal. This city, it's just like any other city, there's arrangements made. The men at the top stay at the top because they have a pact with the ones who really run the show. They leave 'em alone, let 'em have what they want, who they want, and in return their own stay safe. You don't fuck with that. Ever."

"Even if someone's going to die?"

"*Especially* if someone's supposed to die."

Outrage flooded Kyle's jacked-up system. "You know, I can't tell you how many times I've sat outside that courtroom waiting for a verdict, and some rich asshole who got subpoenaed because he happened to witness something leans over and says, 'You know, they ought just let these drug dealers kill each other off.' Except he doesn't mean drug dealers. Not really. He means the poor people. The people who don't share his skin color. And you're just like them, aren't you? And I thought you were different."

Roache turned and walked away. "I can't talk to you anymore. I shouldn't even be here."

THE PAIN PHYSICALLY withdrew from behind his eyes, between his temples. He'd never felt anything like that in his life before, ever. Like something outside his mind had forced its way in, started rifling through. Had that dealer sold him insecticide instead of powder? He knew snow lights from experience; this was nothing like that.

Maybe when Roache decked him that meaty fist had left more than just a couple bruises.

Kyle regained his feet somehow, lurched toward the shoe. The so-called bait.

It was in pristine condition, could've been swiped off the shelf rather than a body. Good, thick soles that resisted when he squeezed. Size 11. He'd heard that square-jawed jarhead of a prosecutor cite that number a triple-dozen times during the summary of evidence at Audie Long's plea hearing. The same size that Kyle's own son Aaron wore. Big feet for such a short, stocky kid.

When he stood up he faced the mouth of the alley that led to the Boneyard, with its insane graffiti, its madhouse of birdsong, a place where the homeless froze to death in the winter and drug kingpins carried out grim executions where no cops would ever stop them. Kyle's internal crime reporter diary ran through name after name after name.

The way the buildings blocked out the moon, he might as well have stared into a cave. Yet as his eyes adjusted, he noticed a column of deeper darkness at the alley's far end. A person, standing unsteady, swaying.

"Jeremy!" Kyle shouted. "I know that's you."

Kyle's ears rang, and his vision doubled. The figure split in two as it strode forward. He heard laughter. It sounded like the cops, the way they joked as they cleaned up after yet another small slaughter, chortling despite the reek, whether blood or body fluids or rotted meat. *Shotgun blew her jaw clean off. That's one hell of a blowjob!*

Kyle groaned, temples throbbing again, as more slides shoved unnaturally into his mind, detailing scenes that hadn't happened yet. He saw himself swipe the cards in the gutter aside with his foot, make a gap in his own name, walk through it. He saw himself standing in the alley, placing the shoe in the figure's proffered hand.

He wanted to run back to the truck, to grab a weapon, any weapon, but he was in fact walking forward. He tried directing his feet to back up, to turn around, but forming those thoughts hurt like hell and instead he took another step closer. And another. The figure paused, waiting. Kyle couldn't make out a face.

He wasn't sure when he started babbling, though he listened to his own words with growing panic, because his mouth moved, his lungs worked, of their own accord. "You picked the perfect place to hide, Jeremy. You did. No one wants to admit this place even exists. It's like the biggest open secret in the world. It's where the disposable people go to be disposed. But you're not disposable. You're not dead. Why are you letting an innocent man rot in jail? He didn't do anything to you. It doesn't make sense."

He fumbled with the high-top, tumbling it back and forth in his hands. The words kept spilling as if reeled out of his throat on fishing line. "This shoe. My son would love it. I know he would. It's too bad you don't have the match anymore. It's his size. Crazy, that you and he wear the same shoe size. I couldn't stop thinking about it. About what I'd do if you were him.

"My ex won't let me see Aaron anymore. Maybe she's smart, because this whole city's against me, and the alcohol, it's not enough to help me anymore. But my boy. He's like me. He'd want to know what's going on here. He's a good boy. He's smart. Smart enough to look at my example and run the other way."

At last he could sort a face out from the dark. Without a doubt the allegedly murdered Jeremy Sellars stood before him, buzz-cut hair, chin scarred by a moped wreck. The bone ridges in his face jutted out sharp as axe blades. The boy hadn't eaten in a long time.

Jeremy's chest heaved as he breathed. A smell wafted from him, like oil from a hot engine. His feet were bare and the weeks unshod had deformed them somehow. They reminded Kyle of socks pulled on with the heels misaligned.

Despite his pounding skull, he found focus. "You let an innocent man go to prison. A man too mentally ill to defend himself. Why did you do that?" He stepped closer. He gripped the shoe by its toe, an awkward impromptu club. "You revealed yourself to me. Only to me. Tell me why."

No answer.

"I ruined my life." His voice rose as his rage gathered steam. "Because of you. Because of what you did to Audie Long. To an innocent!" He dropped the shoe, grabbed Jeremy by the shoulders and shook him with all the fury he could muster. "Why?!?"

At first he thought the sleeves of the boy's jacket had torn off in his hands. He didn't understand what he was holding, why the boy's head both tilted and stood straight, until Jeremy shrugged and shifted his arms and let the rest of his skin fall away. It lay in a puddle around the ankles of a wet and glistening mannequin. Veins pulsed in the membranes stretched between its ribs.

Kyle again heard the cops' crude laughter.

He punched the thing in its blank face—and screamed at the chemical burn that seared his knuckles, like he'd punched roofing tar coated with battery acid.

The courtyard erupted with bird cries and the sound of many claws scrabbling. A blast of skull-breaking pain threatened to buckle Kyle to the ground, but he fought it, stayed upright.

More noise behind. He turned his yammering head, beheld others like the thing in the alley, squeezing up from the storm drain like cockroaches, three, four, a dozen.

Even more were coming out of the courtyard, creeping into the alley behind the thing that had posed as Jeremy.

Kyle stared wide-eyed at its faceless visage, and white hot agony split his brainpan. More scenes shoved into his head, one after the other, and he finally understood it was the creature that was putting them there, that rifled through his memories, made him move in ways he didn't want to.

Now, it showed him the future.

At first light, crows and pigeons swarmed from the Boneyard, massed in the gutter, pecked at his name, flew off with the little white cards like so many breadcrumbs, removing every trace.

The morning sun glinted off the chrome of his truck as its engine finally died. A public works employee dragged the abandoned vehicle onto a tow truck bed, bore it off to the city impound to rust unclaimed.

Sunlight shone low through the city hall windows as the city manager and police chief shook hands and nodded in satisfaction. Uniformed officers, all faces Kyle knew, arrived in the newsroom. Towering Tom watched as they emptied Kyle's desk, packed everything into evidence crates.

Penny, looking the best he'd seen in years in a smart skirt and short business jacket, perched cross-legged on the desk in the prosecutor's office. Her shoulders relaxed as the jarhead put a hand on the small of her back, let the other slide from hip to breast as they kissed.

Aaron paused on the greenway during his walk home from school to tighten the buckles on brand new black high-tops. His father's absence did nothing to dull the spring in his step.

Two big men wrestled a third through a doorway into Boneyard shadow. Roache, his hands cuffed behind his back, his sin, trying to warn Kyle away. *You don't fuck with that. Ever. Especially if someone's supposed to die.* One of his fellow men in blue pinned him against a wall while the other pressed the barrel of a Taurus 9 mm right against the back of his head, and things formed of shadow and hunger shuffled forward.

Audie Long shuddered on the metal cot in his fourth floor jail cell, the crescent moon blotted out as a face made from black void peered through the window slats.

"Lies," Kyle sobbed. "Oh, God."

He cursed his luck, his lot, his utter lack of foresight, that placed his voice so far from anyone who might hear it, that left his weapons in the truck, that left so much distance to cover. That left him so outnumbered.

I tried to be your voice, he said, to Audie, to Jeremy, to the names in his crime reporter diary. The way his brain burned, he couldn't tell whether he spoke the words aloud. The pain in his head fused in an unyielding wall, and yet he turned to the creature that had duped him, closed his hands around its throat.

Not all the screams were his.

CONDOLENCES

Tarissa had seen enough newspapers on the rack in her father's store that she knew who she didn't want to be. The weeping girl behind the witness stand, contorted face wailing from the front page at every casually curious passerby.

She watched the trial from the front bench, sandwiched between her grandmother and the grim-looking little woman who worked as victim witness coordinator for the prosecutor's office. A TV cameraman and a newspaper photographer stood side by side across from her in their designated corner beside the judge's chair. Most of the time they kept their lenses aimed at Ballinger, the man who killed her mother and father, as he glowered at each witness who took the stand. Sometimes, she'd catch him staring right at her, expression a harrowing blank. Sometimes she'd notice the cameras turned her way. She let nothing slip. Not a flinch, no tears, not even a frown.

That poker face, that's what the city saw as the trial coverage unfolded. Black curly hair kept in a neat ponytail, a cream button down, the best her parents could afford, dark eyes focused on the testifying policeman. Only she could see the white hot pillar of anger inside when she regarded those pictures.

So much to be angry about. That this awful man with his bestial underbite drifted in straight from Interstate 484 and chose her parents' store for the holdup. That he thought her mother and father's lives a fair trade for the $20 and change he took. That he dared to take the stand on his own behalf and claim her father threatened him, got in his face yelling and forced him to respond in self-defense. Then when her mother tried to duck behind the counter he thought she was going for a gun, he said. Lie after lie after lie.

Tarissa watched the jurors' faces as Ballinger spoke, amazed none of them laughed at these vile tall tales. She feared to contemplate what might happen if even one of them believed the bastard.

But her fury stretched in another direction. The customers who witnessed the slaying all gave similar accounts, that Ballinger pulled the gun, told her dad to empty the fucking register, and instead of complying, like he'd told her to do a thousand times, he smiled and waved like it was no big deal, said, "Hey, put that away. Just tell us what you want." That he came out from behind the counter, with her mother whispering "No, Zach, no," and actually tried to take the gun away, like the whole situation was a joke. If he'd just done what he'd always told Tarissa to do if a stickup happened, he would be alive now. So would Mom.

The prosecutor called her name. Wanted her to tell the jury what it felt like when they called her to the principal's office, where the officers were gathered to deliver the news that she'd been made an orphan. It's okay to cry, the prosecutor had told her. It might even help.

But she wasn't going to shed tears. Not for the camera. Not for Ballinger.

She ignored the murderer's unblinking stare as she answered the prosecutor's questions. A camera shutter clicked as she talked. A woman on the jury sniffled, eyes moist, perhaps soaking in on some alternate channel the emotions that Tarissa bottled up.

Then came the defense attorney's turn. Bald, pot-bellied and sweaty, Ballinger's counsel had no intention of picking on a grieving thirteen-year-old in front of a jury. "No questions, Your Honor."

But as he sat down, Ballinger cleared his throat. His lawyer waved, No, shut up, but the defendant talked anyway. "Young lady, I just wanted to say, I really am sorry for your loss. I didn't want any of this to happen. I didn't. But I did want to offer you my condolences."

His words were horrible enough, but as he spoke them something inexplicable happened. She heard a different sound underneath, underscoring each syllable.

She had nothing in her experience to compare the sound to, no way to classify it. She could only frame it in terms of the pictures that formed as the noise tore her mind open. A dead body dried to paper in a pit of scorching sand. A crack in the floor of the ocean where no lava burned, no sea worms bred, colder than absolute zero. A space outside the universe where no light would ever reach.

The camera captured the look on her face as Ballinger addressed her: wide-eyed, open-mouthed terror.

Never in the city's history had a jury taken less than an hour to sentence a man to death.

Back in the conference room, the prosecutor, a beautiful but stern Asian woman, told Tarissa that the look on her face alone had won the case. As if she'd somehow planned it.

Perhaps in response to Tarissa's bewildered stare, the attorney put her hand over Tarissa's on the table and said, "I'm so sorry you had to go through all this. And I'm so, so sorry for your loss."

Tarissa screamed. Because she heard the sound again, grinding underneath the prosecutor's words.

Tarissa's grandmother hugged her harder than she ever had in both their lives. "Oh Lord, child, what's wrong, what's wrong," a comforting litany, not a question. As the prosecutor stammered, Grandma said, "Why don't you just leave us alone for a little bit."

Once they were alone in the room, Tarissa finally let those tears flow. "I heard—" she tried to say. "I heard—"

"Shh. You don't need to explain. You don't need to worry 'bout nothing."

SHE MOVED IN with her grandmother.

Grandma Davis's house was older than her parents' had been, bigger and more decrepit. Tarissa's grandmother dwelled in every corner of this rambling den, a sweet-tempered badger who marked her territory with odd groupings of porcelain saltshakers, from apple-cheeked Dutch children to Heckle and Jeckle.

Photos from her parents' wedding hung in the main hall. It took a long time for Tarissa to be able to walk past them without tearing up and trembling.

She tried to explain to Grandma what she heard when Ballinger spoke, but her grandmother insisted on her own interpretation. "You heard that man's evil. God let you hear it, and he got what he had coming to him."

Tarissa wasn't so sure, because she'd heard it other times since. When people tried to talk her about her parents. Always the same things, they said.

I'm so sorry for your loss. My heart goes out to you. I'll keep you in my prayers. My condolences.

Some said it with passion. Some by rote. Her teachers. Her school principal. The reporters who tried to talk to her after the trial. The ladies at church. Her classmates, the ones who cared enough to try to understand.

Language wasn't designed to address what she endured. How anyone suffered through grief. The anguish. The outrage. The fury. The abrupt sorrow. The emptiness. The sinking realization, when she saw a movie advertised and thought, Dad would love that, when she passed a math test with a B+ and thought, I've got to show this to Mom.

Those repeated phrases, those stopgaps meant to give comfort or maybe just ward off the bereaved. When she heard them, she heard that background echo. A black hole bleeding through the syllables.

She began to avoid the topic like her life depended on it. In desperation she asked her Grandma to let her stay home from church. She couldn't take that good-natured chorus of condolences any longer.

Her grandmother scowled at her across the kitchen table, motes of dust blazing between them like warnings in the Saturday morning sunlight. "Alright, child," she said. "But don't think you're going to be sleeping in late."

Tarissa was more than happy to do Sunday morning chores. Even the ones that left her back sore and her clothes soaked with sweat, trimming hedges, weeding the vegetable garden, scrubbing the kitchen and bathroom floors. Anything was better.

Afterward, exhausted, she thumbed through her grandmother's Sunday paper—something she'd never have done otherwise, no one her age did—and she discovered she could summon the noise when she read. It wasn't as intense, but it was unmistakably there.

She developed an obsession with obituaries. She noticed, in stories about the dead and somehow significant, the people quoted tended to say the same things. *She had a great sense of humor. He'd do anything for anybody. She always had a smile. He'd give you the shirt off his back. She never had a bad word to say.* When the words sounded in her head, they could have been an incantation. Beneath them, she heard the noise, that sigh from the bottom of the world, though nothing disturbed the air, though silence wrapped the kitchen tight.

So she questioned, more and more, where the sound came from—the newspapers provided incontrovertible evidence that it happened in her head and only in her head. But she refused to believe it.

She didn't imagine that sound. It didn't originate in her mind. So she told herself, over and over.

She didn't talk about this to anyone else. Not even to Grandma.

One day her grandmother walked in on her as she was using a black magic marker to obliterate the offending words in a story about a woman, president of the arts council, who'd died unexpectedly. ("She had such a great sense of humor," her secretary told the paper.) Tarissa couldn't explain what she was doing or why. She withered under Grandma Davis's glare and never touched the paper after that.

FOUR YEARS WENT by before she heard the noise again.

She begged her grandmother to go to the clinic. The pain in Grandma's stomach grew worse and worse, but still she wouldn't see a doctor, refused with a little more snarl in her voice each time. Tarissa never let up. Nothing her Grandma could do to her could possibly be worse than what she had already been through.

A tall hook-nosed man with a gentle Mr. Rogers demeanor, Dr. Keller ordered a barrage of additional tests, then told Tarissa, "I'm glad you nagged her to come in." He said little about what might be wrong, but his eyes spoke volumes. "I'm so sorry you're going through this."

The way Dr. Keller recoiled, her expression must have rivaled the one in that horrible newspaper photo.

She learned at last not to wince when the sound rasped in her ears, because from that moment on, she heard it again and again and again, from so many sources. The nurses. The technicians. The insurance guy. The ladies from church, who insisted on helping out. The cousins who never used to visit before word got out Grandma had cancer of the pancreas.

From the attorney and the notary. From the preacher. From the hospice workers. From the funeral director.

In most, she sensed no malice. Yet those words—*I'm so sorry. My condolences*—always summoned the noise, an incantation that never ever failed. At times she thought of it as the voice of her grandmother's cancer, broadcasting stronger and stronger signals as its tendrils spread into stomach, intestine and bone. The new avatar of a monster that first spoke to her through her parents' murderer, that was determined to never leave her alone.

Tarissa's great aunt Olivia stayed with her in Grandma's house during the final days. She kept offering words of comfort, and nearly came to hysterics herself when Tarissa hid in her bedroom and locked the door, shrieking, "Stop it! Stop it! Please, please stop!"

"Honey, I'm sorry," Aunt Olivia hollered. "I can't imagine what you've been through—"

Tarissa screamed back, "GO AWAY! GO AWAY! GO AWAY!"

AT LAST SHE heard the sound unaccompanied by words.

Sitting vigil in the hospice beside Grandma's bed with its short, sturdy rails, listening to her labored breathing over the hiss of the oxygen tank. And then something else slid up from underneath, pulsed in time with the rise and fall of her grandmother's chest.

Panic jelled. The noise grew louder. Tarissa wanted to flee the room, but she forced herself to stay. Plugging her ears did nothing to help. Her grandmother's eyes moved beneath her eyelids, but they never opened.

She kissed her grandmother's hand. Her cheek. Her forehead. "Goodbye," she said. "I love you."

The sound stopped when her grandmother did.

SHE DIDN'T WANT to brave the funeral, but for her grandmother's sake she steeled herself and weathered it. The noise ground at her start to finish.

Her relatives invaded the house, packed away the saltshakers. She had no legal right to stop them. But they weren't unkind. Days later, as Tarissa huddled in her bedroom, Olivia knocked. She didn't say anything to Tarissa—for better or for worse, she'd learned her lesson—but her great aunt handed her a piece of flower-printed stationary.

Dearest Tarissa,

I hope this letter finds you well. Don't be sad for me. I'm in a better place.

I want you to know I love you and always have loved you. You've made me proud so many times. You have a strong soul and a smart mind. I think you'll be able to do anything you set your mind to do.

I'll miss you, child, until I see you again.

Love,

Tarissa heard no sound within those words, no void behind the universe.

Just her grandmother's voice.

CECILIA HAD HEART surgery before she was even a day old. And again at two months. Tarissa was drowning in debt.

Providence took her side in one significant way, for which she was especially grateful. Lamont didn't run. He stayed with her, stood by her on the deck of the sinking ship. So many men wouldn't, especially men who hadn't planned on becoming fathers.

They celebrated Cecilia's six month birthday with convenience store ice cream. That night, the sound that Tarissa had attuned her entire being to detect began again: her baby gasping, grunting, struggling to breathe.

Lamont was up the moment she was. The alarm clock, the only light source in the room, shone a cruel 1:22 AM.

He drove them white-knuckled to the emergency room. By the time the goddamn doctor actually came to see them, Cecelia's breathing had calmed, and this quack who came off more like a bureaucrat than a physician told them he could find nothing wrong.

But when he said, "I'm so sorry you had to go through all this trouble," and Tarissa heard something else in his voice, she wanted to howl.

Lamont, God bless him, said, "Thanks for nothing, Doc."

By the time they got Cecilia to sleep in her crib and crawled into the too-small double bed, the clock on the nightstand read 4:03 AM.

Tarissa woke exactly twenty minutes later. Lamont snored softly beside her. A hollow thrum lurked beneath the ambient nighttime murmur. She didn't hear Cecilia. No crying. No breathing.

She vaulted from the bed, almost stumbled headfirst into Cecilia's crib. Lamont moaned but didn't wake. She wanted to shout, *Don't you hear that? Can't you HEAR that SOUND?* but she didn't. She knew he couldn't.

Cecilia's face was warm, her breathing a whispery hiss. Her poor heart beat bravely in her chest. Amazing she didn't wake up bawling, with all the ruckus Tarissa had just made.

The noise. It fluctuated ever so slightly with Cecilia's inhales and exhales.

She thought about those words, the ones that always held the taint. *Sorry for your loss, my condolences.*

She never wanted to hear those words again, couldn't bear the thought. No. Not for Cecilia. Those words weren't for her. That sound wasn't for her.

Her ears rang with it, amplifying the crackle of night. She couldn't pinpoint a single source. Any source. Where was it coming from?

She closed her eyes and concentrated, thought she could glean a hint of a direction. Opened her eyes, immediately lost the focus.

So be it. She would search with her eyes shut.

She took shuffle-steps, arms extended in front of her, the carpet harsh against her bare feet. Her hands found a dresser, a stretch of wall, groped to the door, creaked it open. She kept her eyes closed as she stepped into the hall of the apartment, and yes, that awfulness sounded slightly louder, angled just a fraction to her left.

She had no way to go but straight ahead, down the short passage to the combination living room—kitchen. She pressed herself to the left-hand wall and inched forward, mindful of the long, heavy box Lamont had left on the floor, a cheap plyboard bookshelf still in its packaging. She found it with her feet, managed not to trip or stub her toes.

She didn't think about what she'd do if she did in fact find a physical source for the noise. She kept listening, the air cold against her legs, the wall colder against her arm.

And the sound grew stronger, closer. She forged on. Soon she heard nothing else. An absence of music, an opposite of laughter, as if a throat sculpted pure mourning, emitted waves that drained away power and life as they washed over whatever they touched. Her body didn't shiver, but a sensation akin to ice on skin invaded her flesh, chilled her sinuses, her tongue, the spaces in her belly. The wall she leaned against could have been sheered from a glacier.

She connected, then, how long she'd walked, an astonishing distance. She should have stumbled against the love seat in the living room several minutes ago.

Yet the the space leading to the noise kept on going.

She raised her right hand, immediately discovered the opposite wall, equally cold, closer than it should have been, just inches from her body. No carpet roughed the soles of her feet. She walked on ice. She had not noticed the transition until that moment.

Nowhere in her apartment was there a passage this long or this narrow. Gut intuition shouted down the impulse to open her eyes.

She continued forward. The noise should have been shaking her teeth with its volume. But she experienced its intensity in a different way, as a relentless electric current that affected something other than her physical nerves.

An obstruction barred her way. When she placed a palm against it, the barrier shifted away from her a fraction of an inch, and the sound increased. She heard nothing else, not even her own heartbeat.

She groped with featherlight fingertip touches, careful, so painstakingly careful, and gradually determined from its angle, its texture, its edges, that this object she dared not look at was a door, hinged on the right, open on the left, slightly ajar.

The sound came from the other side. She needed it shut.

It had no handle.

The only way to close it, she reasoned, was to grip its edge, jerk it toward her, pull her fingers free before they were caught in the jamb. She imagined herself with her fingertips caught and crushed and the door sealed, trying to free herself in this unearthly place. She wished she hadn't.

I'm sorry for your loss. My condolences.

She couldn't leave it open.

She braced herself, slid her fingers along the door with the barest of contacts until they passed through the crack. The corner of the doorframe brushed her knuckles. She curled her fingers through the gap, creeping as slowly as she could manage.

She couldn't do it as is: she needed more room. She had no choice but to ease the door open wider, give herself clearance.

The noise grew louder.

She didn't recognize what was happening, not at first. As she secured her grip, the tiny hairs on the back of her right hand pricked as if tweaked by a feeble breeze. The pressure became steady, the settling of a gossamer weight. It felt like long and emaciated fingers touching her as gingerly as she had touched the door.

She opened her mouth in a gasp that made no sound at all.

Fingertips dug down on the back of her hand.

She jerked the door toward her and pulled her fingers free..

The door sealed. The sound stopped.

She didn't open her eyes until, in her hasty retreat, her heels hooked the back of the bookshelf box and she tumbled hard to the floor.

In the bedroom, Cecilia started to cry. So did she.

LAMONT, BETWEEN CONSTRUCTION jobs, at least could mind the baby while she went to work. Thank goodness. At some level she still had trouble gifting him with her full trust; but this morning, as always, he acted more than willing to do his part, tolerated the early morning feeding, tolerated being up with Cecilia in the hours before dawn.

The noise really was gone.

Tarissa's shift at the 24-hour big box hell store started at 7 a.m. Despite being even more shortchanged on sleep than usual, she hummed to herself, tuneless, joyous, a noise to cherish. And every movement suggested a smile. Lamont even noticed. He laughed and shook his head. "What's with you this morning?" After a kiss, "Whatever it is, I like it."

She just shrugged.

Then she saw herself in the mirror, under the bright bathroom light.

She almost called to Lamont. But they'd just spent an hour together tending to Cecilia and he'd said nothing.

She didn't know what was wrong, what it meant, but she couldn't afford to call in sick. They needed every penny.

She finished putting on her uniform, rode the bus to work. Few of the other passengers spared her a second glance, though the one that did, an elderly woman bundled in half a dozen layers despite the heat, stared a moment, eyes almost as wide as Tarissa's had been in that years-ago photograph. When Tarissa's eyes met hers she swiftly looked away.

Her boss frowned at her when she reached the time clock to swipe her badge, but that had to do with her timing, right on the dot instead of the preferred ten minutes early.

At the cash register she might have been a ghost, or, more apt, a machine spouting prices and phrases such as "Cash, check or credit?" and "Have a blessed day." Some shoppers huffed their impatience when the lines grew long, but paid Tarissa the person no mind at all.

She passed the time during the lulls studying the marks on her hand where the being behind the door had touched her. An ignorant person might have mistaken those splotches for vitiligo. There were plenty of ignorant people in the world.

"Oh my God, honey. What happened to you?"

The woman's name was Hildred, a store regular. She dressed in frumpy blouses, often flecked with paint, or with food, or both, sweet as could be with no sense at all as to when it was appropriate to talk or not talk, especially in a crowded checkout lane during the rush hours, never sparing any details of her diabetes or her bone spurs or her many other ailments. Yet she seemed to genuinely care about the people she repeatedly struck up conversations with, whether they were receptive or not.

Now Hildred stared at her, gape-jawed.

Others in line, even the other cashiers, were starting to look.

"I woke up this morning," Tarissa stammered. "And it was just...I feel fine, but..." She flailed for something to say to diffuse the situation. "I'm going to see a doctor. Soon as I can. But I feel fine. Really."

"Oh, honey," Hildred said, and with just a little hesitation, trepidation, she put a comforting hand on Tarissa's wrist. "I'm so sorry. My condolences."

Tarissa's gaze focused somewhere far away.

"Don't worry," she said. "It's okay."

DRAWN SHUT, TORN OPEN

LET THERE BE DARKNESS

The past eludes me—yet I know the future with the clarity of vivid memory. A grand contradiction in my Father's design, that remains to me a mystery...

A DAY WILL come when the sun's pale yellow stare starts to fill with the taint of blood.

Among the confused and tremulous hordes of mankind, amidst the endless processions of grand towers forged from metal stolen from the moon, I will walk. One knowing face, one unique being traversing the rivers of humanity that flood this world.

Unknown now: unknown when it begins. But I shall not remain unnoticed. When the time comes, I will not hide what I am.

My life, a long cycle of waiting, to make the offer I must make.

At first my words will be mere rumor, circulating among the residents of the underdepths. My message will find its way among the filthy creatures dwelling in the sewer networks deep beneath our urban blight; creatures whose only light comes from the poisons that make their eyes phosphorescent. Whispers will find the ears of the affluent and mad who seal themselves away in underworld vaults, hording treasures from every age—hiding from some real or imagined cataclysm, yet striving to hold control of the lands above.

I will wait. Through one path or another, bubbling up through the earth, my message will emerge into day's dimming light.

Those who seek me shall find me. My misshapen face—for by human eyes it is so perceived—printed in two dimensions, projected in three, shall form the center of every conversation: rotating slowly atop the great round tables where corporate councils meet, regarded in puzzlement and awe; placed on private altars and worshiped; precious oil burned, rare beasts slaughtered, even—most horrible of all—children slain to gain my favor.

Against a growing chaos, I will speak the same words, over and over, the network of technology that wraps the world in its web providing my forum. My offer, carried as pulses of light, beamed to the void and back again:

"This world is dying. Very little time remains. Soon all you've become, all you have ever dreamed of becoming, will be scoured away.

"But humanity need not perish. He who first brought you into being didn't intend for you to die with this world. Give me your fealty, ask in humility and I, as His messenger, will strive to grant your kind a second life."

Beneath the flickering light of my burning effigy, religious despots will thunder ridicule, and their followers will chant murder in the streets. Through communication channels wired straight into the heads of their desperate listeners, the rationalists and analysts will call me mad: an exploiter, a charlatan, a parasite. Yet many more, hearing whispers from shadows of memories too ancient to be understood, will know my creed for Truth.

Knowing this, despite my visions of the imminent future, my heart will fill with hope—a human sentiment, surely, gained from so many eons among them.

Is it possible, with so much of the past behind me, that I will have forgotten the hideous service mankind grants its saviors?

The sensations, so vivid: the terrors, so real. I feel them now as I will then: Rough hands roust me from a dreamless sleep, seize my wrists in crushing grips, tear at the folds of my gown; fingers twine in my tangled locks, drag me out into a moonless night. My scalp screams as the follicles tear out—black fluid covers my eyes, clogs my vision. My assailants fill my ears with angry babble; their fingernails strip my gown away, strip skin from my back, belly, breasts…

Outside this frail vessel that carries my soul, a flurry of sensations: of being bound, held high in the air, bleeding; a crowd's chorus of jeers; traveling swift in a craft along an ill-made path. Descending: a shower of blows, a rough grope that ends in a cry of disgust. Ascending.

Inside this vessel, a mounting shrill of fear—knowing what I will see when my vision clears.

When my blood-crusted eyes can finally open, a terrifying vista below: the twisting neon spires of the tallest towers of man glow ethereally in the darkness, seen from the rooftop of the tallest tower of all. Painfully harsh grips keep me doubled-over, force me to my knees, dangle me head-first over the edge....

But when I twist my neck, I glimpse the stars. This night, their clusters shine brighter than any stellar panorama I will ever see with these eyes. I gaze heavenward, and know my silent appeal is useless.

Beneath my terror, a sorrow blooms. Whether mankind itself chooses its final course, or a mad, misguided few, it will not be mine to know. I make no protest at their mishandling: I leave their angry accusations, their hysterical demands, their threats of violation unanswered.

The blade of light pierces me between the breasts—thrusts upward, parting the walls of my belly. My only sound—a gasp—as my body cavities empty into the abyss; a black, viscous flow baptizes the darkness beneath me.

Those who clutch this emptied vessel—who see what flows from my gutted corpse—will know then that I was never human. Even as they let my body fall, they will know.

All will feel my passing from the flesh.

My sorrows, an affectation from my time among humans, left behind with the shell I once wore. Liberated, I shall grieve no more. I—a tiny mote of nothingness, a vast discorporeal consciousness enveloping the world—will dance through the torrents of wind and weather; swim in the gulfs between atoms...and wait.

The energies that bound me to my body, loosed in a massive burst, detected by the instruments of my destroyers, defying analysis. Their learned ones will flounder for explanations—a reverse in polarity? A warning from God, a message from the Spirit Mother? A formation of a white hole; the opening of a wormhole?

A beacon call.

Their radiologists will marvel, their astronomers will speculate at a grand disturbance in the cosmos, a surge in background cosmic rays. They'll mutter in alarm at a tremendous dark mass discovered by their forests of radio telescopes, appearing spontaneously at the galaxy's edge, generated from nothing, emerging from nowhere. A drifting mass of dark matter—a dark nebula, perhaps—spilled through a rift in the fabric of space?

Only my Father—aroused by my dying call; awakening for the first time after a billion human lifetimes of sleep.

Their scientists shall whisper among themselves about the missing piece of the night sky—a widening blotch along the path of the Milky Way, invisible at first to the naked eye. A strip of stars the same age—formed from a nebula parsecs wide—all dying, all winking out at once? A dense cluster of gases, propelled toward Earth by the force of the titanic black hole in the galaxy's center?

Only my Father, swimming between the stars, drawn to the planet where His daughter died.

Their priests and priestesses will offer shrill prayers—beseeching their Lords to impart the meaning of the horrendous dark shadow that swallows the night sky, blotting the stars until nothing remains but pitch black. An omen of Armageddon, a dimming of Light before the Celestial Spheres rend? The Second Coming arrived at last, the vast darkness but the underside of New Jerusalem's greater glories?

Only my Father—closer to His destination than any Earth-bound dreamer in the most twisted of nightmares could ever conceive.

Constellations, occasionally glimpsed in the black night, wavering, fading—the stars that define them dancing around each other; shifting, merging—their shine distorted as their light passes through my Father's translucent flesh. Auroras cavort in twilight hours—horizon-spanning fans of blazing iridescence, triggered in the ionosphere by the winds of radiation that compose my Father's breath. In midnight hours rolling waves of mad color burst across the heavens; widening, spreading, vanishing—stars flickering within them like glowing fish seen in the abyss. Moon-sized spheres like raw red suns appear suddenly, cast aside the darkness, paint the world like an open wound—then are gone.

The Children of Earth will babble, scream and shriek at what they see in the night. Some will panic, hide, resort to murder, or suicide. More tragic yet, some will welcome the sights, thinking them signs of some wondrous new contact—the start of some long-awaited dream of rapture.

But the greatest tragedy of all will be the shroud of ignorance that smothers every one of them. The Power that could have given them new life, here to end the cycle of their evolution. Those who will suffer for the murder of His daughter, doomed never to understand the cause.

When dawn ends a new moon's night, my Father's single six-lobed hand shall appear opposite the sun, a monstrous billowing deformity dwarfing that stained yellow eye. As the world spins, my Father's hand will rise in the western sky, ascending to meet the sun in the east.

Pouring from their towers, crazed masses of humanity will reach undreamed-of peaks of barbarism: Men of the urban blight will parade their dismembered children and women through the streets; military engines will sweep their killing lasers through the crowds, bringing rains of blood and severed limbs; the skyscrapers that pierce the stratosphere will spill human flesh from every window, bodies piling hundreds of feet deep, those trapped beneath crushed by the sheer weight of their fellows.

But despite all supplications, despite all attempts to escape, my Father's hand will eclipse the sun.

As my Father's fingers close, that star's golden corona will shine out between the narrowing gaps, struggling still to give light to its daughter world. Then, absorbed in His nebulous substance, the sun's light will die; the Earth, cast in darkness; and the whole of humanity will see my Father's true face.

The face of their Creator, blotting out the Cosmos.

Then the fires will come. Shockwaves from the dying sun—stellar matter loosed from my Father's fist.

The Earth's surface, purged of life, its crust cracking open, vomiting its innards into the void, turning itself inside out.

But mankind will not die.

Mv Father, governor of energies and forms, will bind them to their bodies. Cast out into the cold of space—blood boiling—still they will live. Buried in the molten floods, trapped inside the cooling rock, still they will live. Burned and hollowed-out shells wandering the lifeless, airless hulk of their planet, still they will live.

The energies fueling the minds and spirits of the human race bond stronger, break brighter than those of any other species blessed by His intervention in their evolution.

My Father will not let His creations go to waste.

The shimmering, ragged pucker of my Father's maw will rise above the ruined Earth—so enormous no human still possessed of eyes will ever glimpse the whole of it. Then His mouth will open, and yet another behind it, and one behind that—infinite tunnel of billion-fanged mouths, receding into His star-swallowing gullet.

Yet the Earth will not be consumed.

Instead, He will draw one great breath… Stripped from the planet surface, pried from the rock, snatched from space, all His creations will be drawn into Him. All the men and women and children, their bodies boiled, broken and burned, hurled through the endless procession of stellar mouths. Even the energies of the discorporated dead—from the apes whose minds first awakened to those who perished during the sun's death—drawn into the labyrinth of tunnels through Time and Space that compose my Father's pulsing veins.

And where will I be?

When He comes, I will rejoice; and when He begins His journey to a new universe, I will join Him—the humans, their writhing shapes howling, endlessly digested, reformed, digested, reformed, to fuel my Father for his travels. Their screams, to me, only music…Celestial Child, I will cavort through the time-streams that carry my Father's blood, delighting in the perpetual-motion machine that is my Sire.

The past eludes me—yet I know the future with the clarity of vivid memory. A grand contradiction in my Father's design, that remains to me a mystery…

Each night I lie awake, pondering why He would bind me here, to play Savior to man, to offer them all the chance to evolve beyond the limits the universe has given them—yet leave me with the certain knowledge that His plan will fail.

A lesson, perhaps, that I once understood, its significance denied to me now, that will prepare me for my eons as a world maker?

How I long for our reunion, that at long last He may enlighten me.

THE QUILTMAKER

prologue: the pattern

You never imagined you'd be in a place like this again.

Mothers. Fathers. Schoolteachers. Children. All about you, children.

To a tiny part of you, this setting is familiar. These hard chairs built a little too small, with their desk flaps scarred by years upon years of pocketknife graffiti, rows on rows slanting down between aisles of threadbare carpet to the stage with its smooth-worn planks and its decades-old curtain and its faded elementary school logo marring the cinder block at the front of the stage platform.

You're packed in tight among these people that the bulk of you finds so alien. To your left, a plump mom in a fancy black coat shushes her sullen son. To your right, a thick-bellied dad with a ridiculously long mustache makes no effort to hide his boredom. In front of you, a younger woman, slender, wearing a tacky spotted top, reveals a hollow, haunted look as as she leans in to listen to whatever her towheaded daughter is trying to tell her.

The lights dim. The curtain parts.

The play is something scripted from a children's picture book, and the set matches the source, all garish pinks and greens. Adults in the cast are dressed as children, with ponytails and long white socks and overalls. They speak in exaggerated childspeak, with loud slurred words, and jump and skip with over-the-top excitement. There are children on stage with them, playing at being playmates. They're singing that old tune about the woman who swallows everything, the fly, the spider, the bird, all manner of beasts. Around you, the parents laugh and laugh, especially the moms, even the haunted mom in front of you.

You pay the story no mind, it's all just screechy noise.

Except it isn't.

If the school auditorium affects you like an alien moonscape, then this sensation is even more alien, this burning moistness behind the eyes you've chosen to use, this pressure in your throat like a tightening fist, this weight pushing down inside your chest, the pain there that billows and unfolds and billows.

You don't understand. Thoughts echo confused inside the marble hall of your mind, whisper amidst infinite layers of tapestry.

Your vision blurs. You bring a hand to your face, unable to believe until your fingers touch your lower eyelids that you're shedding tears. That you're sniffling.

It makes no sense. You're not moved by this squealing travesty on the stage. Not at all.

How many parts of you remember being read to at night? The drone of a father's singsong voice, the sprightly coo of a mother reading Alice or the Grimms? Sharing in your wide-eyed delight with shining eyes of her own.

This agony in your belly uncurls layer after layer. You are a mask of mourning in a garden of mindless giggles, listening to voices from stolen memories, watching a tableau of unabashed, unselfconscious innocence that you will never belong to, can never be part of again.

It's a miracle you don't sob aloud. You have to get away, get out of this crowd, before someone notices.

You excuse yourself. Once upon a time, these people would have had to stand up and press themselves as far back against their seats as they could to let you pass. No such problem now, you're so compact they hardly notice you.

It's no matter that you left early; your plans are still on track. You know what you're looking for and where you want to go. But it's this tide of emotion sloshing inside you, disrupting your concentration, that's unexpected and unwelcome and potentially dangerous.

It takes an uncomfortably long time to find the car, and the slice of you that remains in control frets about how you must look, wandering aimless among the rows of spoiled suburbanite SUVs with tears smearing your face. In another life, you might have called the cops on such a freak, or at least run like a goody two-shoes to tell a teacher.

When you spot that little red hatchback with all its charming dents and rust spots, it's like the day your father arrived at the park just as the sixth-grade bullies had you cornered, a signal of safety, an end to fear.

But not an end to sorrow.

You produce the hand that holds the right key, you open the hatch and swing it up, climb in with a creak of old shocks and seal yourself inside. There's a thick tattered quilt of yellow and green crumpled behind the back seat, where you knew it would be; you pull it over yourself and squirm into the darkness underneath, as small as you can make yourself.

But you want to shrink further, crawl into the purest darkness that's found only in the spaces between atoms and the void outside time and never come out again. The empty places inside you rustle at this longing, trickle echoes down into the sickest pits of your soul, and you allow a sob to escape. But only one.

You can't still the trembling, not completely. Though you smother this ghost chorus of despair in layer after layer, you can't quite force yourself to still, no matter how silent you become, enveloped in warm black misery that doesn't abate even as the young mother with the hollow stare opens the passenger door. You can't see her, but you know she's there.

Her towheaded daughter chirps Shotgun! as she climbs onto her seat to be buckled in.

Maddy, don't be silly, scolds her mom, and hold still, damn it. Hold still.

Madeleine, you say, too soft for either of them to hear.

Somewhere inside you, someone's heartstring stretches past the breaking point.

The little engine that could starts up after after several cough-and-hack tries, and as the asphalt rumbles beneath you, Maddy starts to talk. She tells her mother over and over again about the play's funny parts, the parts that make her laugh again to think about them, prompted along by her mom's disengaged Mmm-hmms and Yeahs muttered at the right places. And that little girl's laughter, that indecipherable Rosetta stone from a land with all its gates barred to you forevermore, makes you want to plug your ears and howl.

Even in your state, tactile memories tell you when the final turn arrives, when the tires bounce and trundle over the gutter and onto the gravel drive. That's when you do move, when you sit up, when you stretch out.

As you draw your magic pouch from your neck, your bulging button sack, and dig fingers into your writhing faerie beads, far more addictive than any crystal Maddy's mother was ever tempted to try, you glimpse your face in the rear view mirror, so distressed from your pathetic weeping that it's peeled in strips like wet wallpaper, and the stuff beneath has sagged like softened wax, a paper-mâché horror show.

You could scream at the sight, as you slide forward. And so could Madeleine and her haunted mother, but soon they have no mouths to open.

In your hands, it shudders, this thing plucked from a little girl's limp shell, this eye-searing, beautiful thing.

You wail as it flutters against your fingers.

first square

In the cobweb-garnished shadows of his living room, Benjamin does what he does every morning at this hour, creeps to the bay window where he keeps the gauzelike curtains pulled almost shut but for a gap of an inch or two.

And he watches through his remaining eye.

His living room is dim and cavernous, and yet he never turns on the lights here. There's no need, because he never has visitors.

Binoculars rest on on a doily atop the lamp table beside the window, next to a telescope on a tripod that bows its heavy magnifying lens in a show of mock shame.

For now, with the sky cloud-free, he has no need for such tools—perched on the hill at the end of the circle, his house commands an ideal view down the short length of the street, with split-level domiciles lined up to either side, four to the right, three to the left, triplets and quadruplets clad in beige and white vinyl siding. He has a surveyor's command of the neighborhood, and the people in it, what they do in their yards, what they do in their cars.

He only needs assistance when he wants his gaze to reach through a few choice windows.

Already there's sights to behold. Second house on the left, Maria the single mother is outside washing her car in cut-off jean shorts and a bikini top, a good use of an idle May morning. Her son is probably in school, true, but even if school was out she'd still be idle—her ex has custody on weekdays. A loudmouth talk radio DJ, that pinheaded tub of lard was no prize in any box, but she was the one who got caught cheating. Let her boss's nephew nail her on top of the manager's desk in the very restaurant where she worked as a hostess, or so Benjamin heard. Just one unseemly bead on a string of terrible decisions that stretches across her entire life.

Maria is not a young lass anymore but the wear has all been on the inside. It's no wonder that even though she's almost twice his age, Lance the redneck brute has emerged from the first house on the right to make a show of trimming the hedges. He stares at his neighbor whenever her back is turned, sometimes even when she's facing him.

Surely she knows he's there, what he's doing, but whenever Maria looks up, it's to steal furtive glances at the house directly across from hers, third house right, where Clive and Francene's troubled prodigal son has just been returned to the nest.

Benjamin had been witness a couple afternoons ago to the sad procession, as the unhappy couple brought wayward Shaun home from rehab, rushed him inside like handlers hiding their charge from paparazzi.

What a delectable mess that household is. Once upon a time they were four, with stiff and proper Francene, demure wife number two, agreeing to help Clive raise a granddaughter produced through his first marriage. So little boy Shaun acquired a niece, Denise, who started as a sweet tomboy in a softball uniform, graduated from there to full-blown teen crackhouse queen, then vanished without a trace.

And now, Shaun, their perfect son, their honor-roll-scoring son, is headed down that same route. That special hell paved behind pressure-washed siding and meticulously fertilized lawns.

The fact is, hollow eyes and needle tracks serve little perfect boy Shaun just dandy, as far as Benjamin is concerned. Benjamin knows the boy was never what he seemed, he saw the backyard parties when mom and dad weren't home, the toking, the drinking, the groping. Kept a lot of things hidden from his parents, that boy did. Benjamin always had a suspicion that bad things happened to little Denise when Clive and Francene left her alone with their bright-eyed boy.

Then Denise went missing, Shaun charged off looking for her, and not only did he fail, he came back an utter wreck, a babbling addict, the candy wrapper removed to reveal the turd that was always there.

But why is Maria so invested in Clive and Francene's intimate misfortunes? Why the worried frown when she stares at their house?

There she goes, stealing yet another concerned glance, herself a central pattern in the fabric of that perfect family's unraveling lies.

Invisible at the window, Benjamin smiles, witness to the long hours Clive has spent inside Maria's house over the course of years. He's noted with lascivious glee the times of entrance and exits, and that sometimes these day-after-day repetitions of arrival and departure occur through the back door rather than the front—usually when she's between other lovers, and their on-off is on again, and Clive feels pressed to avoid his wife's gaze. Sometimes he even comes over when her sniveling whelp of a boy is visiting, on loan from his overbearing disk jockey dad.

Benjamin has devoted much space in his imagination to what happens inside Maria's house, with its wildflower gardens always on the verge of riot.

She's hardly the only sad soul in this neighborhood whose imaginary exploits keep him awake long into the night. There's the ripening teenage redhead being raised by her milky-eyed grandmother in the fourth house on the right, who Benjamin knows with his own eyes and the aid of his telescope to be turning in the direction that most offspring of strict church upbringings turn. The things she does in her blank-eyed boyfriend's truck, parked right in her grandmother's driveway—surely she wants to be caught, surely it will be only a matter of time before she gets her wish.

And then there's the cop in third house left who comes home from nights spent arresting drunken and abusive husbands to beat his mousy wife if she doesn't fix his breakfast fast enough. Or the heartthrob weatherman in second house right with his endless procession of lithe young men brought home well after dark, kicked out in the wee hours of the morning.

The door opens first house left, and Benjamin's smile changes, to one of fond indulgence. Here's scrawny, feisty, nosy Patsy, trundling down her ramp in her motorized wheelchair.

It's been years since he was inside Patsy's house, with its Christmas tree always lit in the dining room and its overpowering smell of cats' piss. But hers is the only other home in this cul-de-sac he's ever set foot inside. And she's the only neighbor he ever speaks to, though it all happens over the phone.

She has never been inside his residence.

Afflicted by a cruel degenerative brain disease that's taken more and more of her mobility away over her fifty years of life, Patsy will never be a part of the harem in Benjamin's inner sanctum. Yet amidst the dingy rooms inside his mind, he keeps a shrine to her that's pristine, bathed in light.

She waves to Lance the white-trash thug, who beats a retreat like a pitbull nailed with pepper spray, unable in his hardwired hatred to cope with his neighbor's half-paralyzed body and relentless good cheer, not so bold a bully as to mock a handicapped woman when the parents he still lives with might find out about it. To Lance, Patsy is wolfsbane.

At the window, Benjamin smiles, as Patsy glides her slow and steady wheelchair up the street, to where Maria wipes a towel over her tiny car's back bumper. She doesn't seem to mind the interruption at all as Patsy hails her—she stands up and steps over to chat, despite being drenched head to toe from her labors.

This is the one thing that that raises Maria higher in Benjamin's esteem than all the other pathetic human lumps making their nests along this street. She's always kind to Patsy.

The way both women keep looking over at Clive and Francene's house, Benjamin guesses they must be chatting in stage whispers about the drug addict's return. He longs to know what they're saying, but doesn't trouble himself. Sometime this afternoon, the phone will shrill, and Patsy's adenoidal voice will tell him everything.

And he will share things too, things he's seen. He will never tell her everything, never that, but enough to keep her coming back.

They've been entwined in this relationship so long, he and Patsy, that he no longer remembers precisely how it started, other than that it must have begun all those years ago when she invited him to her house and he accepted, even then not entirely understanding why. Possibly because no one else had ever asked such a thing of the creepy old man on the hill.

Though they had almost nothing in common, they immediately recognized the one thing they shared, an outsider's perspective on everyone else, that delectable twist of longing and contempt. And an unspoken and yet soundly understood acceptance that directed a gentle breeze through the torn rags of each others' psyches.

Dearest Patsy, who like him lives off disability checks, who like him has a ravaged face to show the world. When he was younger, he would tell people his eyepatch covered the results of a war wound in Vietnam, where he never served. He would never admit to anyone his puddinglike eye and prematurely arthritis-crimped joints resulted from venereal disease.

Patsy, for all her chatty nosiness in the neighborhood, showed no interest in learning about his embarrassments. She just wanted him to feel at home, she once said.

Her empathy had actually freed him to make the play he most desired in the game of human interaction: to drop out, to give up trying.

Maria turns her head, and Patsy hers. And now Benjamin looks too, and squints his one good eye, and shuffles to grab the binoculars.

That drug-addled boy, Shaun the Formerly Perfect, has just turned onto the circle from the cross-street, walking with shoulders hunched in a jacket too warm for the weather, like he thinks that will stop him from being seen.

But when did he leave his parents' house? And where on earth is he coming from?

Benjamin presses the binoculars to the window.

* * *

second square

Maria knows something has gone terribly wrong the moment she spies Shaun trudging up the street, shoulders hunched, the skin around his eyes puffy and raw, his expression unfathomable.

Speak of the devil.

He looks like a devil, doesn't he? Like someone consumed inside by fire, any moment his skin will blacken and the flames lick through.

Sweet Patsy stops her soft-spoken prattle mid-sentence, thank goodness. She has to sense it too, how wrong this is.

The boy's not supposed to be out of the house, Maria knows this. Clive told her last week, during a brief, jittery-nerved visit. It had been a Wednesday before sunup, her son Davey staying with his accursed father, Clive dressed for work in his button-down, her in her violet nightie. They'd shared nothing more than a quick kiss on the lips. Her on-again off-again lover had been wound tight enough to snap a spring.

That in itself wasn't so unusual for Clive these days—his family had unraveled, his granddaughter Denise gone without a trace, his son plunged down the same path of addiction and self-inflicted psychosis.

And worse, Shaun's stay in rehab had gone about as poorly as could be imagined. His second night there one of his podmates at the Langan Center had gone missing, presumably bolting back to his life of crack and crystal, but the third podmate had made wild accusations that Shaun had assaulted his fellow junkie—they weren't taken seriously because what the guy described sounded like something straight out of a peyote delusion.

The accusations stopped when the third podmate staged his own disappearing act the next night, but the seeds of suspicion had been irrevocably sown.

That morning, they sat pressed together on the couch in her den, her shoulders tucked under his arm. They're kicking him out, he said. I have to go get him today. It's either that or the streets, and I'm not letting that happen again.

She frowned up at him, but he was staring somewhere else, staring through the paneled wall.

Did I tell you about the things he said?

I remember. Maria shuddered involuntarily, remembering the night Shaun came home, how he'd pounded on the windows of his parents' house, screaming about things crawling inside him, things like little living needles.

No. When I saw him yesterday, when the staff called me in.

She looked into those eyes that weren't focused on her. No, you didn't.

So the director leaves me alone in the pod with him for a couple minutes, and he's had this hangdog, sullen look on his face the whole time, but then, as soon as the door shuts, he cuts loose with this smile. I've never seen a look quite like that on his face before. It's not a nice smile. It's like he wants to take a bite out of me. And he says, You don't have to grieve for Denise anymore, Dad. She's right here. And he taps his chest. I found her, and you'll see her again and so will Mom.

And I'm so freaked out that I don't know how to even respond to that. And I'm thinking about how when he disappeared, so did one of my handguns. So I ask him, Shaun, do you know where your roommates went?

And he just smiles that same way and says, They didn't go anywhere.

Good God, she said. They can't let him out. Not like that.

That's what I tried to tell them. But they wouldn't listen. Clive bit his lip like a child. I think they're as afraid of him as I am.

They had ended the visit by clinging to each other in a desperate hug. There'd been no closing kiss.

Shaun trudges down the street between these passive rows of cookie-cutter split levels, a feral dog stalking the hen houses in the open. She knows he's never been the stand-up chip off the block her lover believes him to be. She'd been the subject of too many more-than-cursory glances from the little creep over the years. How much did he know about her, about her and his father? What did he imagine when he looked at her that way?

Maria knows something is wrong, and she's burning to know what, and she is not afraid of Clive's pup. Hey, Shaun, she says, how's it going?

He draws up short, and his face lights up in a manner that makes no sense, like a trapped miner who has just spotted a pinprick of light, but this glow goes out almost as soon as she notices.

And then he turns to her, to Patsy, and he's walking over to them with his mouth compressed into an anxious line, and Maria wonders why she couldn't just leave well enough alone.

Hi, ladies, he says. He glances over Maria, still dripping from her not quite finished carwash, before he turns to Patsy, scrawny and wide-eyed in her wheelchair, and Maria's heart starts to pound, her fists to clench.

Are you feeling okay? he says to Patsy. You look pale.

Patsy, bless her heart, recovers quickly from the shock of being addressed by the creep she was just whispering about. I don't feel any worse than I usually do, Shaun, but I appreciate your concern.

I know you've both heard things about me, he says.

Maria sees her own cold trepidation mirrored in Patsy's round face. Her wheelchair-bound neighbor's thick glasses, framed by graying curls, magnify her pop-eyed shock.

I'm sure everybody heard me screaming the other night. I don't even know what I was saying. He hangs his head. I know Mom and Dad had to tell all of you why. I didn't leave them a choice. And that's no one's fault but mine. Everything that's happened to me is all my fault. All of it.

The pain on his face is so frank that Patsy has gone misty-eyed. Maria feels that urge, too, gathering behind her own eyes, but it doesn't gain momentum, because something in her doesn't believe in what she's seeing, as if it's staged, a movie trick, as if she's staring at the most perfect rubber mask ever molded.

I know I frightened everyone, he goes on. And I know I caused my mom and dad a lot of pain and confusion and worry. I have to make it up to them. And I want to make it up to all of you.

How are your mom and dad, Shaun? Maria doesn't think she kept the suspicion completely out of her voice.

Oh, man, he says. They're so unhappy right now. Unhappy as they can be.

The way he looks at her, when he says it.

I know dad helps you around the house sometimes, he says. Maybe I can do that for you. Help out some.

The thought makes her skin crawl. She's shaking her head before she even comes up with words to blurt out. I can always lean on my ex if I have to, she says, with what she hopes is a jaunty smirk. He doesn't know jack about squat, but he can afford electricians and plumbers. And the courts made sure he has to pay for them. Don't you worry about me.

But he's already turned to Patsy. Same offer stands for you, he says. My mom's told me about how much trouble it is for you, keeping things up inside your house. I know I can help. I want to help. His voice grows even more urgent. I've been so selfish. Putting my needs above all others. That needs to stop. I want to do something that I know is worthwhile. Give to a good person.

Oh, Shaun, poor Patsy stammers, that's, that's so sweet…

He keeps speaking to Patsy, even though he's looking at Maria sidelong. Mom told me what she said to you. About talking to myself all night. In different voices. How they could hear me through the floor. About the fight I had with Dad. How they locked themselves in the bedroom to keep me out. I know. Yes, it's all true.

This is exactly what Patsy had been telling Maria about when Shaun walked up. The things she'd heard from Francene.

But I'm done with that. I'm done with the DTs. Too much has happened to me these past few weeks, and I've made a lot of mistakes, and I can't take any of them back. But I want to make good now. I want to show everyone that I can.

Maria has backed away a little. You don't need to try so hard, she says. Just be the person you want to be. And quit being bad to yourself.

He ignores her, kneels beside Patsy. Come on, Patsy, please. There's got to be errands I can help you with. Chores?

The sheer force of his need bends her will. She nods, flashes a nervous smile. Sure. Sure. Tomorrow. Let me think about it.

And he takes her hand. Thank you. Kisses her fingertips. Then stands, and grins radiantly at both of them, a smile so heartbreakingly genuine that Maria feels ashamed for a moment that her hackles were ever raised.

And then he turns to his house, and goes inside, without knocking—the door isn't locked.

Immediately she's at Patsy's side. I don't think you should do it. Don't let him in your house. It's not…he might be looking to steal something. For money. For drugs. It's what happens.

She fears something worse, but she can't imagine or articulate what.

I want to help him, Patsy says.

No, no, you don't have to do that.
It'll be fine, she says. I feel so bad for him.
Well, If you notice anything funny, you call.
A shy smile. I will. Don't you worry.

third square

Lance crouches behind the peeling picket fence that stretches from the side of his parents' house like a molting wing, and peers between the slats, watches the woman in the wheelchair roll back home, watches Maria finish up her chore, plucks idly at the crotch of his jeans.

He doesn't know which of the two women he hates more, the freakish one that gives him the willies with her cheerful, slurring speech and owl eyes and spindly frame slumping all the wrong ways, or the sad sexpot bitch who thinks she's too good to give him what he wants.

That latter hate has been with him a long time, planted in puberty, growing poison vines. A tower of athletic-numbered-and-school-lettered muscle in high school, he never had trouble reeling in pussy at the rich-kid parties despite his own humbler origins—and he couldn't count how many times, when he'd had some dumb bitch squealing beneath him while he hammered her with his hips hard enough to leave bruises, he'd shut his eyes as he spurted and groaned and pictured his neighbor across the street in all her latté-skinned glory.

As for the former, he'd only ever imagined choking her to death.

In truth, his loathing for either woman means nothing special, given his quick slide into obscurity after squeaking through graduation, his father who still calls him a lazy cocksucker, his father's cheapskate friend who owns the oil-change shop where he works but doesn't pay him enough to let him move out, the friend's microskirt-wearing slut of a daughter—his withered, leathery heart holds plenty of hate to spare for all of them, and most everyone else besides.

When Maria finally goes inside, Lance stands up, adjusts his jeans, and notices with an angry blush that the creepy kid from two doors down is staring right at him. The gall of that boy, prissy Shaun, offspring of perfect Clive and Francene, standing beneath a tree, not averting his gaze at all. And fucking grinning.

Lance meets him stare for stare, getting angrier by the second. What the fuck are you looking at?

The little prick grins and shrugs. Actually grins and shrugs.

You want me to come over there? Want me to beat your junkie ass?

No, that's okay, he says. As if this is fucking funny. But he trucks toward his house like the plucked chicken he is.

Lance thinks about shouting after him, but he knows that little prick has been acting all bugnuts, he knows that family has guns, and his entire life has been about walking the edge of discretion, only hurting others when he knows there will be no repercussions.

That little prick had been a recipient of some of that hurt, once upon a time. You'd think he would remember how it felt, surrounded and petrified in the little park down the hill, blubbering on the ground while Lance's friends circled him and laughed, while Lance himself pretended he was going to shove the pipe wrench in his grip handle first up Shaun's prissy little asshole. He had no intention of doing so, but the fact that the little faggot believed it and was terrified enough to piss himself, and too humiliated afterward to ever tell—that was what mattered.

You'd think he'd remember that, and know who not to fuck with.

Recalling the scene brings Lance to a quick boil, but not because of his crybaby neighbor's defiance of the pecking order. Lance remembers how that confrontation ended, with perfect daddy Clive, who seemed so much bigger then, driving his Pontiac right over the cement parking block and onto the playground grass, stepping out with a tire iron gripped in one hand as all the big kids scattered. Lance hating little Shaunie even more as he ran, not because his wuss ass had to be rescued by his dad but because he knew his own dad would never do anything like that for him.

Think of the devil. Inside the house, Lance's dad starts shouting, and he freezes, and fucking hates himself for doing it. His dad's just screaming at his mom again. Nothing for him to care about.

Lance saunters all supercool back to the garage and resumes the task he had planned to start when Maria popped out her front door with all that skin showing. He has his Cutlass Supreme's front tires up on ramps, the oil filter wrench and the oil tray and the new filter already in easy reach. He lies down on his back on the mechanic's creeper he swiped from his employer and glides under the engine.

This chore is child's play, and as he clamps on the wrench, his mind wanders, because the smirk on that little prick's face still pisses him off. His rage is like a hydra made from rattlesnakes; it wants to sink all its fangs into its target, any target, and never let go.

He mutters under his breath as he awkwardly twists the wrench. I know what would wipe that smile off your face, you little prick. He twists. That crazy bitch niece of yours showed up at Mickey's party stoned out of her mind. He twists. She gave every motherfucker head that was there. He twists, harder. The filter's not coming off. I had my turn in line, little prick. I had my turn. What do you think of that, prick? What do you think?

But then his stomach is in knots, because the fact is he'd been so drunk he barely remembers what happened that night, only Denise's eyes staring up at him, bloodshot to the point of pink. And the memory makes him sick—

The filter tears apart, spraying oil all over him. Fuck!

It takes him a full second to realize that in his distracted state of mind he was turning the wrench the wrong way, and then he cusses that much louder.

And that's when he notices the shoes. There's someone standing in front of the Cutlass, two nice high tops parked right by his left thigh.

What the— he begins, but he doesn't get to finish, because something shoves what feels like a fist-sized rock in his mouth. He thrashes, smashes his forehead into the bottom of the engine. The thing in his mouth shoves down, slams the back of his head into the ground. It tastes like snotty flesh. It pulses and thickens, and his muffled scream becomes a shriek as his jaw pops out of its hinges.

The shoes never move. Dark, mottled ropes blur with cobra speed around the tire ramps.

The engine drops, embeds itself in Lance's body. His chest and ribs cave in. His pelvis splits. Beneath him, the caster wheels pop out from underneath the creeper. The weight of the Cutlass pins his head sideways against the concrete of the garage floor. So many nerve signals are roaring that he doesn't feel his right ear tear free. He's shrieking, shrieking, shrieking, but the sound can't get around the fleshy obstruction swelling in his mouth.

He doesn't have enough mind functioning rationally to wonder how Shaun is with him, under the car with him, somehow slid under to join him, bright green eyes boring right into his as he once again displays that maddening smirk.

You remember my niece, then, Shaun says. Turns out, she does remember you. Just barely.

Something balloons out. From Shaun's neck. Like a sack. Except it's also a face. A girl's face. Bright things crawl from her eyes.

stitches

You were so lucky.

Your father never told you, No you can't, never said anything was out of your grasp. Your mother never laughed at you when you talked about writing poetry for a living, starting a band, hitchhiking the country just to do it. They always told you that whatever you wanted most was the thing that was best for you.

You had to take things into your own hands to learn what a waste you are, what a repulsive excuse for a human being you turned out to be, even before you could no longer call yourself human.

At rare intervals, such as now, shuddering on your parents' king-size bed, stifling your whimpers with the barrel of your father's .357 magnum, you congeal in some rough approximation of your old self.

Most of the time you are not—you are a creature of unbridled longing, unstoppable hunger, lacking even the discerning predilection for the weak and unwanted that kept the monster you have now become hidden from the light for long ages.

You no longer know where you begin or when you began. You can crawl inside yourself like a silverfish skittering through the coils of a rolled-up tapestry but no matter how deep into the dark you crawl you will never find the other end.

You are every god that ever had the raw remains of a sacrifice stretched over its shoulders, every monster that ever wore its victims' skins, stitched them into capes, coats and masks. The soul is a bright morsel sealed in an envelope of flesh, and you are the unbinder and the weaver, the one who adds new patches to the ever-growing quilt. You carry the motes that, when cast upon your prey, reveal the seams by which you unhook and unbutton, but never rip, never draw blood.

You are a nightmare from the grimmest of all fairy tales. Call your true name, and you'll simply unhinge your jaw to swallow the shrieking princess and her squalling baby whole. You are a throat that can never be stoppered, a hole that can't be sealed by sunlight or stake or bullet.

Sometimes the you who once was slides out from the folds to glimpse the surface, but that you is never is control. There is nothing in control.

The only thing you ever had control over, was Denise. Until she fled. Right into the arms of another monster, and led you right to it, led it to you.

She ran from your probing hands, from the sickening price you exacted for a false show of brotherly love, and to addiction, to alcohol, to sex, to Ecstasy, to the archdemons of crack and heroin and meth and finally into the grasp of something a million times worse.

When you tracked her down at that quaint little shop, innocuous front for a methadone empire, it was waiting for you. It had a name, Lenahan, and a sweet public face, and an awe-inspiring profile in the drug-running underworld. And an even older pedigree and an even more terrible purpose, a hunger it fed so carefully, so thoroughly.

And you thought you were so clever, when you bested it with its own button-hook magic. But as it died, it opened you up, it made you understand what you were, a pathetic, predatory scavenger, a belly-crawling degenerate, feeble clone of its own black-stitched glory.

You're draped in its hunger, in its lust, in its skins, but not worthy of the mantle. You're the will-o'-the-wisp struggling to steer the whirlwind.

You're the fly swallowed alive, helpless, wriggling.

In the dead of night, blubbering on all fours on your parents' bed, you press the tip of the brutal metal barrel hard against the back of your mouth and squeeze the trigger.

The bullet bores through your palate, out the back of your head, punches into the ceiling. You feel nothing but a hard tug.

You start screaming. The screams are in Denise's voice, in your father's voice, in the voice of an innocent little girl, in voices you don't recognize and never will.

You push your mouth down on the barrel, jam it in your throat, you gag on it but shove it in deeper, you squeeze the trigger in your fist again, again, punching holes through your head, the entire clip, ten spent shell casings spit from the chamber one after the other. And you wail and you keen as each bullet does you no more harm than a needle shoved through a cloth sack.

Your cries leak through the spiral coils inside you and you can feel the responses in kind, a muffled chorus of despair croaking for release.

You're just one more voice at the crest of this crypt, the thin-stretched shroud wound over and through a mass grave packed with thousands, pressed on each other in layer after layer.

Your father's gun has gone impotent but you keep clicking the trigger, screaming into an empty chamber.

Still later in the night, when the cops come to the door, you calmly tell them nothing's wrong. You let them search the house. They ask about the bullet holes in the bedroom ceiling. You say your son did that when he was drunk and alone in the house, before you had him taken to rehab, and right now you don't know where he is.

They can see there's no blood. Finally, they leave you. And you resist the urges. You leave them alone. You let them leave.

The crushed shell of your mind leaks with other urges, more pressing lusts to slake.

fourth square

Truth be told, Patsy gave no credence to Shaun's strange, tear-stained speech of the previous day, expected nothing to come of it, which makes the knock on her door so early this morning that much more of a surprise.

Everyone promises to call on Patsy and her cats. No one ever does. And she makes sure they don't need to. Every warm day, she makes sure they all have to see her bright-eyed, smiling face.

Most of her neighbors pretend to be kind to her, and she's not blind to the pretense. They smile too long, won't look her in the eye, say goodbye before she's done talking. She's always gracious about the subtle abuse—a compromise she offers to those who might be happiest if she gave into the disease slowly rendering her paralyzed, if she simply stayed in her home and withered away, died helpless and forgotten in her bed, a sacrifice to the flies.

One of the consequences of being inconsequential, a person looked past rather than seen—she has been cast as the neighborhood's cheerful confessor, its motorized wheelchair-bound repository of secrets.

If she wanted to, she could make the whole neighborhood come apart at the seams. But, because she never breaches trust, never shares these sacred scraps, and because of the pity those with a glimmer of a conscience feel toward this woman with no friends, she is entrusted with so much. She knows so many things about people who care little to nothing about her.

She hears the elderly woman at the end of the street complaining about her tramp of a granddaughter. She hears Francene's frettings about missing Denise, and her not-so-perfect son, and the suspicions about her husband that she doesn't quite dare face head-on.

She hears Maria's gripes about her many obnoxious boyfriends, enough that she can tell when someone's about to get dumped. She hears about the fights with the ex, how he lords his custody of Davey over her, how he deprives Davey of things like comic books and field trips just to spite his mother, to show her how powerless she is.

Patsy even hears about the break-ups and reunions with Clive—Maria has never kept this secret, not from her.

And she hears from Barry the bulked-up, hunky weatherman about the annoying and adorable quirks of his latest boy toys. She hears the resentful whispers of the cop's wife, and many, many more, even sometimes speaks to Lance's withered and hateful mother, aged to twice her years, about what goes on in that hell of a household.

There is only one person with whom she shares these treasures. Withdrawn, crazy Benjamin, with his fenced-in house on the hill past the dead end. She talks to Benjamin because of all the ones she knows, he's the one she pities. Because the rest of the neighborhood has forgotten him, the way they'd love to forget her. Because she has vowed to never be what he became, a thing so cut off from the world his blighted soul is barely recognizable as human, the way he eats the morsels of other lives that she feeds him the way a starved dog gobbles leftover fat.

Though he came to see her once in the mildew-blotted house she can't keep up with, she has never been so naive as to mistake his alien fascination for kindness. Others have shown genuine kindness, Maria for one, Barry for another in his self-indulgent way, sometimes calling her to warn her about the weather when he thinks of it. Even distracted Francene has at times remembered her with tiny gestures, cheap porcelain kittens given at Christmas to match her octet of living ones. Patsy places Francene's gifts in the living room, under the plastic Christmas tree that she never takes down, set up when she was more mobile.

When the knock comes again, she wonders if one of her occasional benefactors is making a rare house call. Maria, most likely, though she hardly stops by anymore, and she can't keep from wrinkling her nose when she does. No one ever asks if she wants to live with this stink, no one ever offers to help. She can't afford in-home care. They look at the stains on the carpet, the turds on the floor, and assume this is something she wants. And if she asks for help, that leads to the cold stares, to the questions, Why do you keep so many cats? Can't you get rid of them? She doesn't dare ask for help.

The knock again.

Who is it? she yells, commencing her struggle to get out of bed. Her crutches haven't slipped out of reach, that's a good start.

Muffled through the door, It's me, Miss Hale.

Francene and Clive's boy has kept his word. He's really at the door. The depth of her shock can't be sounded, especially after all that commotion last night, noises like firecrackers and police cars parked out front, their blue rollers bathing the street in submarine light.

She wonders what that was about. She wonders if it's safe to have that boy on her doorstep. She wonders if Benjamin watched last night, what he saw.

He knocks again. I'm coming, she says, you'll have to wait.

Okay.

Getting dressed is an ordeal that requires careful coordination. In forty-five minutes, she is clad in slacks, shoes, an oversized, faded floral-print blouse, and rolling her halting way to the door. She hasn't heard a peep from Shaun, but when she peers through the spyhole, there he is, standing at the top of her ramp, those piercing green eyes gazing off into nowhere, a slight frown creasing his forehead.

Her voice quavers slightly as she unlocks the door. Bless you for being so patient.

Not a problem, Patsy. He slips inside, closing the door behind him, deftly maneuvering around her wheelchair. She rotates the machine to see where he goes but he just stands in the middle of the living room, doesn't raise his eyebrows at the Christmas tree, doesn't show any sign he notices the reek.

What a lovely house, he says.

Patsy starts. She could swear that when he spoke, the voice she heard was Francene's. Yet the illusion breaks when he speaks again. I can get started if you show me where you keep your cleaning supplies.

They're in the kitchen, beside the sink. You'll see them right away.

He doesn't move. Actually, before I get started, there's something I want to talk to you about.

Now she understands. He wants what everyone wants: to make a confession. Yet still her unease grows, blood rushing in the parts of her that still have functioning nerves to feel. Well, anytime, Shaun.

This isn't easy for me. He takes a deep breath. Maybe you can show me around the place, give me a little tour, so I can see what needs to be done. While I think about how to start. It's a painful subject.

And raw pain wrenches in his voice. Patsy doesn't know what to say other than, Okay, then.

Go ahead, I'll follow you, he says.

Well, okay. There's not much to see. I don't use the basement much.

He doesn't laugh at her joke. His red-rimmed eyes glisten.

Oh, Shaun, she says, what is it?

He just shakes his head. She finally pushes the lever to guide the chair toward the hall, and from there into the kitchen. Beneath her the floor creaks. Something is egregiously wrong about all this, his unprecedented frankness, his claims to want to make amends, his presence here so early, but she can't deny that he's genuinely upset over something. In fact, behind her, he's starting to sob.

The kitchen linoleum is filthy as the living room carpet. Three of her babies hunch under the table, mute witnesses with wide slit-pupil eyes, eager for morsels and charity. Were she alone, they would have it.

She's almost afraid to speak. He's crying behind her. Whimpering. Maybe she should suggest he leave, but she doesn't have the heart. I do have a table in here with a couple extra chairs. I don't use them much, but maybe you could…sit down?

Then her head snaps back as he shoves her out of the chair, as her chin smashes against the floor, her mouth blooming with agony as she bites her tongue.

She's spitting blood as he flips her onto her back as if she's no more than a porcelain doll. Her babies all pitter-patter away in panic as he straddles her stomach. The sounds coming out of him—he's bawling like a child with his hand slammed in a door.

His face. The skin of his face is sliding loose. And there's another face underneath. And that too is peeling along a previously invisible seam, splitting to reveal yet another layer that starts to slide free as soon as it's exposed.

He's not heavy, not a big man, but her traitor muscles can't help her, she can never hope to get out from underneath. Her blows against him are kitten-weak and she hates that even more than she hates him.

He claws at his throat, which splits open at the Adam's apple. His sobs don't stop as he draws out something like a kerchief that expands into a sack, into a limp mask. He bends toward her, with this mask clutched beneath his sloughing face as if it's a bag on a necklace, and the mask's mouth is shaping silent words. The face, it's familiar, she would know it if it weren't so distended, if her mind were not on fire with fear and pain.

Stop.

He shakes the mask. Bright beads fall from its mouth, eyes, into his cupped hand.

Stop. Please.

He jerks her up by her collar and shoves his hand with its fistful of bright crawling motes down her blouse. She wails up at him in outrage as her aching chest goes numb. Beneath the peeling onion of his face, the gasping girl mask opens its mouth in a silent scream that mirrors hers as he rips her blouse open, the fabric tearing like tissue paper.

The bright beads have arranged themselves in rows down her heaving ribs. They look like buttons, multihued buttons of all shapes and sizes, but they also look like living things, beetles or ticks, aligning themselves along invisible seams.

His fingers trace those seams. As he gropes, his breath hitches, somewhere deep inside the ruin of his head.

She cannot be seeing what she is seeing. Her flesh parting under his manipulations as if he's unfastening another blouse.

She swallows a copper gob of blood. Why?

I can't fight them, he sobs. It's what they want. I can't stop.

fifth square

Barry winces as he gets out of the gleaming Volvo he can't actually afford and limps the six yards from his driveway to his house, still dressed in the sweater and button-down he wore during the early morning forecast.

Sometimes his face aches from the smile he has to hold steady the entire time the cameras are at risk of rolling. He kept it on through the 5 a.m. and 6 a.m. shows. Even sat there grinning beside the anchor, her adipose-padded hips safely hidden behind the counter on the set, as she rattled off a sad script about a young single mom and her daughter reporting missing yesterday, and how police wanted to question her ex-boyfriend, a doozy of a catch with an easily checked-on criminal record who vanished without a trace from a rehab center just days ago.

That poor woman and her kid, last seen at a school play, probably already dead at the hands of psycho Romeo. How is it that people never have their guard up, never recognize the signs, he wonders.

Of course, the cheerful weatherman act was even trickier this morning, thanks to that beautiful peacock of a hookup from the night before. An exquisite young buck from the club with plush pouty lips and not an ounce of cellulite on his slender frame, with cheekbones high and sleek as an elf's. But he'd pleaded an over-reactive gag reflex, insisted on sucking and chewing only on the very tip of Barry's cock and making up for it with his hands. Oh, they did the trick, yes—his thighs were still sore—but he'd also woken up with the tip of his penis bruised purple as a plum. He had to look forward to an entire day pretending in front of a camera that every step wasn't accompanied by an excruciating pinch of pain.

Ordinarily, he would head straight for the basement and the free weights, to pass the couple hours before he had to drive back and prepare the noon forecast. Instead, he fills a sock full of ice from the fridge and climbs straight to bed. He doesn't know if the ice will help, but he has to try.

He lies there in a fugue, mind shifting between the day's labor and the not at all unpleasant memory of the face of that evil Adonis bobbing at his groin. He sits up with a yell when the scratching at the window starts.

Obscured by the shade, there's a dark shape in the window's bottom corner that could be the curve of a head in silhouette.

Get out of here, he hears. Get in your car and never come back here.

Patsy?

Barry's window is at the back of his house, on the second floor. There's no deck, no tree, nothing below it to stand on for support. And Patsy....

I'm sharing a secret, she says. He wants to fight it but he can't stop. He's too weak. You have to go.

He springs to the window, jerks the shade handle. It slams up onto its roll, flapping hard against the wall, one, two, three.

Nothing out there but the sun dappling his tool shed and the tiny square of his vegetable garden.

Before he gets back in his car, he notices a curtain moving in Clive and Francene's bedroom window next door, the fabric stirring as if caught by a breeze, even though the sash is closed.

sixth square

Late for work, Maria freezes with the side door to the carport half open. Clive stands by her Hyundai, clean-shaven in a short-sleeve button down and tie, face vacant as a zombie's.

Then he sees her, and that square-cornered grin of his brings all his smile lines out.

Inside her the spike of alarm melts, and for a moment she doesn't care that they're out in the open. Oh, baby, she says, where you been?

His smile falters. I'm so sorry I haven't been in touch. I swear, that crazy kid's going to be the death of me.

No he won't. You'll get through to him. She knows this role, the comforter. She's played it for him many a time. She locks the door behind her. Your timing's terrible, I have to get to the restaurant, I'm going to be late.

I know, I just…I had to get out of there a minute. I had to see you. He stares hard at the ground as he says this.

Now she's beside him. He happens to be blocking her driver's side door. It's okay baby. I was worried, really worried, you've been silent as the grave. I just can't do this right this minute. She holds up her car keys in a clear I'm-about-to-unlock-the-door gesture. He doesn't move, just studies her face. His Adam's apple bobs up and down above the knot of his tie, as if there's a word stuck there that won't come out.

Um, baby? I have to go.

He reaches up, strokes a warm finger under her jawline. She leans into his hand out of reflex a split second before her brain kicks in. Then she recoils. Clive, what the hell are you doing?

He grabs her shoulders, pulls her in for a kiss.

He's never done this before, not this way, and not where everyone can see. His fingers dig in hard enough to bruise, and with a hiss she punches him in the solar plexus. Jesus fucking Christ!

Her knuckles sting from the impact. He doesn't flinch but he lets go.

What the hell are you thinking? You want Francene to see?

She's never seen his face assume a configuration like this before, a snake flickering its tongue above a quivering mouse. You really think she doesn't know, Maria?

For a moment, his eyes are green, like his son's, like Francene's. She blinks and they're dark brown, like they should be.

She grips her ignition key like she's holding a knife. I need to go.

She vowed a long time ago not to let men bully her any more, not to let them use her, not when she has a choice. She's not going to tolerate this kind of bullshit, not anymore, least of all from Clive. She'll do what she has to do, even if it hurts.

He's not moving. For a breath-stopping moment she's certain she'll have to make good on her threat. Then he shudders, and gives way.

A higher power blesses her at that instant, keeps her from fumbling at the lock, lets her hop into the driver's seat in a fluid motion without ever having to look at him, even though he's just inches away. She pulls the switch that locks all the doors.

As the car coughs to life, he starts shouting. Maria, I'm sorry. I'm sorry.

She floors the accelerator, screeches straight out of the driveway. At the end of the street she checks her side mirror. He's still standing in the same spot.

seventh square

Binoculars pressed against the window, Benjamin witnesses the whole brouhaha, Clive the Perfect Husband attempting to draw Maria the Single Mom into a kiss right there on the front lawn, his not-so-secret lover-on-the-side responding by thrashing out of his grip and holding her car keys like she intends to stab him in the eye.

Obviously having Junior home has pushed Mr. Perfect Husband and Father over the edge. Benjamin can't help but feel little thrills, of titillation, of anticipation.

It makes up some for not having seen Patsy out and about today despite the sunny glow outside. It's not time for her to call yet, though. When she does, he'll learn what's happened, what new twist in her ailment has laid her low. And he'll listen as if he's interested, because sometimes one must make an investment to keep the returns you want coming in.

Clive the Perfect stands in the driveway as his mistress zooms off. This Benjamin can actually hear, the sulky tramp lead-footing the engine. Surely all that noise has brought meek little Francene or even wild son Shaun who caused all that police ruckus last night to come to a window, to see.

Maybe they'll have a confrontation right in the street. Benjamin can only hope.

He watches Maria's car disappear around the corner at the far end of the circle, then turns his attention back to Wayward Daddy.

Who is staring right back at him.

Benjamin utters a little girly shriek and stumbles back from the window.

Then he pulls himself together, because it could only have been coincidence. He did not see Clive the Perfect Father with a smile like a serpent about to swallow a nest of eggs, looking not at his house or even at his window but right at him, meeting his single-eye gaze across the distance. It did not happen. No one ever looks at him in the slit between the bay window curtains. He's never caught the neighbors doing more than idly scanning what little of the overgrown yard they could see behind his fence.

He returns to the pane, puts binoculars to the glass.

And finds himself looking right into bright green eyes, glistening mad eyes, eyes like aurora fire.

Clive hasn't moved an inch, except he has to have moved, and with astonishing speed. Because it's not the father standing there now, in his bland blue button-down, it's the son, the drug addict, in an unwashed black print t-shirt, standing in the exact same spot in Maria's driveway, in the exact same hands-in-the-pocket pose, staring at Benjamin with the exact same predatory smile.

Where has the father gone? Benjamin doesn't know and he never finds out. He can't look away from those green eyes. Seconds turn into minutes.

Shaun winks. And blows Benjamin a kiss.

And the old man cries out, and pulls the curtains shut.

eighth square

Lance doesn't understand the place where he's been, or the condition he now finds himself in.

If his mind ever connected to the concept of a card catalog, he might have explained the raw sensations in those terms—he had been as a sheet of flesh compressed against other sheets in a claustrophobic drawer, waiting for fingers to pull open the narrow space, page through the pink membranes of exposed nerves. But Lance lacks the vocabulary to explain how it felt, just as he has no words to articulate how awareness, sight, smell and hearing have returned to him as abruptly as a sack pulled over his face.

He stares at the ominous circular grill directly over his head for several seconds before his addled brain tells him it's in fact the cover over a drain set in a concrete floor. Though his eyes tell him he must be hanging upside down, he feels no corresponding upset of balance. When he tries to bend his neck, he learns something doesn't work right. It's like his muscles find no spine to pull or push against, but his gaze swivels enough to see a water heater, a tool bench, saws and hammers hanging on a wall-mounted peg board.

Somewhere, perhaps in another room, the sound of a tea kettle boiling to a whistle, quickly subsiding as a hand removes it from the stove.

He doesn't know if he should call out or keep quiet. He tries to look up at the ceiling, find out what the hell he's hanging from, but he can't make himself bend. His back, his arms, his legs—none of these things cooperate.

Unbidden he remembers something awkward, something awful. Hanging upside-down in a smoke-filled bedroom, his mountain of a father dangling him, crushing both ankles together in a sandpaper-rough hand. Lance was tiny then, so tiny, and when his father used his free hand to punch him in the back, the fist that struck him was almost as wide as he was. He wailed like a siren, wailed red-faced at his momma sitting on the bed, who took the cigarette out of her mouth to say, Hit him again! The impact felt like it cracked him in half, and when he screamed his momma yelled, Shut him up! Again!

When the mist clears from his eyes he connects with a start that he's in a utility room, just a plain old utility room like any you'd find in the houses all through this neighborhood where he's lived all his life. Those blocky things in the darkness beneath the lowered shade are just a washer and dryer, those jars on the shelves across from him hold nothing more than jam and canned beans.

A door opens somewhere he can't see, and the overhead light clicks on. Someone pads into the room. Lance tries again to turn his head, can't. Then he tries to call out, but he can only push out air, no matter what he tries to say, Hey or Help me down or Who are you or You fucker.

Striped athlete's socks, no shoes, slender legs covered in blond fuzz, white boxers, the bottom hem of a black T-shirt. A hand gripping a large silver stovetop kettle, thumb fiddling with the lever that controls the lid over the spout, making it open and snap shut. The bastard stands that way, the spout not inches from Lance's nose, flicking the lid open and shut, muttering something Lance can't quite hear.

His course of action ought to be a no-brainer. Knock that kettle away, grab hold of the little fuck however he can with his own massive hands, twist with arms thick as his puny captor's legs, hell, tear the freak's balls off if that's what it takes, make him weep, make him beg, make him Let me down!

But he does nothing of the sort—the most he manages to do is sort of tremble in place.

Now is when it occurs to him to be afraid.

And even that feels all wrong. His heart should be freaking in its ribcage like an inmate with the DTs. Instead he feels an unnatural and sickening chill, like ice is cracking underneath his chin.

The guy bends down to look him in the eye. It's Shaun, staring with wild green eyes. His hair is matted, bird's-nest crazy, as if he hasn't slept in years. And there's something wrong with his face, not just that the pussy's been crying, but his skin looks like it's straining, on the verge of bursting.

It isn't enough, he says. Don't try to tell me it's enough. It isn't enough. He deserves so much worse. So much worse than what we can do. Don't tell me it's enough. Don't tell me what to fucking do, I want this, I want this.

He grabs Lance by the hair and lifts his head. Lance's head and shoulders shouldn't be able to bend and fold the way that they do.

His eyes tell him things. He doesn't understand or accept them.

His eyes show him that he's hanging from nothing more substantial than clothesline strung from the bare ceiling rafters. Something is wrong with his skin. It's loose, neither stretched by muscle nor distended by belly fat. His eyes tell him he has no arms—they're simply not there. His body truncates at the waist, no cock, no legs. Odd black pins clip him to the clothesline. If his eyes are to be believed, he's hanging like a pillowcase of empty hide in the drug addict's basement.

For a second, his captor looks him in the eye, face peeling like wet wallpaper.

The kid lets him go, and his head flops down so he's staring at the drain again.

Shaun walks around him, still talking. So he never did this. That makes me an innovator. Taking things to the next level. Shaun stops behind him, tugs at him, tugs at his back, where he can't defend himself.

Now Lance is really struggling to form words, saying Don't, don't, Daddy don't…

Tell me if this hurts, the addict says.

Then the water sluices in, poured through the opening at his waist, scalding him from the inside out. It burns worse than a hand on the burner, than a blowtorch in the throat, gushing through his empty insides, and he screams and screams, but only water pours out, searing his tongue, searing his nostrils, cooking his eyes like eggs as it leaks out through the corners of his eyelids.

stitching

You can't control the whole, but you can control its pieces. You can break off parts, you can make them long for a voice to scream with. You've never loved loss of control so much, you're high on it, laughing as the tornado lifts you.

Surely a sin eater can also sin. You say it to yourself, over and over, despite the whispers of alarm deep within. Eventually all those whispers shift along the spectrum, no longer voices in unison, no one could understand their thousandfold overlapping syllables, especially not you.

ninth square

Maria has too much to think about when she gets home.

The confrontation with Clive really rattled her, has her pacing through the house, paying only half-attention to her evening routines as she rehearses how she'll tell him she never wants to hear from him again.

She's only indulged their clandestine trysts this long because he's been so sweet to her, oftentimes the only help on hand when she really needs it. And he's smart in a way that most of the men who chase her generally aren't. She never sought out a relationship with a married man, but she fell for him anyway. Her feelings are what they are and she knows the good things in life are fleeting, so she enjoys them when she can.

And she knows that as soon as something goes bad it must be thrown away. No matter what excuse he concocts.

So many men are just like children. They push boundaries. It took her a few bouts with abuse too many to learn that lesson, but boy has she learned it.

She ditched graduating high school to become a wealthy older man's toy, to learn a toy's life is torture when one's owner never lets you out of the box and never wants you to ask what he does while you're trapped inside alone. The bad boy who helped her escape turned out out be even worse, a charming wild-man guitar player with a heart-melting grin and a honey tongue, who'd get her drunk and stoned and show off what he could make her do, with other men, with other women, with people watching. And then Ralph the disc jockey, who turned out to be the worst of all, like marrying Hitler disguised as Casanova. The only thing worthwhile that came from all of it was Davey. For her son, she'd do anything.

Everyone else could go to Hell, and if Hell came for her and her boy, she'd stand in the fire and hold him out of reach of the flames.

She's wandered into Davey's room, the one he uses on weekends. She sits on his bed with its Spiderman-patterned comforter, idly thumbs through the books stacked on his short metal bookshelf. Bartholomew and the Oobleck. He's a little old for that one now. Alice in Wonderland. Something Wicked This Way Comes. That's a little better. Bulfinch's Mythology. She's wondered if that would be too fat and wordy for him, but he loves it, loves those old tales of weird Greek heroes and gods and goddesses always doing terrible things to each other, just like life.

What was the one they read together that punched her so hard in the gut? The musician and his wife. Orpheus.

No man was ever going to lure her down into the dark and trap her there, accident or no. She thinks of Clive again, starts telling him to go fuck himself a hundred different ways, then snaps out of it. Laundry. All her uniforms are dirty. Laundry, now.

There's a note taped to the basement door. She doesn't recognize the handwriting. A woman's, curvy and meticulous. It just says, I know now.

She freezes as if every drop of blood in her body changed to ice crystal.

Who the fuck has been in my house, she thinks, although the message itself points to one particular person, which is impossible because Clive doesn't have a key to her house. She learned never to make that mistake again many years ago.

With a slow-motion avalanche of denial at war in her mind with an inferno of curiosity, she opens the door.

When she spies the heap at the foot of the basement stairs, at first she thinks it's a pile of clothes, and she wonders how it got there, because Davey's with his father.

Another step down after flipping on the light and her confusion grows, because these are women's clothes, but not like anything she herself has ever worn. A no-nonsense, non-revealing skirt and a clean, pristine blouse, when she is totally a jeans-and-T-shirt person, if even that formal.

The disconnect resolves itself when she takes her next step, and she understands someone is wearing these clothes, someone lying motionless at the bottom of the stairs.

Down a slow step further and she realizes she knows who it is, recognizes the outfit. Francene, who is always at home, because

Clive makes enough she doesn't have to work. She's had any number of reasons, ranging from seething envy to sympathetic pity, to give Francene more than casual scrutiny on multiple occasions.

It looks for all the world like Francene is lying with her head wedged under the bottom step.

The illusion doesn't come apart until Maria stands on the bottom step and softly calls Francene's name. When no response comes she toes the other woman's arm with her slipper, and the body shifts.

She appeared to have her head wedged under the step because her shoulders were flush against it. Francene's head is missing.

What's even stranger about it, what pushes Maria right past the need to scream, leaves her sitting silent with mind in freefall, is the sheer absurdity of the fatal wound—or lack thereof. Francene's starched collar doesn't encircle a gory stalk of severed neck. Instead it reveals an expanse of smooth skin, as if Maria's unknowing romantic rival had never had a head, was somehow born without one.

Immediately Maria convinces herself that she's the victim of a prank and her own overactive imagination. She grabs an arm of the dummy and her fingers circle flesh that's still warm, still has a pulse.

The next thing she knows she's on the floor herself, back against the cinder-block wall in the furnace room, kicking at headless Francene, who does nothing in response but flop and loll. The shrieks ringing in her ears are no doubt her own.

A rap on the basement window startles her into new silence.

The squat window in question is set high in the wall above the dryer. On the outside of the house, the sill of that window is set in a shallow concrete well, its floor about six inches below ground level. Shadows move outside that could be legs and feet, someone in the backyard retreating from the window, impossible to tell in the dark.

There's another note, taped to the window. She can see writing. WE NEED TO TALK—in the same hand she saw before, that neat feminine cursive.

She should call the police.

She can't. Her cursed brain shows her the consequences all too clearly.

Her rival's still-living headless body lies sprawled at the foot of her basement stairs. Either Clive or his son left her there. One of them is responsible for Francene's state, somehow. She doesn't understand what's happened to Francene, she knows that she's alive, somehow, and that means there's hope. Whatever has been done, she doesn't understand it, but she needs it undone.

She can't call the police.

She could have before, and she didn't. When Denise showed up on her stoop crying late one night, wanting to talk. Maria will never forget the conversation they had over warm tea that graduated to straight shots of Jack, as Denise spilled her guts about things that happened in that house. She made Maria promise never to tell.

It weighs like a hot brick inside that she kept that promise. But the consequences of breaking it are too painful to think about.

The loud-mouthed father of her sweet little bookworm of a son already has far too much power. What would happen to her life, if she exposed this squirming mess? How would Ralph exploit it?

She can't give up. For Davey's sake, she needs this fixed.

But she's not completely without her senses.

When she crosses over to Clive's house, nonchalant as if she's planning to borrow a bag of sugar, there's a little extra pressure in the front hip pocket of her jeans, a gift from one of her previous paramours, a big-bellied trucker with a wicked sense of humor and too much of a mean streak to be a keeper.

The gift: a silvery folding knife with molded black grips and a ten-pound spring that causes it to flip open and lock with the speed of a switchblade when she depresses a button with her thumb. Hardly an assurance of even odds—Clive owns guns. And there's Francene's body, still living somehow without its head. She can't comprehend how something like that is possible, can't deal with it in any rational way, so she just doesn't.

All the neighborhood's cookie-cutter houses gleam ghostly in the lamplight. The street is empty. Somewhere down the cross-street, a kid shouts, a basketball bounces on a driveway.

Upstairs, to her right, in the room where Denise slept, the curtain moves. A face glimpsed.

Francene? Francene's head?

She watches her finger push the doorbell as if she's dreaming. Footsteps on the other side, but no one answers.

She hears Clive call. It's open.

She hasn't set foot in this house in years. Hasn't dared.

As promised, the door's unlocked. Inside the house is pristine as ever, shoes arranged neat as soldiers on the split-level landing, a wooden plaque carved with the words Our Lovely Home mounted above the short stairwell to the basement, and to the side, above another plaque that reads Home Is Family, hangs a huge photo of the family in their younger years, Denise in her softball uniform, Shaun in glasses and an Izod shirt, Clive in a sweater and Francene in a pink blouse with puffy sleeves.

Maria regards them all, their phony smiles. Clive, what the hell is going on?

No answer.

Clive?

A noise from downstairs, a creak, something banging on a metal surface, and a wet sound she can't quite place.

As she descends the stairs, more homilies await on the walls. God bless this house. Home is where the heart is. Forgive us our trespasses.

The door to the utility room stands ajar. That odd, wet flopping sound wafts through it. She contemplates pulling out the knife, decides against it.

Through the door, past the furnace, and at first she's puzzled by what she sees hanging from the short clothesline attached to the ceiling beams.

Her mind translates it as a large, shapeless sack of untanned leather, with a swarm of something inside it, making it twitch and ripple up and down its length in a truly disgusting way. Insects? Mice? The creaks come from the clothesline cord as the thing's weight tugs and shifts, the bangs occur when the cord snaps up against a metal air duct.

When she steps closer, the sack shivers even more violently. Her stomach knots as she notices the thing is leaking, a thick, foamy, snot-like string dripping out a hole at its tapered bottom. A hole that looks disturbingly like a mouth. With lips that stretch and contract.

She can make out more features. Nostrils. Ears. There are eyes. Rolling to stare at her as the drooling mouth shapes words.

She recoils, and bumps into someone standing right behind her.

A warm envelope of red, glistening flesh engulfs her head. A bear hug crushes her arms to her sides, and what feels like another arm crooks around her neck. She kicks, kicks, kicks as she's dragged upstairs.

one stitch loosens

A voice, louder than the others. *Not her.*

tenth square

Her struggle ends when she's hurled like a Barbie doll thrown in a tantrum. She lands on a mattress.

Maria wants to laugh. She's in the master bedroom, sprawled on Clive and Francene's king-size bed, with its layers upon layers of floral comforters, its pillows color-coordinated to anal-retentive perfection.

The ceiling is riddled with bullet holes.

Shaun bars the way between her and the doorway, eyes bulged, teeth bared in an extraordinary grimace. Tears slick his cheeks. Snot globs his vestigial mustache. He's panting so hard, it's like his whole body is pulsing.

She scrambles away from him, to the opposite corner, between Francene's delicate white dresser and an immense oak wardrobe.

The boy thumps his chest with a fist. You belong in here.

No I don't, she says. What the fuck's wrong with you?

Everything, he says, his voice breaking.

She's on her feet in the narrow space between bed and wall, wardrobe and dresser. He's crossing by the foot of the bed, moving toward her as he claws at his throat with both hands, his lips stretched in an agonized rictus.

Stay away, she says, and flicks the knife open.

He looses a sob, and steps closer.

* * *

stitching, undone

You're a forlorn cry of despair, echoing and echoing down through the spirals of flesh and darkness.

You're an ant atop a mountain crawling with severed and recombined horrors, the mountain itself built on layers of half-mad, half-alive remains. You're battling against other fanged and pincered mites as the entire mass beneath you begins to move.

As legs kick. As arms scrabble. As skin inches and bunches and slithers. The coils of the tapestry plunge deep, deeper than anything remembers, so many strata crushed one onto the other, all sewn together with the darkest magic, all alive.

You are the cork shaking loose above a building geyser of hunger. A thin membrane that swells, ruptures, leaks.

You are staring at the parasite who drained your father's love away, your husband's sperm away, and as you reach for your thronging faerie beads, your black magic buttons, your ultimate drug of choice, other fingers pluck at yours, other wills rip at yours, other longings disrupt yours, and the bright motes slip into the cracks inside you and scuttle the wrong way.

Your father's voice, cutting against the grain of yours. Not her.

And other heads lift inside the coils of this endless, overloaded patchwork of stolen sin and severed lives. Uncounted mouths cry out, even as voices both yours and not yours hiss in your ear.

Not her.

Somewhere inside you a little girl wails.

And you're in a fight to keep your own mind intact as a multitude strains for freedom, pushing and pulling in all directions from their places in the quilt. The only thing these fragments have in common is appetite.

You are the head torn almost free, dangling by a shred of flesh no thicker than a thread.

You are the pattern that can no longer hold.

eleventh square

Through the gap in his throat something bulges, another mouth, whispering not her not her not her...

Shaun screams and lurches forward another step.

Even his eyes split, another pair bubbling up behind them.

Backed up against the wall, Maria has forgotten to breathe. Forgotten she has a heartbeat. Forgotten she has a weapon.

Beneath his clothes, beneath his skin, Shaun's flesh is swelling.

Just as with his face, his forearms begin to split.

Inside his left arm, there's another mouth, and it starts screaming too. In Patsy's voice. Run, Maria! He can't control it!

The thing that was Shaun gasps NO! and stumbles closer.

Get away, she says, but she can't even hear her own voice over the many, many others that join Patsy's, yammering over top of her. Run run help me not her help me RUN…

Worst of all, she hears the ear-shredding screams of a terrified little girl.

Folds of skin slide out from underneath Shaun's shirt, from inside his sleeves, pour out like foam from an overflowing cup.

His face is a shattered nesting doll, a peeling onion of mouths and eyes. His arms, too, peeling back like corn husks as he reaches toward her, his soft shell rolling back to reveal clots of squirming fingers, gobs of knotted flesh between them mushrooming out into even more faces, the empty eye sockets abruptly filling with eyes, bright mites flowing through the creases between the tumorous blooms.

He's filling the space between wardrobe and bed, sealing her in. She peels herself out of her paralysis, stabs him in what's left of his face.

The knife sticks in his molting forehead as if plunged in a grapefruit. It draws no blood. Above and below it, his head yawns apart. The knife slips into the widening hole and vanishes somewhere inside him.

She scrambles onto the bed, flailing pillows out of the way as every bit of Shaun's mutating body begins to unwind.

He comes undone, a thing made of unreeling tapestries, every panel sewn together from writhing, bleating human remains, every single tortured sheet unrolling.

You belong here. The words waft out of his partitioning face before the length of his body splits and yawns wide open.

One of the thousand voices she hears screaming must be her own.

What had been a body, however chimerical, is now a tunnel gaping down into another space, a spiraling channel into somewhere completely outside the confines of reality, its walls formed of peeling patches of skin knitted and merged in suppurating layers, of thrashing limbs, of lolling heads, of flopping genitals, of twisting intestines and latticed bone, all fused in brain-bending Picasso distortion.

She could laugh. She does laugh. The thing fills half the room, every part of it like a window shade flapping open, like fleshy tongues of carpet unrolling, speeding to a blur, every new fractalling tendril opening out and uncoiling, spewing even more patchworks of flesh. The babble of voices echoing out of that otherwordly tunnel of fused-together body parts has reached such a crescendo that she can no longer make out any individual one.

Somehow she's crawled backward onto the floor by the bedroom door, as a curtain of swarming skin covers the ceiling in a single motion like the tossing of a sheet, as a twisting tendril of flesh slithers out from beneath the bed, its tip opening in a polyp of arms that rises to embrace her.

She scrambles backward into the hall. The tendril formed of grasping arms lashes at her like a striking snake. Her cries have moved beyond words.

She's up and running, down the hall, down the stairs, out the door, into the night.

twelfth square

Outside, the bright streetlights cast the neighborhood in friendly amber. In the distance, Maria hears traffic. Closer, the springboard sound of a basketball hitting a backboard, the game she heard before continuing into the night, in someone's floodlit driveway.

From the house behind her, not a sound.

A pickup truck turns onto the street, pulls up to the curb by the first house on the right, engine idling. The headlights momentarily blind her—she steps hesitantly out of Clive and Francene's yard, feeling as if she just woke from a nightmare to discover she's been sleepwalking.

She can see redhead Jillian and her peach-fuzz bearded boyfriend, necking in the cab of the truck right where Jillian's grandma could see her if she chose to look.

She wants to warn them but her mind can't wrap around what to warn them about. What did she see in that house? Did she see anything at all? Her heart could be sprinting in place.

She turns.

The house stands silent, front door sensibly shut, lights on behind the dark curtains in the windows.

A rustling catches her ear, and she backpedals to the road until she can see its source. Clive and Francene have a juniper beside their house that they've allowed to grow up until its crown crops just beneath their bedroom window. The branches are waving back and forth, ever so slightly—but even as her heart attempts to leap into her mouth, she can feel the quickening breeze.

A new flicker of motion makes her glance back up at the living room window, on the second floor, on the left side of the house, above a neatly trimmed hedge of cedars, black boxes in the night illumination. Again, the curtain in that window moves. Is moving.

Maria peers closer. The way the fabric is moving.

What she sees in the window, illuminated by the truck headlights, is a continuous glistening sheet, sliding up the glass. It flexes and expands until the window goes black.

Maria backs away as the rustling in the trees grows louder, joined by new noises from the back yard, as something starts moving in the hedges that shield the basement windows.

An exit plan is forming in her head. Get back to her house, grab her keys, get to her car, roar as far away from this place as possible, pausing only to pick up Davey from his father's apartment. She'll take him by force if she has to, somehow. And then just keep driving. What's one waitress job? She can always get another. And she's blessed enough that she can always find a place to live, even if it means shacking up with someone disposable for a while.

A voice whispers, Maria.

She can't tell from where.

She's off at a sprint.

* * *

thirteenth square

When the telephone rings, it's as if a banshee breaks the silence in Benjamin's dank cavern of a house.

He's lain in his own bed under the covers most of the day, shivering, but not because of any cold. He wants the courage to spit in those green eyes that sought him out in his hidey-hole. He wants the courage, the rage, to say to that smugly predatory face, You have no right, to seize that smug head in his bare hands and squeeze that all-too-knowing stare out of existence with his thumbs.

He wants to put the bricks back in the wall that's been blasted through. But the most he has the strength to do is hide and hope the rock he's under gets left alone.

The phone shocks him out of his withdrawal. He's so deeply shaken, San Andreas fault shaken, that he's only in the most passing way noticed that Patsy's afternoon call never came. He has not wondered why, or what might be wrong.

Patsy. He needs to ask her what's gone on down there, why Shaun the Drug Addict has taken notice of him.

The phone continues to shrill, a deafening nag worse than any his long-gone mother had to offer him.

He pads into the kitchen with increasing hurry, so used to the dark he navigates without need to see his way, wanting as much to quiet that hideous ringing as to hear from his partner in spying on the neighborhood's sad dregs.

The receiver is cold in his grip. When he picks it up the noise is astonishing, like someone's called him from a room where everyone is shouting.

The volume dims as he places it to his ear, but as he speaks Hello! Hello! into the phone, it takes many seconds before he can hear Patsy talking to him.

Her voice sounds strange in the receiver, like she's having trouble breathing. And even once he can make her out she's hard to hear. Though he can't fathom why, she's whispering, even though it sounds like she's still in a crowded room, a cocktail party where hundreds of people are speaking softly.

What? he asks.

You have to come to the window, the woman's voice whispers. You won't believe your eye.

new stitching

If he could still breathe, Lance would breathe a sigh of relief when the bright motes stitch him back into the seamless sheet of the greater body.

He's never been a beast of strong will or secure mind, governed from childhood by primal, petty instincts, a creature crushed beneath his father, forced to grow unnaturally in what little space remained under that flabby oppression. He has no identity to clutch to beyond the scrub of hate, cannot hold his own against the torrent and doesn't even try.

And yet in the expanding corpus of the quilt, hunger trumps all, and the desires of its individual parts become guiding urges, adding eddies to the current, that scrabble and claw into tributaries.

Perhaps it's only chance that his gibbering remains are among those disassembled and rearranged segments that push out through the crack in the utility room window.

Yet as he and his companions slither as one across the weatherman's backyard, grope not quite blindly toward his own home, this tributary of fused-together flesh gains momentum, gains purpose, speeding even faster as he leads the squeeze through the hairline gap beneath the garage door, faster yet as he tracks the muted sounds of emphysema-roughened moans and animal grunts.

He finds them naked in the den, their shriveled, sagging flesh bared and animated with full rut, his mother on the couch on all fours, his father kneeling behind her, red-faced, veins bulging in his neck just as they did during a prelude to a beating.

Neither has time to squawk a syllable as the tide washes over them, as Lance's hands find his mother's neck, as his mouth locks with his father's mouth.

The bright motes unbind them and Lance is inside his mother and father and both are inside and part of him, and all the pathetic and mean secrets they kept from one another are known for one brief moment before they're all absorbed and swept away.

* * *

fourteenth square

The higher powers are not smiling on Maria.

Neither her purse nor her keys are on the lamp table by the door where they're supposed to be. Nor are they on the coffee table in front of the TV. Nor are they on the spare chair in the kitchen. What the hell did she do when she came home, before she found Francene's body?

She finds them on the desk in Davey's room, her keys glittering like stray treasure beside a stack of coloring books he hasn't touched in years. She vaguely remembers thumbing through the books and daydreaming before heading down to start laundry.

She snatches the keys and she's sprinting again, breath hissing through her nose. Her mind alights briefly on the headless not-corpse in the basement, regrets there's no time to hide it, to somehow make it go away. But if someone finds it, if someone wants to ask her about it, so be it. If God really does love her she'll be far away from here by this time next day, with Davey sleeping in the passenger seat.

She dashes outside, keeping her mind restricted to the practical, the need to leave, not letting herself dwell on the unexplainable. Stay focused, get away, get to Davey. One foot on the sidewalk, she pauses to wonder if she should bother locking the house. A hand waves to her from the grass alongside the driveway.

Her mind tells her someone's lying there, though she sees no body. The arm waves again, protruding straight up from the ground, a pale, thick and disconcertingly lively flower.

A second arm lifts up nearby. And a third, this one terminating in a smooth knob at the wrist rather than a hand.

Someone else starts to scream.

The pickup truck's shock absorbers groan and squeak as it rocks back and forth with tremendous force. A mass of churning, meaty darkness blots and flattens against the windows of the cab. The girl's screams continue, muted underneath. The waving headlights sweep a road flooded with travesty, a boiling river of wet glistening eyes, gasping mouths, floundering limbs.

What the fuck!

From the house on Maria's right, that boulder-muscled hulk of a cop has come out onto his front deck, his scalp reflecting white beneath the halo of his crew cut, wearing only his boxers, his coal black Glock 22 clutched with both fists.

Her own yard is smothered in serpentine motion. Inside the truck cab, the girl is still screaming, though her voice sounds like it's coming from down a long hallway, someplace far distant. The passenger window rolls down and something pale and inhumanly long wiggles out of it.

The cop swears again. His gun cracks and flashes.

Hundreds of limbs, a forest of arms, rise up from the cop's yard, from Maria's, in eerie synchronicity. They sprout beside her car. They grope out from underneath it.

She hears a laugh, Shaun's laugh. One of the arms holds up a pale bag of flesh that fills into a woman's blond head. The woman whose body lies in her basement. Francene's head bares teeth, her jaw unhinging to stretch her mouth in a baboon's insane scream.

Maria runs straight toward Patsy's house, where she saw no animated remains raise their hands. She aims for the treeline behind, the railroad tracks beyond.

Behind her, more gunfire.

new stitching

Francene knows anger. She knows betrayal, she knows rage, she knows the urge to murder. For good or for ill, she has known these things for years, and kept them buried deep.

Now they're all that's left of her.

The thing that used to be her son claimed both her and her sham of a husband just hours after Clive brought him home from the rehab center. So funny, so funny, when he started wailing that he couldn't resist any longer, they thought he meant the drugs. But, oh, the thing their boy was addicted to, one taste and hooked for life, it wasn't drugs. Oh, how soon they learned.

Since then Francene has been nothing, a speck of plankton swallowed by the whale, not even a party to the cruel game of bait and lure to which her body had been put to use. Until this spark, this ignition that renders her a particle of positive charge, drawn with increasing power to a negative target.

When she was gobbled by the monster, her husband did nothing to keep it from happening, nothing to fight it, nothing.

When the monster came for Maria—he fought for her, used what was left of his will to delay the strike, buy her time to escape, break her son's crumbling will. *Not her.* He fought for Maria.

Francene's anger swells. Her hunger snowballs.

The prey is on the run.

The forest of arms bends toward Maria's retreating back like flowers pursuing sunlight in time lapse. The pool of flesh gushes as the limbs swarm after her.

The bulk of the chaos she's part of surges in ravenous bloodlust toward a different morsel but the impulse spreading through the tide of flesh has no hold on her. Francene rides her own frenzied engine, her wrath outpacing the momentum of the greater body. She hardly feels the plucks of stitches parting, nerves separating.

This time, her beautiful rival won't be spared.

fifteenth square

Benjamin can't tear himself away from the window.

As Maria the Mistress runs, the Uniformed Wifebeater clutches his gun and wades into what looks from Benjamin's perspective like churning floodwaters, only it's too pale, too patchwork, too alive and deliberate in all its motion to be water or any other form of fluid.

Through the disc of his monocular vision the entire street seethes with twisted life. The mouth of Hell has vomited up all its squirming scrapple of damned.

The cop shoots again, shouting in a voice uncharacteristically high-pitched. The visual makes no sense at all: hands clutch at the cop's waist like he's a rock star attempting to stride across a crowd of rabid fans. Something like glitter sparks between the scrabbling fingers. Then the cop drops straight down as if a trap door opens under his feet, disappears up to his bare heaving chest in the chaos, shrieking nonstop as his arms flail wildly.

Then, as if he were an iceberg melting, his head, his shoulders, his muscle-knotted arms simply drift apart—one arm slapping the air, the other with the gun firing straight up, his face contorted like a pug, still shrieking, as each part drifts at speed in different directions, separated by feet, by yards, still moving, still alive.

I told you, a voice whispers. The best show of your life.

He drops his binoculars. They break on the hard oak floor.

A woman's voice. Watching, always watching. Never one of us.

He peers back into his darkened cavern of a house. Patsy?

The woman laughs, softly, and her voice is joined by another, and another, a chorus of mockery.

We know all about you now.

Never one of us.

Always watching. Always peeping.

He thinks he hears weeping. He thinks he hears Patsy's voice, a moan of warning. Something plucks at the hem of his dressing gown.

He cries out and stumbles back, into a host of waiting arms.

Lips press against his ear. Nasty little spy. You will never be one of us.

He's yelling, Leave me alone, Leave me alone, and struggling against the hands that are all over him, palms sliding across his body, fingers digging in. There are mouths, teeth nipping pinches of flesh.

Never part of us. Simply…apart.

His feet leave the floor.

His gown torn away, his eye patch gone, arms squeezing him, pinning his own arms, fingers probing his mouth, his anus, his blind eye, squeezing his cock, his balls, his throat, grabbing fistfuls of his flab, more fingers grabbing at his tongue to replace the ones he bites through, stuffing his mouth as he tries to plead for mercy.

His joints are being bent the wrong way. The pressure, unrelenting, unbearable.

And the hands tighten their grips to stone-crushing force. And pull until they tear, as joints pop loose, as teeth force themselves through skin.

* * *

sixteenth square

As Maria bolts past the fenced-in house where that weird recluse lives, a horrible noise rips from its dark depths, screams fed from a level of pain she's never encountered in the whole of her life, never even been able to imagine. The very sound makes her want to weep and cover her ears.

When she reaches the treeline, they still haven't stopped. She's tuned them out. She has to. And she doesn't notice at first that there's another voice, screaming her name.

Her mind is racing far ahead of her wheezing body, thinking about what she needs to do once she's on the railroad tracks, once she's off them, who she'll call and who she'll recruit, how she'll get to the apartment where the father of her child lives to snatch Davey up.

She doesn't understand any of the things she's seen over the past hour, doesn't understand what happened to Shaun and Clive and Patsy, doesn't need to. She knows she can't go home, knows she can't leave this town without her son, knows she can't leave him vulnerable in a place where the pylons of reality have ripped free of the ocean floor.

She's a survivor. Someone who lands in bad situations and then springs out again under her own power, whether it's through the possessive clutches of a beefy, jealous boyfriend or through the snags of untrimmed brambles and disease-slimed trees with the mouth of Hell open behind her.

The fence guarding the rail yard has barbed wire strung along the top. Twenty years ago, she would have climbed it without thinking twice. Tonight the sight makes her hesitate, just for a second.

Maria.

And now she can't mistake the sound.

Maria.

She turns to meet Francene's green-eyed glare, not three feet away, illuminated by the rail yard lights, peering at her through the crown of a sumac tree, her oval head cross-hatched by the shadows of the compound leaves. Maria doesn't see a body—she knows Francene's body isn't with her head—she can't tell how Francene's face is hanging there.

She picks the only obvious option, and flees. The treetops rattle and rock above her as Francene follows. The rustle of the leaves could be thunder.

No more hiding, Francene says.

She lowers down from a cedar that's directly in Maria's path.

Not anymore.

Francene's head with its blond hair once wound back in a tightly braided bun now grins at the tip of a slender twist of flesh that thickens out into a column, a many-limbed worm cobbled together from the still-moving parts of other people. They clamber through the branches with no concern for injury as Francene lowers her head further—there are so many of them, the branches heavy with motion all around her, the coils of the creature winding from trunk to trunk, hands grasping everywhere as the circle tightens.

She's surrounded. Francene's head lifts toward her, the mutant head of a caterpillar. Maria wants to laugh.

More rustling of leaves, and she's confronted with the tail of the serpent. This too sports a face, gasping like a fish. Shaun, Francene's son.

My disgusting son wants to know you from inside, the way my disgusting husband did.

The boy's voice whimpers. I'm sorry.

The crazy quilt monster of torsos and arms and legs and eyes has closed in on all sides, steadily inching through the branches and brush. Francene's head nuzzles against her weeping son in a twisted show of affection. My little sweetheart should always get what he wants most.

Everywhere Maria could lunge, arms await.

She kneels. I just want to see my son again. You understand.

Mine wants to see inside you, Francene's mouth hisses. The coils unite, become a wall, a chimney.

Maria knows Francene's hatred is just. I never meant to hurt you. I never meant to hurt any of you, she says. I'm so sorry.

Fingers pull at her hair, her clothes. Most of her body goes numb as glowing mites crawl from the monster's skin onto hers, arrange themselves in orderly rows.

Arms encircle her, lift her shirt as Francene's face lowers to her navel, pulls one of the bright fasteners loose with her teeth, then another, then another, opening Maria's belly like a baby doll's. What's inside flitters in mind-bending motion.

Shaun's face disappears inside her as the serpent invades tail-first. She can feel its length folding up inside her, folding and folding, feel the blind eyes along its length flutter open.

the pattern

You are so lucky.

Your life and hers connect in one long worm of memory, and with full understanding hate can only transmute into sadness.

You learn all you ever needed to know about the man you have in common, how he kept feeble ghosts of love alive for both of you, one shade comatose and dying, the other leprous and selfish, based on a stunted waxwork of desire. He never wanted you close enough to have for keeps but never wanted you to stray out of reach. In your shared soul, you see he always wanted you in your proper place, loved you for your usefulness but demanded that you stay out of sight, carry out what you were charged to do without ever getting in the way. And for this empty, manipulative homunculus of a man you've waged a war of wills, burrowed into one another in life and after.

You are so lucky.

That her furor, her desire to rend you piecemeal so overwhelmed that she tore away from the great body and found you on her own.

That as she stitches herself into you and fastens you around herself, as the scraps and tatters she dragged with her fuse into you, as that insatiable hunger for the stains of flesh and spirit becomes your hunger, as her mind buttons itself to yours, she understands everything, the web you had lived in together all these years, understands your surrender, your genuine repentance, and loses the willpower to do anything but grieve.

And as she howls, as she curls into herself, you smother her, you swallow her, you unravel the bits that remain and weave her into your new pattern.

You're a survivor, with a drive, a cause that devours all others.

Your belly closes over the tapestry of horror rolled up inside you. A thousand half-memories loop around your thickening thread, add their feral undercurrents.

You are every goddess that ever wore the skins of her followers. You are every witch that ever stole a man's damnable shape. You are an innocent girl molested, you are her pathetic, cowardly abuser, you are every docile loved one who ever kept silent and looked the other way. You are the woman on the side, the woman scorned, the woman bent on murder.

You are a new pattern sheared from the old quilt.

You find what's left of the weak, mewling man-boy, the one who tried to be the monster and failed, and fold him into nothing, into something even less.

You can feel the great body's resonance in your weave of nerves, the wonderful agony as it spews and stretches with no end in sight. The slavering delight at finding new patches to absorb, new secrets, new nasties, hunting them as they run through the streets, hide in cellars and closets and clutch their button-eyed dolls under their beds, winding tendrils around the punches they throw, circling fingers around their ankles as they try to climb into their cars.

You could return to it, yes. Perhaps you could become its new nerve center, new master pattern, the quilter who stretches all the layers across the frame and binds them with the strength of living skin.

Or perhaps you'd simply become lost and reabsorbed in its folds. Or perhaps you'll snip away all you can steal and set out on your own, a new colony.

You have nothing to fear, everything to learn. You go to meet it.

the piece trimmed free

A little girl kneels in the center of a quiet street.

As below, so above. Asphalt washed by streetlamps. A bright moon muffled by clouds. All the same gray.

Empty houses stand to either side of her, dead sentinels, skulls of concrete and plaster picked clean of all human parasites. The girl has never seen any of these houses before. She still doesn't see them. She stares at the ground between her hands, posed as if she plans to puke, as if she's pressed her hands to the plate glass above a view into the craw of Hell, and she can't stop watching, no matter how much she wants to.

Around her the neighborhood lies silent. In the distance, somewhere well out of sight of this deserted cul-de-sac, a brief scream, a sound that could belong to anything, human or animal.

Off to one side, in the front yard of one of the abandoned houses, a woman rises from the grass. In the gray ambiance her hair flows black as strokes of ink, her skin dusky, her eyes glistening pits. Every bit of her is alive, flesh, clothing, layers sliding over one another as might snakes in a nest, before she settles into one shape.

She steps onto the road, walks to the girl, who doesn't move, doesn't look up.

Maria stoops beside the girl, cups a hand under her chin, forces her to raise her head. She whispers the girl's name. Maddy. She speaks in another woman's voice.

The girl who was Maddy stares at nothing, starts to shudder.

When Maria speaks again, it's with a voice akin to her own. She whispers in the girl's ear. You don't belong in here.

Maddy sings softly, without melody. She swallowed the spider. To catch the fly.

I gave you back everything I could.

She swallowed the fly. I don't know why. Maybe she'll die.

You'll have to find the rest on your own.

Maddy's mouth moves but makes no more sounds. Maria stands and backs away. Now her eyes are star-bright. Maybe I'll see you again. When you're older.

When Maria drives away, the little girl is still hunched in the road, neither laughing nor crying as she speaks. Funny, Mommy. It was so funny. Mommy, don't you think it was funny?

the scrap left over

Mom, what's going on?

Davey stands at the end of the dark hallway, his silhouette ludicrously tall and wide for a boy of ten, especially one as sedentary as he is, but these days that's how they grow them.

Maria has just stepped out of his father's bedroom, carrying a bulky juggernaut of a purse that's packed to the point of overflow.

She pushes past her son and sets her bag down on the breakfast bar that delineates the kitchenette. Its handles flop to one side and its contents take a while to settle, stirring quite a bit of noise as they rattle about.

Jeez, Mom, you got mice in there?

She laughs. In the background, the voice on the TV changes. The panicked newscasters have actually stopped hogging the airways long enough to let that hunky weatherman talk about the thunderstorm sweeping in ahead of the cold front.

Davey bites his lip as he peers down the hall again. Where's dad?

Oh, he's still here. He just can't see you right now.

Huh?

He's not feeling well.

Oh. He wanders over to the TV, but he's still eying his mom. Did Marcie know you were coming over? You know how she gets, if you come over without telling her first.

A smirk. Oh, she knows I'm here.

And now his mother grows thoughtful.

Davey, remember that story we were talking about the other day, that thing you read?

More specifics, Mom?

That story about the harpist.

Orpheus?

Yeah, that's the guy.

How he couldn't stop from looking back and left his wife in Hades forever?

No, no, there was something else. About his head.

Oh, that. I told you, these women who were like demons tore off his head, but he was immortal, so he couldn't die, and when they threw his head in the river it was still singing, and it floated away.

Yes, that exactly, she says. I really like that part of the story. I think it's my favorite. I was wondering if it could work in real life.

The contents of the purse shift. There's a noise inside, like a hiss of air, a gasp.

Her son cocks his head, but his mother seems to take no notice. Instead she snatches the handles. I need you to wait here just for an hour or so, okay. Just stay put. Play a game or something.

Where you going?

Don't worry about it. I'll be back for you soon.

And she totes her burden out the door.

MONSTER

Since I grew tall enough to sit at a classroom desk, I've longed to be a monster. There is no reason for this that you or your friends in the department will ever be able to find, should you have an opportunity to delve into my history. My mother and father loved each other. They were neither too lenient nor too strict. The bullies in my school, the ones who introduced my fellow gifted students to cycles of humiliation and pain, paid no attention to me at all. My teachers never singled me out for praise or discipline.

Perhaps you'd find this of note: I never courted the opposite sex and never considered my lack of interest a shortcoming, and never drew down any mockery because of it. It would be fair to call me a loner, though I've never suffered from the affliction of loneliness.

I had learned to make things disappear by the time I could drive, but the only proof you'll ever have that speaks to what or whom I've vanished is my word. Just as an example, nowhere in that building will you find a single body, no matter how many tons of charred debris you remove. And yes, you found me in the ruins after the blaze, but it's not because of those flames that I look the way I do.

Missing? Oh, but they're not, dear friend. Help you find them? Of course.

Here's some useful history. Just before the European empires carved up Africa and Asia, their mathematicians confronted a phenomenon that their small white minds struggled to get their greedy grips around: the possibilities of curves that are infinite in length, even though they occupy a finite space. They viewed these puzzles as freakish mysteries and, in keeping with the spirit of the age, dubbed them "monsters."

I have long been fascinated by the concept of a universe that can contain infinitely many things within its borders, and yet outside be no larger than this table. Or you. Or me.

I started with an equation brutal and repetitive as razor wire, with variables that grew in complexity and instability with each new iteration. I learned the craft of trance. I sliced pieces from my soul in a symmetrical pattern and replaced the portions removed with the entire model copied in miniature, then wounded each of them in the same way I did before, and filled in the holes with copies smaller yet, carving into those and grafting yet again, on and on.

For years I dedicated every waking moment to making new folds, new incisions, new growths. And I never lost my precision, no matter how small the surgeries or how large their number. I have mutilated myself for so long the process now self-perpetuates.

When I passed puberty the changes no longer manifested in mind alone. They took hold, first in the folds of my brain, in my yellow globs of adipose, at last in the pink layers of my living skin. And deeper inside as well. You look at me, seated across from you in this tiny room with its walls painted flowery colors to keep the inmates calm, and you see a walking scar, a melted mass of tissue, an arsonist who earned his just deserts. But you've wondered how I can see, for you can see, can you not, I have no eyes? And yet, I do see. And I know you've also wondered how it is I speak. Your partner watching from behind the one-way glass, he fears for your safety, even with these manacles on my arms and legs. Your partner, I believe, has perceptions you lack. Though you may yet come around.

To you, I am a shriveled lump, but I speak with pride when I tell you that I'm a self-made monster, a Mandelbrot set, a Koch curve, a Menger sponge, and inside I have no boundaries. When I decide it's time to teach you, you'll have no more hope of unlearning the lesson than you do of finding these others whose pictures you've spread here on the table.

My good man. Your laugh inspires me. Let me give you more to laugh about. I have a shaggy dog story to tell. Let me explain how it unfolds.

When you turn to aim that look of disbelief at the mirror that your partner lurks behind, you'll see me standing between you and the mirror, my shackles gone. I'll bet you won't take the time to study what my reflection looks like, what hints that will give you. Instead you'll shout, and when I don't move, you'll shoot. Your brain isn't equipped to accommodate what you'll see next. Your eyes will tell you that the bullets never reached me. No burst of flesh, no impact, no reaction at all, no matter how many times you squeeze the trigger, no matter how close you hold the gun.

When you finally turn to run, there I'll be, in the way. Wherever you look next, there I am, closer. Finally, you'll charge at me, because there's no other direction to move.

Were you as smart as your partner, you might glimpse for just an instant a chaotic lattice of wax-flow flesh, an interlacing weave of soft honeycomb forms that billows about you like a cast net. Most likely you'll just find yourself in among them, these biomorphic vistas that open and open and open before you, repeating themselves in scales large and small, patterns that on close observation yield segments of the same half-formed face or slats of ribs or curls of hair or pillars of fingers, growing more and more complex and cavernous as you stumble and slide, as you scream like an junkie in the throes of withdrawal, piss down both legs of those tasteful flat-front slacks your detective status grants you the luxury of wearing.

I've seen it before, the way your partner will react when he follows you, pausing to inhale the fractal wonders even as knowledge of what it all means dawns in his more sophisticated cortex. You eventually regain your head, lean against one of a thousand identical strands of pulsing flesh thick as sequoia trees. You do what a good cop does, you draw a grid in your mind across your surroundings, methodically parse out the squares to deduce the logical way back, valiant in your failure to comprehend how space now flows one way.

You're a practical man, not as brave as everyone who's known you believes, but you apply assertiveness the way a carpenter wields a saw, and your sense of duty remains as fixed in its proportions as Planck's constant. It takes a long time, doesn't it, in the face of the latest endlessly repeated face in my Escher landscape, for your resolve to approach zero. You're thinking about your wife, the look on her face at the table this morning when you snarled at her about the unpaid electric bill, and about your arthritic dog who you absently struck when he pressed his head under your hand at the height of the argument. I see down into that moment in the track of your life, and your simple little mind revisits it now. And you're thinking about your father lying in his back room bed, the oxygen tube hissing under his nose, and how it always falls to your wife to bathe his sores and empty his bedpan because this job you so love and so hate keeps you out at all hours. You're thinking about all of them, about how they'll remember you, and what will happen to them now.

This is new, an experience I've not had before. You try your cell phone. Wonderful!

The connection's faint, she can maybe understand one word in three as you tell her how sorry you are. Both parts of the conversation are clear to me, my strings of synapses stretch forever, my ears are without number. Odds are that somewhere within me, some semblance of a heart is moved to beat faster in a manner not unlike the breathless effect I sometimes feel when contemplating the perfection of numbers, or the efficiency of tissue breakdown in a starving human body, or the cosmological processes of decay mirrored in the moist disintegration of a corpse. I am stimulated in a new and delightful way until the battery in your device dies.

Screaming your partner's name isn't entirely futile—there is a chance, though astronomically small, that he will find you.

Yet your despair is based on illusion, my friend. Here, you will never be alone.

And no matter how long you wander you will never be lost. Not to me, my weeping friend. Never to me.

ABOUT THE AUTHOR

On weekdays, Mike Allen writes the arts column for the daily newspaper in Roanoke, Va. Most of the rest of his time he devotes to writing, editing, and publishing. His first novel, a dark fantasy called *The Black Fire Concerto*, appeared in 2013, and he's written a sequel, *The Ghoulmaker's Aria*, that's in the revision stage.

He raised more than $10,000 through a Kickstarter campaign to revive his anthology series dedicated to boundary-blurring work, *Clockwork Phoenix*. That Kickstarter funded *Clockwork Phoenix 4*, released in 2013 to much critical acclaim. He also edits and publishes *Mythic Delirium*, which began in 1998 as a poetry journal; a second Kickstarter campaign in 2013 rebooted it as a digital publication for poetry and fiction. In other words, 2013 was a big year for him, and 2014 isn't far behind, with the release of his sixth poetry collection, *Hungry Constellations*; an eponymous paperback anthology of stories and poems from *Mythic Delirium*; and his first collection of short fiction, *Unseaming*. Somewhere in there he squeezes in time for an audio column, "Tour of the Abattoir," which appears in mostly monthly intervals at *Tales to Terrify*.

He receives a ton of help with all this editing from his wife, artist and horticulturalist Anita Allen. Their pets, Loki (canine) and Persephone and Pandora (feline) provide distractions. You can follow Mike's exploits as a writer at descentintolight.com, as an editor at mythicdelirium.com, and all at once on Twitter at @mythicdelirium.

CPSIA information can be obtained at www.ICGtesting.com
Printed in the USA
LVOW07s0025181214

419284LV00007BA/1142/P